Books should be returned on or before the last date stamped below.

29 JAN 96

30 MAR 1996   11 APR 1997

31 MAY 1996

17 JUN 1996

31 JAN 1997

19 AUG 1997

15 SEP '97

15 OCT '97

-7 NOV 1997

13 JUL 00

29 AUG 2000

11 DEC 2001

16 JAN 2002

12 NOV 2002

-9 DEC 2002

03 MAY 2003

18 NOV 2003

28 APR 2004

19 MAY 2004

13 JUL 2004

NORTH EAST of SCOTLAND LIBRARY SERVICE

MELDRUM MEG WAY, OLDMELDRUM

WISHART, DAVID

Virgil

ABERDEENSHIRE
LIBRARIES

WITHDRAWN
FROM LIBRARY

SFR

F

888351

I, Virgil

'It's a very long time since I've read a first novel written with such assurance and style. David Wishart is clearly a born storyteller. His knowledge and love of Classical literature shines luminously throughout the book and his characters have a vividness and clarity which renders the narrative as lively as a contemporary thriller.'

Hugh C. Rae

SCEPTRE

I, Virgil

DAVID WISHART

SCEPTRE

Copyright © 1995 David Wishart

First published in Great Britain in 1995 by Hodder and Stoughton
A division of Hodder Headline PLC
A Sceptre Book

10 9 8 7 6 5 4 3 2 1

The right of David Wishart to be identified as the Author of
the Work has been asserted by him in accordance with the
Copyright, Designs and Patents Act 1988.

All rights reserved. No part of this publication may be
reproduced, stored in a retrieval system or transmitted,
in any form or by any means, without the prior written
permission of the publisher, nor be otherwise circulated
in any form of binding or cover other than that in which
it is published and without a similar condition being
imposed on the subsequent purchaser.

All characters in this publication are fictitious
and any resemblance to real persons, living or dead,
is purely coincidental.

British Library Cataloguing in Publication Data

Wishart, David
  I, Virgil
  I. Title
  823 [F]

F
988351

ISBN 0-340-62817-0

Typeset by Hewer Text Composition Services, Edinburgh
Printed and bound in Great Britain by
Mackays of Chatham plc, Chatham, Kent

Hodder and Stoughton
A division of Hodder Headline PLC
338 Euston Road
London NW1 3BH

To Rona, Mairi and Maggie –
uxori optimae liberisque optimis

Acknowledgements ∫

With thanks to Roy Pinkerton and his colleagues at Edinburgh University's Department of Classics and Ancient History for their invaluable help and criticism.

Dramatis Personae

(Purely fictional names are given in lower case.)

AGRIPPA, Marcus Vipsanius: Octavian's friend, colleague and principal general.

AHENOBARBUS, Gnaeus Domitius: Republican general and admiral, who later supported Antony.

Albinus, Titus Lutatius: young aristocrat with whose murder Cotta is charged.

ANTONY (Marcus Antonius): Caesar's lieutenant, triumvir. Later (with Cleopatra) Octavian's principal opponent.

BARBATUS, Furius: prosecuting lawyer at Cotta's trial.

BRUTUS, Decimus Junius: Tyrannicide, Republican general, brother of the more famous Marcus.

BRUTUS, Marcus Junius: Tyrannicide. Leader, with Cassius, of the Republican forces in the civil war. Committed suicide after Philippi.

CAESAR, Gaius Julius: warlord, triumvir (with Pompey and Crassus) and eventual dictator. Octavian's adoptive father. Murdered in the conspiracy of 44 BC and later deified.

CASSIUS (Gaius Cassius Longinus): Tyrannicide. Leader, with Brutus, of the Republican forces in the civil war. Committed suicide after Philippi.

CALVUS, Gaius Licinius: orator and poet admired by Virgil.

CICERO, Marcus Tullius: writer, statesman, and Rome's finest orator. Opposed Antony and Octavian and was executed on Antony's orders.

CLEOPATRA: queen of Egypt and, with Antony, Octavian's principal opponent.

CLODIUS (Publius Clodius Pulcher): demagogue, opponent of Milo, by whom he was murdered.

Cornelia: wife of Proculus, and Valeria's mother.

Cotta, Marcus: Valeria's fiancé.

CRASSUS, Marcus Licinius: triumvir, with Pompey and Caesar. Killed at Carrhae.

CYTHERIS: Gallus's girlfriend.

EPIDIUS: Greek rhetorician. Taught (at different times) both Virgil and Octavian.

Eupolis: Virgil's secondary-school teacher.

FULVIA: Antony's first wife.

GALLUS, Gaius Cornelius: poet, soldier and politician. Friend of Virgil and Octavian. Committed suicide after being recalled in disgrace from his Egyptian command.

HORACE (Quintus Horatius Flaccus): friend of Virgil and, after him, the greatest of the Augustan poets.

Latro, Afius: the orator under whom Virgil studied in Milan.

LEPIDUS, Marcus Aemilius: triumvir, with Antony and Octavian. Discredited after Philippi and retired from politics.

MAECENAS, Gaius Cilnius: Octavian's friend and political/cultural adviser. Patron to Virgil, Horace and other Augustan poets.

MAGIUS: Virgil's maternal grandfather.

MILO, Titus Annius: right-wing opponent and murderer of the demagogue Clodius.

OCTAVIA: Octavian's sister and Antony's second wife.

OCTAVIAN: grand-nephew and adopted son of Caesar, triumvir and eventual first emperor. Given the name 'Augustus' by the Senate in 27 BC. He died in AD 14, thirty-five years after Virgil.

PARTHENIUS: Greek poet and critic. Virgil's friend, host and teacher in Campania.

PHILO, Caesennius: defence counsel at Cotta's trial.

POLLIO, Gaius Asinius: poet, author, orator, general, politician. Virgil's first patron.

POMPEY (Gnaeus Pompeius Magnus): Caesar's erstwhile ally and the Senate's champion against him in the civil war.

POMPEY, Sextus: son of the above, opponent of Antony and Octavian.

Proculus, Quintus Valerius: Virgil's 'second father', with whom he stays while studying in Rome.

SIRO: Greek Epicurean philosopher, Virgil's friend and teacher in Campania.

Valeria Procula: Proculus's daughter.

VARRO, Marcus Terentius: polymath and prolific author. His work on agriculture was a prime source for Virgil's *Georgics*.

Virgil and his Poetry

Several short *Lives* of Virgil exist, the best and fullest being by the fourth-century AD grammarian Aelius Donatus – probably based on the much earlier (second century AD) historian Suetonius. I have used this *Life* as the framework (it is no more) for my story.

Virgil was born in Andes, near Mantua – perhaps the modern Pietole – on 15 October 70 BC. His father was, by different accounts, a potter or a servant to the local official Magius, whose daughter he married (the Magii, although they had never held the consulship, were a very respectable family at Rome). He had two brothers, the elder of whom died in boyhood, the younger as a young man. He studied in Cremona, Milan and Rome, speaking in court only once: his speech was so slow and laboured by nature that it almost gave the impression of mental backwardness.

As a very young man, he tried his hand at various poems in the light, clever Alexandrian style, and finally (between 41 BC and 39/38 BC) wrote the *Pastorals* – we now call them the *Eclogues* – in honour of Pollio and Gallus, who had regained for him his father's confiscated farm. They imitate the style of the *Idylls* of the Greek poet Theocritus (c300 BC-c260 BC), but have a completely unTheocritean social and political slant. The famous *Fourth* (known as the *Messaianic Eclogue*) was seized on by later Christian writers as prophesying the birth of Christ, and went far in establishing Virgil's popularity during the Middle Ages (the *Aeneid* was used, like the Bible, in bibliomancy). Around this time, Virgil met the young Horace, and although very different in temperament they remained lifelong friends.

With the publication (and success) of the *Eclogues*, Virgil was taken up by Augustus's 'minister of culture' Maecenas. Under his patronage he began the *Georgics* (c38 BC) a four-book poem on agriculture which chimed with Augustus's attempt to revitalise Italian farming. Although it contains a great deal of practical detail – the fourth book is still a standard work for beekeepers – it was probably politically motivated: in style it imitates the didactic, philosophical poem of Lucretius (94 BC–55 BC) *On Things as They Are* (*De Rerum Natura*). The *Georgics* were completed around 31 BC (when Actium was fought), and Virgil began his greatest work, the *Aeneid*.

The *Aeneid* is what is called a 'programme poem', i.e. it has a political purpose which underlies and pervades the straight narrative. Like the *Georgics* it is written in iambic hexameters, the elevated, didactic metre reserved for really serious poetry, especially epic. On the surface, it describes the wanderings of the Trojan Aeneas after the fall of Troy and his eventual landing in Italy which led finally to the founding of Rome; however, its contemporary importance was monumental, recalling as it does the *Odyssey* and *Iliad* of Homer.

To the Greeks the works of Homer had an almost sacred significance; passages were cited, for example, to settle legal disputes between the city states over who owned what territory, and Homer's ruling was regarded as final. The *Aeneid* was intended – by Augustus, at least – to fulfil a similar role in justifying the rightness of his political and social policies. The fact that this was to be done in poetry, not in prose, elevated the justification far above the simply mundane: a common Latin term for 'poet' is *vates*, which can also be translated as 'priest-prophet', while *carmen* has the force, not only of 'song' or 'poem' but also 'charm' or 'spell' (*poeta* and *poema* are imports from Greek, not the original Latin terms). All this would have given the *Aeneid*, to Virgil's contemporaries, a significance far beyond the story itself.

The circumstances of Virgil's death are as I have described them. He set out for Greece intending a three-year absence to edit the poem, leaving instructions that any 'Italian' copies be destroyed. At Piraeus, he was met by Augustus himself, who persuaded him to return immediately with him to Rome. On a sightseeing trip to Megara, Virgil caught a chill, which grew worse on the voyage. He asked for the manuscript to be brought to him so he could burn it, but permission was refused. Virgil died at Brindisi on 21 September 19 BC.

Of the incidents I have manufactured from whole cloth (i.e. those affecting his private life rather than historical events) I should mention the death of his brother Marcus, and his relationship with Proculus and Valeria. I needed the Marcus incident to establish the theme of fratricide, so relevant to Virgil's time. Valeria's death (and Proculus's) echo another contemporary theme, fundamental to the *Aeneid*: that of *furor* – mindless, undirected violence totally geared to destruction. Also, according to Donatus, the poet 'left half his property to Valerius Proculus, his half-brother by a different father'. I have tried to reconcile this with my story by equating Donatus's Proculus and my Proculus's son Lucius, who would naturally have inherited the house on the Esquiline if it had not been confiscated.

Finally, a short note on Virgil's private life. He was almost certainly homosexual – partners quoted are Alexander, one of his slaves, and Cebes, probably also a slave, who wrote poetry – but I have played this down for reasons of plot.

Donatus says that 'his personal conduct was so respectable that at Naples he was given the name Parthenias (Virgin)'; and a consciously chosen sexlessness fits better (I think) with the character I have tried to create.

Childhood: Mantua and Cremona (70–54 BC)

I

I was born on 15 October in the first consulship of Pompey the Great and Marcus Licinius Crassus in a ditch near Mantua.

I don't think Mother ever forgave my father that ditch. She certainly would not have forgiven me, if I had not gratified her social ambitions by showing an academic bent.

Why a ditch at all, you ask? Was Virgil's mother a drab, a no one? Did he even have a father for his mother to forgive?

This was precisely my mother's point. Such stories tend to stick.

The truth is less dramatic. My father and mother were visiting friends in the village of Andes, just outside Mantua. Mother had wanted to put it off, for obvious reasons, but my father insisted (why I do not know), compromising only over the hire of a litter. The shaking may have had something to do with it, or it may simply have been my proper hour. Whatever the reason, my mother's waters broke on the way back; and my father, being more at home with delivering ewes than women, hustled her out into the most convenient place away from prying eyes and performed his office of midwife.

At least the ditch was dry. At that time of year, that was a miracle in itself.

Perhaps here I should discount one story of my birth which says more about my mother than about me. Later she was to claim (probably to counteract the ditch story) that in her last month of pregnancy she had dreamt of giving birth to a sprig of bay. The sprig took root, flourished and produced all kinds of berries and flowers. This, although flattering to my poetry, is false. Apart from a passionate craving for pickled cucumbers (so my father told me) her pregnancy was a perfectly normal one. In any event, she did not 'remember' the dream until long afterwards.

My parents did not get on well together. Take a cup of Rhodian wine, of no distinction apart from its name. Prink and perfume it with Arabian spices – pepper, saffron and cinnamon. That was my mother. Now take a cup of plain, honest domestic oil from the second pressing, such as a peasant soaks his bread in. That was my father. Mix them. That was my parents' marriage.

Physically they were completely unlike. My mother was fair-skinned and straight-nosed; my father, brown as a nut, tall but stocky as a Slav. I take after both – my father in build (apart from his broad nose) and my mother in character. Which explains why I look like a countryman but have not the countryman's self-confidence. Even today I have a genuine horror of being recognised, and the prospect of giving a public reading brings me out in a cold sweat for hours beforehand.

I was the second son of three. My elder brother Marcus . . .

My elder brother. Long dead now, his death a knife in my side. Marcus is the pale ghost that grins at me from the shadows, his hair green with weed. He is my Remus, a reminder of the ancient Roman curse that goes too deep for expiation. I cannot tell you yet about Marcus.

The third son was Gaius. He is dead now, too, but his death brought no guilt, only grief. There were nine years between us, as if he owed his life to the other's death. I can quite well believe this of my father: although I have no sons myself I understand the desire to see oneself in one's children. It was his sorrow to lose his own image and be left with a milksop for an heir.

Death. Guilt. Sorrow. You see the dark path that mention of that drowned ghost leads me down? These are no thoughts for a dying man. Away with them.

He is poisoning me.

I saw it in his eyes before we sailed, despite the smile on his lips.

'It's only a fever, Virgil.' (Why are hypochondriacs so dismissive of other men's illnesses?) 'And you deserve it for traipsing off to Greece without telling me. What made you think the poem needed three years' editing, you beetroot?'

It is as artificial as it sounds, this bluff heartiness and rustic eccentricity of language. Like so many of his amiable qualities – his republicanism, his dislike of flattery and, not least, his reverence for the old Roman ways – it serves a very practical purpose. Octavian is nothing if not a pragmatist.

Literally nothing.

Strip the layers from an onion. The bit that is left, that is Octavian.

You are shocked. I am committing *lèse majesté*. Warlord Octavian is dead, surely; he died eight years ago, by order of the Senate, and First Citizen Augustus rose phoenix-like from his ashes, to grace the Republic he had restored. But Augustus has had many names: Octavius, Octavian, Caesar. The man shifts shape like a Proteus. I have learned. I shall hang on to his reality, and call him Octavian.

Need I make my opinion of him any plainer? The august ruler of the Roman world is a calculating, ruthless, cowardly, hypocritical opportunist with as much moral firmness as a weathercock.

He is also the greatest man Rome has ever produced, and the saviour of his country. Divine honours are no more than his due.

I have surprised you again, this time by my inconsistency; but I am not inconsistent. Consider.

Marius and Sulla. Caesar and Pompey. The Tyrannicides, Antony. Fifty-seven terrible years from the stoning of the Senate's envoys by the troops at Nola to the victory of Actium. The whole of Italy rolled in blood for almost three generations before we had peace.

Peace.

That is the one great word that straddles all others like a Colossus. Wherever you stand, you have merely to raise your eyes to see its huge hand stretched over you. Peace is the ultimate blessing, and we owe it to Octavian and Octavian alone. If by my poetry I have helped him establish Plato's Mighty Lie, then the Roman in me has no regrets. He condones even his own death.

Not so the poet. He condones nothing, pardons nothing. If he had done, then I would not be dying now.

Plato was right to exclude us from his perfect state. Our poetry is like a poorly broken horse. We may harness it to the public good, but we cannot curb its rogue desire for truth; and when it shies in spite of us and leaves the highway the charioteer – who is the poet – is smashed to atoms.

I tried. Not for myself, least of all for Octavian, but for Rome and the memory of these fifty-seven years. But I could not, when all was said and done, send my *Aeneid* down the centuries with a lie in its mouth. I compromised, as far as was safe – as far as I thought was safe; and my scruples destroyed me.

So I ran from them. Ran to Greece – where else would a frightened, confused poet run but to his mother? – intending a three-year absence. Three years, to regain my soul and destroy myself as a Roman. Three years to burn the golden lie from the poem and give it back its integrity.

The news reached Octavian at Pergamon before I set out. He was in Athens before I was. Then a convenient chill at Megara, an unexpected fever and a boat waiting to carry me back to Italy . . .

I have caught my death. The poem still lies, with its tongue if not its heart, and if I am given the chance I will burn it.

I will not be given the chance.

Consider the lowly dung-beetle that the Egyptian calls a scarab.

Its world is the manure-heap. It cuts out a portion of manure larger than itself, which it rolls into a ball. Then it stands on its head and begins to push the ball of manure with its back legs. Over stones and rocks it goes, labouring behind its huge burden, through thorns and mud, pushing and struggling until at last it finds the perfect place. There it digs a hole for the manure-ball and burrows inside, to feast on dung and lay its eggs.

The scarab is motivated purely by self-interest.

You understand the parable, of course. The manure-heap (O perfect symbol!) is the Roman state, the scarab Warlord Octavian, who let nothing stand between him and absolute power. But wait, that is not the end.

Along comes the Egyptian. He looks at the scarab and sees the hand of God. To him it is divine, its efforts divinely inspired. Manure-heap becomes universe, dung, fire, and lo! the sun is rolled across the sky, giving light to the world, and a divine scarab pushes it.

What if the Egyptian is right? I mean, literally right. Then the scarab, born in dung, living in and on dung, becomes an instrument of the gods, and its self-interested labour is exalted and transmogrified far beyond its own conception.

Scarab Octavian, with all his imperfections, becomes Divine Augustus. Is this not matter for the poet?

However, let us follow the parable further, and give the scarab a voice.

'Clearly, poet,' it says, 'from the beginning my destiny was a high one, and of inestimable benefit to mankind. Sing it, then, justify the ways of God to Man. But let's have no mention of the manure-heap or the dung-ball. They are inappropriate to your theme. And – oh, you should also stress my complete altruism, high-mindedness and lack of mortal frailty. That will be more morally instructive to your listeners.'

What is the poet to say? To him the struggling, the backsliding, the dung and the mud are essentials. How can he leave them out, even when they detract from the dignity of his theme? He temporises.

'Perhaps,' he says, 'someone else could do it better.'

'I don't want someone else,' says the scarab. 'I want you.'

'But what about the truth? These things – the manure-heap, the dung-ball – they happened. I can't just ignore them.'

The scarab frowns.

'Listen,' it says. 'Which is more important? The past or the future? You and I have the chance to build a perfect world. People unborn will listen to your poem and say, Yes, that's right, that's how things should be, fine and noble and clean and pure. That's how we want to live. Who are you, poet, to set doubts in their minds? I need you, Virgil. I have the present, but I need you to give me the future. Forget my past. Help me, not for my own sake, but for the sake of Rome.'

What could I say? You see my problem? You see, also, how important my *Aeneid* is to him, and why he cannot allow me to live?

He is quite right. As am I.
That is our tragedy.

My earliest memories are of clay and fire.

We lived, the four of us, above my grandfather's pottery shop in Three Taverns Street, near the centre of Mantua. Magius was my mother's father. He was an important man in the town, a member of the Council, but he had not a trace of snobbishness – witness my parents' marriage. Father was his steward, his right-hand man, with a nose for business that complemented Magius's skill as a potter. It was thanks to him that you could find our pots as far afield as Cremona – plain earthenware cooking pots, admittedly, but beautifully shaped: I can still feel the cool curve of them under my hand, and see their burning redness as they sat fat on their racks at the shop door. Magius, as well as being an artist, was a generous man; I am sure that my mother was his gift to my father in exchange for prosperity. My mother knew it, too. It cannot have been a pleasant thought, or helped an already mismatched marriage. My father took it as no more than his due. In his own way, he was as lacking in snobbishness as his master; and his wife's obvious contempt for the material possessions he later laid at her feet hurt and genuinely puzzled him.

Clay and fire. The primal elements. I remember the feel of the wet clay, its delicious cool formlessness as I clenched my small fist and watched it spurt like red worms between the fingers. I remember my sense of wonder as it was transformed for my delight by the magic hands of kindly giants into men and horses and oxen and given permanence by its passage through the fire. I remember, too, watching with round eyes and bated breath – unmoving, lest I break the spell – the giants take a lump of clay, throw it on the wheel and conjure from it a perfect pot; the formless, under their cunning hands, given form and meaning.

For me, they were the magic demiurges, effortlessly spinning worlds from shapeless matter, and I worshipped them.

I was five when my grandfather died. Him, I can remember only vaguely: a giant with bright brown eyes and a bristly cheek that rubbed my face like pumice. He smelt like his pots, of rich wet clay and charcoal from the kiln (unlike most potters, he had his own in the yard behind the shop), and I can never see him without his grey homespun tunic, spattered with red earth thrown up by the wheel. Yes, Magius still threw his own pots, although he had half a dozen slaves to do it for him. No doubt he also had a tunic of fine white wool and a mantle to match, for his civic duties; but I have no memory of them.

One image, bright and sharp as a cut gemstone, before I turn to true memories: a great wobbling mass of clay spinning on a wheel. My hands around it, wrestling with this amorphous Pelion, striving to impose my order on its chaos. The clay, a wild beast, thumps against my chest, spurts between my clutching fingers, escapes me in a thousand different ways. Tears come, wave upon wave, tears of anger at the clay's selfish wildness, of frustration at its mindless denial of order . . .

Strong arms behind and around me, a bristly chin on my neck. Huge hands close around mine, pressing with irresistible force, hugging them to the clay. Guiding, controlling, forming . . .

And suddenly the clay loses its wildness, becomes tame, runs smooth as cream between my palms. All is order, rightness.

'You'll make a potter yet,' says my grandfather.

2 ∫

We left Mantua the year after the old man's death.

He had no other heirs, my mother being an only child. My father wanted to sell the pottery business and buy a farm – a small one, no more than six or seven acres. Mother objected. She was not averse to the idea of a farm – farming is eminently respectable, more so than trade – but she was horrified at the thought of what my father had in mind. If she was to be buried away in the country, she said, then at least let it be on a decent-sized estate: they had the money (the shop had gone for a large sum and besides my grandfather had been no pauper) and it would allow her to mix with ladies of her own standing. My father laughed.

'Admire big farms if you like,' he said, 'but never buy one, unless you're rich enough not to dirty your own hands. Big farms swallow money faster than a dog does a pudding.'

Argue as she might, he was adamant. Finally – fortunately – she let him have his way. Business, after all, is a man's concern.

He took months over the selection. In a way, for him it was a time of metamorphosis. I had always seen my father against an urban backdrop: a neat, dapper figure who talked of accounts and orders and was never far from his abacus and wax tablets. Now, looking over prospective properties, his character, even his appearance, began to alter; as if the townsman were splitting up the back like a pupa and giving birth to a different person.

Of course, that impression was false. My father was a countryman by nature: he had been brought up on a farm, and it was only because of a talent for arithmetic that his father had set him on the way to becoming a steward. Besides, his family was a large one – I had five uncles on my father's side – and there had been little land to divide.

For my father, then, this 'back to the land' was a home-coming, and came as naturally as breathing. He spoke the earth's language, knew its soul. I remember him, on one of our tours of inspection, stamping across a field in his laced countryman's boots, myself and my brother trotting behind. Suddenly he stooped, gathered a handful of earth, squeezed it, threw it into the air and caught it again.

'Too rich,' he said, showing us the sodden, compact ball in his palm. 'You see how it hasn't crumbled? How it sticks to the fingers like pitch? Soil like this holds the moisture too well. It ploughs heavy and breeds rank crops.'

Or again, on another occasion: 'This is good earth' (rubbing it between his hands). 'Not too light, not too heavy. A few acres of this and I could match the best farm in Sicily for corn.'

While we tramped about the fields, getting gloriously filthy, my mother would sit prim-mouthed on her mule, or closeted behind the curtains of her litter – Father insisted that we choose our future home as a family. She turned aside all offers of hospitality from the farmers' wives, not brusquely (my mother was always polite), but with a gentle firmness that left them in no doubt of the social gap involved.

'Never forget,' she told Marcus and me on one occasion, 'that your grandfather was a magistrate and sat in judgment over people like that.'

'Did he whip them?' Marcus asked.

My mother fixed with a stare the loutish farm servant who was gaping at us, until he turned away.

'Not often enough,' she said loudly.

If she expected my father to keep a similar distance, she was disappointed. He knew how important hospitality is to country folk, not least where business is concerned; and Marcus and I stuck to him like goose-grass when we could escape our mother's clutches, in the hope and expectation of some honey-cakes or a handful of raisins.

Not that the hospitality was always disinterested. There is always the farmer who tries to mask his farm's deficiencies by plying the prospective buyer with good wine – not his own, but passed off as such. I noticed that my father insisted on making his tour first before accepting anything to eat or drink, while taking every opportunity to help himself unasked to an apple from a tree or a few grapes from a vine.

'Remember,' he said to us, 'you should believe the fruit before the farmer. If an apple is sour or tastes like cinders, then however much he tells you otherwise you'll make no profit.'

After eight months of searching, we bought a farm a few miles from Cremona.

It was a tight little farm, barely six acres. I knew that we would buy it before father told me: I had become an expert in reading him, and I knew the different signs. If the farm turned out not to be what was promised, his tour was genial, uncritical and cursory. The more it pleased him, the less he spoke, except for straight questions; and my mother had a dreary wait in her litter, for which she paid him back later with her sharp tongue.

Our inspection began unpropitiously. For once, we had left Mother behind with an autumn chill. The journey had been a pleasant one at first. Then, all of a sudden, the weather turned colder and a drizzling rain began to fall, stirred up by a gusting southerly wind. Long before we reached the farm, both Marcus and I were at the fractious stage, and as a result no one was in a very good temper when we finally arrived and tethered the mules to a thorn tree.

We had passed through the gate and were approaching the courtyard, my father in front with Marcus, me lagging behind. As I passed the boxwood hedge that bordered the path, I saw something come out from beneath it. I looked, and screamed.

The figure was not much taller than I was: a little old man brown and gnarled and bent as a piece of olive wood. In his hand he carried a raised bill-hook. I had seen him often before: farmers carve him from the stock of a tree-stump and set him up to guard their property against thieves and marauding animals. But this was the first time I had seen him move. I ran towards my father, howling.

My father turned, startled, caught me.

'What's got into you, you fool?' he said. 'Wipe the snot from your nose and behave yourself!' Then, turning to the little old man: 'Forgive my son, sir. Would this be Rufidius's farm?'

'It would.' The small dark eyes were bright with suspicion. 'Who're you, and what d'you want?'

My father explained. The little man unbent with an audible creaking, and his seamed face split across in a grin, revealing four teeth like chips of olive wood.

'I'd best show you round, then,' he said, shouldering the bill-hook. 'The master's not at home, but he won't mind, I'm sure.'

I was still clinging to the back of my father's tunic, half hidden beneath his winter cloak. The dark eyes turned on me, and I caught a glint of amusement.

'What's your name, boy?'

'Publius, sir,' I said. 'Publius Vergilius.'

'You have sharp eyes, my Publius.' The old man's laugh was like the creaking of a branch in the wind. 'Be careful they don't cut you one of these days.'

That was all. He turned his attention to my father, and the tour began. It was almost sunset when we left. My father asked a lot of questions, and nodded gravely at the answers.

I have said that I knew we would buy the property from studying my father, but that is only half true. I had another reason for knowing. To this day I believe (and call me a superstitious fool if you like) that one of the little gods of the place, the guardians of stock and stone and harvest, recognised the farm's future owners, and came out to welcome us.

3 ʃ

We moved to the farm in early spring.

If I take anything with me into death it will be the memory of that first morning. We had arrived in darkness, Marcus and I muffled in cloaks against the cold, half asleep and querulous. My father had carried me upstairs and put me to bed in the room I shared with my brother. I lay awake for a long time, listening to the unfamiliar rustlings and creakings, too terrified to go to sleep or put my head out from under the blanket in case the things that lived in the dark pounced and carried me off.

The next day – that magical first day – the weather had broken. My bedroom, which the night before had been dark and cold and full of terror, was flooded in golden light shot through with green. Instead of the rumble of carts and the braying of donkeys that I was used to, the world outside my window was filled with birds. The air was fresh as new bread.

I got up quickly and put on my tunic. Downstairs, my mother was in the kitchen mopping up some spilt oil.

'Where's Marcus?' I asked.

She straightened, brushed the hair from her eyes with the back of her hand. I noticed that her mouth was set in a grim line.

'Your father's taken him to school in town,' she said.

'Can I have some porridge?'

'Really, Publius, you can see I've enough problems at present without making porridge specially for you. Why your father didn't arrange for a kitchen slave in time for our arrival I don't know. I'm sure I mentioned it to him enough before we . . .'

But that was no day to listen to my mother's complaints. Before she could finish, I had taken a piece of bread and a handful of olives from the table and was out and away.

The meadow was the wide eastern edge of our land. It ended in a stand of alder trees by the river, a side-shoot of the Po that sprawled across the plain like a trailing vine, sluggish, fragmented into deep pools edged with reeds. I ran faster and faster, in great bounds, my arms stretched to the breeze like the wings of a hawk, feeling that at any moment I would lift, hurl myself at the sun and burst through it into the shining heavens beyond, where the gods walked.

Instead, I broke through a screen of bracken into a clearing and saw something that stopped me as if I had run into a wall.

Opposite stood a bear. Its back was to me, and its front paws were laden with branches which it was setting carefully across a little stream that flowed down a drainage channel towards the river. I crouched down to watch, my heart pounding, no longer hawk but fieldmouse.

An insect passed – the air was full of them – and I saw it was a bee.

Its last branch set, the bear turned, flowed, changed into a man. I tensed, poised for flight.

'Here, you!' the bear-man shouted. 'Hang on, boy! I won't hurt you!'

His accent was thick, strange, but at least the words were understandable.

'You're one of the new master's lads,' he said. 'Which one are you? Marcus? Or Publius?'

The sound of my name held me like a spell. I waited, unable to move.

'Hanno.' The man jerked a thumb at his barrel chest. 'Hanno the beekeeper.'

So. He was one of our slaves, and not a shape-changer after all! In my relief, I almost forgot to be afraid.

'Publius,' I said, rising from the sheltering bracken. 'I thought you were a bear.'

The man's face broke into a grin, and he bellowed like autumn thunder. Suddenly he slouched forward. He let his hairy arms swing, shambled a few steps, then sat down heavily on the grass and laughed.

'Thought I was a bear!' he said at last. 'That's a good 'un!'

'These are bees, aren't they?' I felt myself reddening with embarrassment. 'And bears like honey.'

He became serious, nodded his huge head.

''S true enough. You had cause, I suppose.'

'What were you doing with the branches?'

'Eh?' He looked up. 'Oh, they're for the bees. Saves them getting their wings wet when they drink.'

'I thought bees drank from flowers.'

'So they do, so they do. But they like a bit of water as well, so long as it's not stagnant. Bees can't stand stagnant water. It stinks.'

'Do bees have noses, then?'

He laughed again.

''Course they have! You've got a nose, so've I. Every-thing's got one, 'less 'n it's cut off. Why not bees?'

'What about fish?' I said.

'What'd a fish want with a nose? You ever try smelling under water?'

It was my turn to laugh.

'You'd choke,' I said.

'So you would.' He pinched his nose momentarily with

thumb and forefinger, made gulping motions with his mouth, popped his eyes. 'Thass a fish. Fish don't smell nothing.'

I was over my shyness now, but still unwilling to leave the safety of the undergrowth.

'Do your bees sting?' I asked.

'Not unless you're fool enough to touch them.'

'Can I see inside the hives?' They were all around us, in the shelter of the trees: crude little huts of stitched bark and withies.

He shook his head.

'Oh, now, that's another story. They won't have that. Not without a bit of smoke.'

'Smoke?'

'Thass it. Quietens 'em, makes 'em sleepy. 'S how you get the honey. I'll show you come summer, 'f you like.'

'Why not now?'

'Combs is empty this time of year. Bees don't fly in cold weather. 'Sides, there's no flowers growing. They stay at home, same as we do. Bees is smart.'

'Smart?'

Hanno sat down on a tree-stump, pulled a stalk of grass and chewed on it.

'You know what they do in wind? When it's blustery, like?'

I shook my head and sat down beside him.

'Well, they pick up little bits of stone' – he held up his hand, first finger and thumb apart – 'no bigger nor that. Use 'em to fly with.'

'Why do they do that?'

'So they won't be blown about. Like a boat taking on ballast. And something else that's strange. Bees don't f . . . don't have babies.'

'Don't they?'

'No, they don't. They don't have, you know, male and

female like what usually happens. They get their children from flowers 'n carry them home in their mouths. You find them in the combs, same as the honey, sealed right in.'

My eyes must have been like saucers. Hanno grinned and stood up.

'Well, I can't be sitting here yakking all morning,' he said, ruffling my hair. 'Your father'll have my hide, and quite right too. There's new skeps to make and lots of other things to be done, now spring's here.'

'Can I help?' I said.

'Maybe. See what your father says.'

That was the beginning of my fascination with bees. It lasted through boyhood and beyond.

Consider the bee.

It has evolved the perfect society. Each knows its proper place and is happy in the role it plays: worker, builder, soldier, caretaker. Bees have no political ambition. They are motivated by no self-interest. Their passions are controlled and directed to one end, which is the good of the state. When that is threatened, they will fight to the death to protect it. They are fanatically loyal. Having chosen a king, they will stand by him to the end, and if he dies or is killed they will lose all desire for life themselves. Significantly, they are sexless. They have eliminated what Sophocles rightly called the insane and savage master.

That is, as my father would have said, the plus side of the account. There is another, darker side.

Do you know how the Egyptians of the Delta breed bees?

If a farmer has lost his swarm through natural disaster or illness, he builds a small hut with a tiled roof and narrow, slitted windows opening obliquely to the four winds. Then he takes a two-year-old calf. He blocks up its mouth and nostrils with straw or rags and then he and his men beat it to death with clubs. They do this carefully, so as to pound the flesh to pulp without breaking the skin. They shut the corpse up within the hut, on a bed of cassia, thyme and broken branches. The calf rots, and from its putrid flesh crawl the living bees.

Even perfect societies, you see, are born of blood and violence. It is the task of the poet to remind men of that fact, however politically unwelcome the reminder may be to the society's rulers. We cannot divorce ourselves from our own nature by a simple effort of will. The past is always with us: it clings to us stinking, like an importunate beggar.

It is time to tell you about Marcus.

4

My brother was two years older than me, and the golden one of the family in all but looks (he took after my father even more than I did). He was everything I was not: brave, adventurous, open, confident; the ideal boy, his father's pride and his mother's darling.

I hated him.

I would like to say, We hated each other, but that is arrogating too much worth to myself. I was beneath his notice, except perhaps as a thing to torment.

Wait. I must be careful here. In justifying myself, it is all too easy to blacken him, and that would be false. If I am to exorcise my brother's ghost I must be truthful, even if truth hurts. Marcus was not cruel, or no more so than any other small boy. If he tormented me, then it was because I invited it by my own cowardice. I was afraid of everything: of pain, darkness, heights and spiders; of climbing trees and jumping into rivers; of rough games and strange boys; of giving the least offence to anyone, child or adult. The very universality of my fear must have tempted him beyond bearing. Nor was he mean-spirited; if anything, I was the mean-spirited one. At the Winter Festival he would bring out his sweets to share, while I ate mine in secret. When he played with other children, he would take me along with him, greasing the social wheels for me as far as he could. It was not his fault that I quickly made excuses and slunk off to brood alone. As for my parents, he sought them out and enjoyed their company, where I avoided them whenever possible.

If Marcus had most of my parents' love, it was because he deserved it, not because he had stolen it from me.

Truth comes hard, and wounds like a razor-slash. Truth is the source of my guilt, and the reason for its intensity.

That first year passed quickly. Mother saw that my father had been right: the farm may have been small, but everything in it was of the best, and it blossomed under his hand like an opening rose. The weather, too, was on our side. Spring deliquesced with a richness that was almost tangible: you felt that you could take a grip of the air and squeeze it like a she-goat's udder, drawing out foaming jets of milk. The earth stirred beneath your feet with a sussuration of quickening seed. Buds burst from the branches of the trees and covered them with a spindrift of blossom until the open plain was a seashore lapped by creaming waves. Spring changed to summer, and then came the harvest. Crowned with oak leaves, we called the corn goddess into our barns and sang the harvest hymn, old as time itself. We gathered the grapes and the olives, the apples and the green figs, the honey bursting from the comb, and stored it all away until the jars and bins and lofts creaked with fullness. And when the days grew shorter and colder, herons flew high and the frogs began to croak in the marshes, we barred our doors and prepared for the winter storms.

They came from the south with the swooping fury of eagles. For three days they battered us. The wind shrieked and howled about the roof tiles, rain beat the earth flat and turned the fields into swirling seas of mud. We rode the waters like a ship, tossed back and forth, round and about; plunged from crest to trough, sank, surfaced again, decks awash, rigging gone; and when the winds had spent their force, and the sun broke through the lowering clouds, we crawled from beneath our hatches and found that the world had changed.

'It could have been worse.'

That was my father, belittling the damage as a true countryman will. The farm looked as if some giant god had stamped it flat and ground it beneath his sandal. The hurdles had gone, or were buried in mud to half their height. Branches torn from trees lay everywhere, and the trees themselves were gashed skeletons stripped of leaves and twigs. The trellised vine had broken free from its moorings against the farmhouse wall, a single tile from the roof making a splash of colour in its topmost branches.

'It could have been worse,' my father said again, looking about him. 'The harvest is in, the animals are safe in their pens. And the repairs will keep us busy till spring.'

'What about the bees?' I said.

'Their hives are sheltered against the worst of the wind. And Hanno will have anchored them with stones.'

'Shall I go and check?' said Marcus.

My father turned to him and smiled; the special smile he kept for Marcus, not for me, warm, approving. Paternal.

'You do that, son,' he said. 'I want to have a look at the rest of the vines.'

'Come on.' Marcus grabbed my arm. 'It was your idea.'

We ran towards the river, splashing through the pools that covered most of the meadow, Marcus in front as ever, me trailing behind, shivering at the touch of the cold water on my sandalled feet and bare legs.

'Wait for me!' I shouted, and Marcus stopped, turned, grinned.

'Come on, then, you snail,' he said. 'The river'll be full. We can make boats and sail them to India. Publius, come *on*!'

Most of the clearing had gone. The little drainage ditch had overflowed its banks and the floodwater had almost reached the doors of the hives – almost, but not quite: Hanno had chosen the site well, at the top of a gentle slope under the sheltering trees. The hives themselves were well protected, as my father had said they would be, each covered with a mat of woven reeds held down by ropes anchored to the ground by heavy stones. I listened, but there was no sound within. The bees were asleep, dreaming of spring.

'Let's go down to the river,' said Marcus.

I had not believed it could be so wide. Brown water poured past us, thick as soup. Dead branches reached up like claws, or were carried spinning, fast as arrows. Along the banks, and in the river itself, was scattered the debris of its human plunder – an osier hurdle, the smashed remnants of a skiff, the drowned carcass of a sheep. The river mesmerised me, held me bewitched; flexed its muscles like a brown god and dared me to wrestle with it.

I felt sick.

'The whole bank's gone this side!' Marcus exulted. 'Look at that tree!'

It was an elm. When it had been erect it must have been a good eighty feet high. The river had pulled it down, tearing the earth from between its roots, carrying it away and coming back for more, until the tree had slipped sideways and fallen, to lie half submerged along its length, crown to the opposite bank.

'It's like a bridge!' Marcus scrambled towards it, picked up a spar of driftwood and waved it, swordlike. 'I'm Horatius, defending the Sublician Bridge!' He clambered among the exposed roots, walked along the smooth trunk and turned to face the Etruscan army. Beneath him the brown god boiled and raged, catching at his sandals with greedy fingers. 'Come on, Porsenna! Come and taste Roman iron if you dare!'

I did not move.

'Oh, come on, Publius!' Marcus grounded his sword. 'Don't be a spoilsport, it's perfectly safe.' He spun on his heel, crouched; chanted: 'Publius is a cissy, Publius is a cissy!'

'I'm not!' I shouted.

The god chuckled.

'Look! It's solid as a rock!' Marcus jumped up and down. The tree-trunk did not move. 'You don't have to come far out. You can stay near the bank and hold on to the roots.'

'No. It's too dangerous.'

'Cissy! Cissy!'

Slowly I came forward. There was a long, straight stick floating in the shallows – a beanpole, carried down from one of the farms upriver. If I use that, I thought, I won't really have to leave the bank at all.

I climbed on to the bole of the tree, caught hold of a root and held the pole stiffly out in front of me.

'That's better. Now put a bit of life into it. Let's have a real sword-fight. Come on, you cissy! Fight!'

And he whacked at the pole with the full strength of his arm.

The jarring shock of the blow numbed my hand and swung me round, so that I almost lost my grip of both pole and root. I started to cry.

Marcus laughed.

'Call yourself a warrior?' he jeered. 'I don't need anyone else's help to hold this bridge against you, Porsenna! You're nothing but a cissy!'

'Stop it!'

'Cissy! Cissy!'

I lunged at him. Through the tears, I saw the tip of my pole catch the centre of his chest, saw the expression on his face change to surprise, to fear, heard the splash as he struck the water.

I could have saved him, even then. I could have stretched out my pole for him to grasp as he clung to one of the elm's trailing branches, fighting the pull of the triumphant god's fingers. It would have been easy, so easy.

I did not.

Tell it, Virgil. Tell it.

Edging along the trunk of the elm, I placed the point of my pole against his throat, beneath his screaming mouth, and pushed.

We found his body a week later, five miles downstream; but some animal had reached him first, and half his face was gone.

5

No one knew. No one ever knew.

You are revolted. How dare he ask for our sympathy, this murderer, this self-confessed fratricide? How dare he brand Augustus as coward, hypocrite, self-seeking tyrant, when his own soul is damned? How dare this poet preach to *us*?

I ask for no sympathy. I brand no one. I preach to no one. Least of all do I ask for forgiveness.

I simply tell the truth.

Think. If fratricide will damn a man's soul, what must it do to the soul of a nation?

You shuffle uncomfortably. You know what is coming: the truth never-mentioned, the skull at the feast. The dark stain on Rome's begetting.

What other race began with the murder of brother by brother? Tell me that. What other race not only condones, but exalts fratricide?

'So perish all who o'erleap the walls of Rome!'

I met a Jew once in Brindisi, who told me of another such killing as Remus's by Romulus. The killer was marked upon the forehead by his god and driven out from the tribe to die accursed. Surely this was right and proper, said the Jew. Why, pray, did Rome worship her founder as a god?

I had no answer then. I still have none.

Look at your ancient Laws of the Twelve Tables, Romans.

The penalty for murder of father, mother, grandfather, grandmother is to be sewn living into a sack with a dog, a viper, a cock and an ape, and thrown into the sea. On the murder of a brother the laws are silent. Did a brother's murder, then, stink less in the gods' nostrils? Or was it the silence of guilt, of uneasy complicity?

Do you wonder that you have wallowed in civil war like pigs in the mire? An ocean of blood could not wash out that stain. Octavian certainly cannot.

So do not let me hear, Romans, of the glorious destiny of Rome, or the divine mission of the Roman race, or the Golden Age that is to come. These are mere words. I know, I have used them myself. The truth is, that you were cursed at your begetting, and the curse lives on in every one of you. You are like a cracked beaker of Phoenician glass: the fault goes too deep for remedy, and patch it how you will it will never be whole, unless you smash it and melt it down and start afresh.

Do not talk to me, Romans, about fratricide.

6

I was ill for a month after my brother's death.

I cannot remember much about this time, except for the dreams, if they were dreams. He used to come to me in the night. Sometimes he stood in the corner of the room, where the moonlight shone, staring at me, the water running down his face from his lank hair, over his white, open eyes, dripping from the hem of his tunic on to the bare floorboards. At other times he would turn to me from shadow into light, and he would have half a face, the other half gnawed to the skull. He did not speak, and I never spoke to him. Nor did I, as I would have done confronted by another night terror, hide myself away beneath the blankets. Even then, I knew that he was my punishment, and that I must bear it or suffer worse.

He still comes sometimes, especially when I have been working hard and am overtired, or have one of my head-aches. But I have learned to live with him.

I will pass over the next few years, not because I have no memories of them but because they have no relevance. They were like the stretch of road between two milestones – essential in themselves, but unremarkable, undifferentiated one from another.

My brother Gaius was born almost ten months to the

day after Marcus died. His birth helped to heal – or at least bridge – the growing rift between my parents, in a way that I never could. They did not blame me for the death, or not in words. To them, it had been an accident, the prank of a too-high-spirited boy that had gone terribly wrong. They never knew, and I think never even suspected, that I had been involved at all, let alone the prime cause. If I caught my father looking at me sideways, or if my mother's hand lacked gentleness, then it was because of who I was (or rather who I was not), rather than what I had done. When Gaius came, I was quietly edged to one side. I expected, and did not resent, it.

What else? I went to school, of course; learned my letters and my fractions; wrote out *To work is to pray* and the other old lies that I have since helped to promulgate; was beaten by my teachers (not often) and by my schoolmates (frequently), grew taller and broader, both in body and mind. Lived. My father's farm prospered, he bought up a neighbouring property; moved into the timber business and won several lucrative contracts for supplying wood to the building trade. My mother grew older, stouter, sourer and took to wearing expensive jewellery and Egyptian perfume.

Time passed.

I was twelve when I reached my next milestone.

School for me, up till then, had been a converted shop in a side street off Cremona's main square, separated by a threadbare curtain from the eyes (but not, alas, the ears) of passers-by. It was run by two brothers, Arrius Niger and Arrius Postumus, who parcelled out between them (on, I suspect, a purely arbitrary basis) the usual offices of writing master and arithmetic teacher. Both the brothers were gross, red-lipped, greasy men with lank dark hair and broken fingernails, and we called them (behind their backs, of course) Niger and Nigrior (Black and Blacker).

I detested them. I detested, by extension, what they taught.

'All right, boy. What'j'ou get'f you take five-twelfs f'm'an ounce? C'm on, c'm on, make it snappy! I haven't got all day!'

'A half, sir.'

'Rubbish! Take your tunic off an' hand me that cane. You, Fannius's son!'

'A third, sir.'

'Good! Smart lad! No one'll be able t'pull a fast one on you when you grow up, hey?'

If it had been left to my father, I think that would have been the only schooling I got. It was not that I was a dunce – far from it, most of the lessons were ridiculously easy, if pointless – or that he did not take his responsibilities seriously. It was simply that to him practical education began and ended with basic literacy and numeracy, and he was not sufficiently interested in me to mark any higher yearnings. My mother, fortunately, was different, even although her motives were less noble.

'Tertullia the butcher's wife was saying to me the other day that her Quintus was getting on extremely well with his Greek, dear. He's learned half a book of Homer already, and he's only thirteen.'

'What use is Greek to a butcher's boy? People're too busy making sure he keeps his thumb off the scales to ask him the name of Acillus's grandmother.'

'Achilles, dear. Well, I think it's nice. Anyway, if a butcher's son can learn Greek I don't see why our children should be any different.'

Mother got her way. As soon as I was old enough, I went to grammar school.

The schoolroom was only a step up from that of the Arrius brothers: the back room of a baker's shop in Public Baths Street. At least we had some privacy, even if the decor was almost as uninspiring: plaster busts of Homer, Hesiod and (for a reason I did not appreciate until much later) Alcibiades gazed blankly at us from their several shelves. There was also – wonder of wonders! – a map of Greece fixed to the wall behind the teacher's chair.

The teacher's name was Eupolis, and I cannot imagine a greater contrast to the two Arrii. He was a tall, thin wisp of a man, completely bald except for a few strands of hair carefully arranged across his scalp like cracks in an egg. I suppose now he can have been no more than fifty, but he seemed ancient and fragile, like a piece of overused parchment that has been scrubbed with pumice-stone until the light shows through. He spoke softly, barely above a whisper, and you had to bend forwards in order to hear.

He fascinated me. He fascinated me from the first moment of the first day.

'Listen,' he said, without preamble, when he had our attention. 'With the help of the archer god Apollo, Trojan Hector has driven the Greeks back across the plains of Troy to their ships. Achilles, the Greek champion, sits in his tent, taking no part in the fighting, angry because Agamemnon King of Men has taken from him the slave-girl Briseis. Patroclus, who is Achilles's friend, comes to him begging for the loan of his armour. "Give me your armour," says Patroclus, "and I will fight in your stead. Disguised as you, I will scatter the Trojans, drive them back, save our army. Grant me this, Achilles, in token of our friendship." And Achilles grants it, little knowing that he sends his friend to his death. That is the story. Listen now, my children!'

And he told it, line by burning line. I understood nothing, and everything. I heard the ringing clash of bronze on bronze, the thud of spear in flesh, the grating slither of shield on oxhide shield. I smelt the sweat, tasted the dust and blood on my lips. I felt the pity and the glory and the tragedy of Patroclus's death mount to my throat and choke me, gather behind my eyes and spill over into tears.

I have been accused of stealing lines from Homer. That would be impossible. Try it, and you will find that it is easier to take the club from the hands of Hercules than filch one of the Master's lines. Compared with him, we later poets are pygmies.

When my eyes had cleared, I saw that he was watching me. The class was completely silent.

'Publius, you can understand Greek already?' he asked.

'No, sir. Not a word.'

He said nothing more; but from then on he took a special interest in me, and I knew I had found a friend.

7

I studied under Eupolis for four years.

He was, perhaps, the best of my teachers, even including Siro. Oh, he was no paragon. We had our share, as all boys do, of the trivia, or at least what boys regard as trivia, not knowing that they are being grounded in the basic patterns of thought on which they can later build. Just as no house-builder will start with the walls or the roof, knowing that these things make the show but cannot stand alone, but first digs the unseen foundations so that the house will stand strong and have integrity, he had us take the poems apart like dull mechanics, turn them over with our grubby fingers and grubbier minds to examine their construction.

'How many verbs in this passage? How many nouns? Who was Diomedes? Who was his father? His mother? What were Athene's attributes? How did she come by the Gorgon's head? What was the aegis?'

The questions were endless. At times I went home wrung dry like a wet sponge, my head spinning, only to sit hour by hour in the light of a single oil-lamp learning by heart my hundred lines.

I loved it.

Homer, we learned. Of course. Ascraean Hesiod, hard and unforgiving as basalt, stony as the ground he ploughed, sour as a mouthful of vinegar: Hesiod, the misanthrope, poet of the Age of Iron as Homer was of the Age of Bronze. These two were our gods, and rightly so. But there were others: Aeschylus, who hacked his characters from the living rock; Sophocles, who gave them hearts and made them suffer and bleed, and asked us why?, even Euripides, most human of the tragedians, who showed us the gods cloaked in our own frailties and dared to say, 'If these are gods, and act thus, then they are no gods at all.'

Can you imagine what I felt? Can you? Imagine being blind from birth, moving in a world of darkness where only tangible things have reality – the reality of height and length and width, shape and texture. You touch a flower: that is soft and fragile. Fire: that burns. Water: that is wet. Then one day you wake with open eyes. You see a bank of primroses blazing yellow against the green of the grass. You watch the flames flickering in a brazier, see the lightning strike and burn, raise your face and meet the pitiless eye of the sun. You watch a stream run glinting over a bed of pebbles, see the waves crash and thunder against a rocky coastline, sit in the cool of the evening as the setting sun turns the sea to blood.

That is how I felt. That is how I still feel. Eupolis gave me all that, and more.

Do you wonder that I loved him?

I was fourteen when I discovered the truth about Eupolis.

I suppose there had been enough hints, boys being boys; but I had closed my ears to them, thinking that they were only smut. Quintus the butcher's boy was gone now, but most of my classmates were like him: big, red, raw as beefsteak, great clods of Cremona earth sent by their parents to acquire a patina of civilisation. How could they judge someone like Eupolis? How could they even begin to understand him?

As I said, he had taken a special interest in me. He had introduced me to the gentle Alexandrians, who were too late (and too human) to have a place in the standard curriculum: Theocritus, Bion, Euphorion and the others. Homer and Hesiod moved in worlds far above mine, worlds where gods walked and spoke as men in stately hexameters. Before them I could only bow my head and worship. These younger poets were part of my world. They spoke of things I understood, like trees and fields, rivers, sheep and shepherds; but dignified, raised beyond the mundane, as if washed clean of their earthly imperfections, caught in crystal and preserved in timeless serenity. Unlike my gods, they were approachable. Reading them, I felt that, although to equal them was impossible, emulation at least was within my reach.

You see, I was even then dreaming of becoming a poet.

Class had just finished for the day. I was packing up my things when I felt a hand on my shoulder.

'Ah, Publius,' Eupolis said in his low, dry voice. 'I have just acquired a copy of the *Epigrams* of Callimachus. Perhaps you would like to read it?'

I blushed with pleasure.

'Yes, sir. Yes, indeed!'

'Good.' He hesitated. 'I usually bathe at this hour. Would it be possible for you to meet me at the bath-house? I must call in for the book first at my lodgings. We could read a little of it together.'

I thought rapidly. My father had delegated Hanno the beekeeper to take me to and from school; even although we had house-servants in plenty now, and it was no job for a field-slave, I had begged him that favour early on, and Father, being Father, had readily agreed and turned to matters more important than his son. Hanno, as usual, would be sitting over a pot of wine in the tavern round the corner. I could easily persuade him to wait half an hour or so.

'I should like that very much, sir,' I said.

'Good.' Eupolis gave me a cool smile and walked off. I returned to my packing.

'Make sure you keep your backside covered.'

'What?' I looked up, startled. It was Titus, the son of one of our neighbours. He was eighteen months older than me, and already had the sharp, knowing look of his father.

'Or maybe you don't mind?' he said.

I prepared to close my ears. As I say, I had heard this smut before.

'He's a queer.' Titus grinned. 'An arse-bandit. Understand?'

'Shut up, Titus.' I picked up my satchel and turned to go.

'Famous for it,' Titus yelled after me. 'Have a nice time!'

Hanno was no trouble. I doubt if he even listened to my facile explanation of having to take a message to a friend's mother.

'You take your time,' he said, pouring himself another beaker of wine. 'I'll be here when you get back.'

The bath-house was further up the street, an ancient, crumbling building whose outside walls had once been plastered but now showed their wrinkles like an old woman's face under make-up. The public slave on duty stopped me at the door.

'Hey, sonny, where d'you think you're going?' he said.

'I have to meet my teacher.'

'Not in there, you don't. Not unless you pay your penny like the rest of them.'

'But I don't want to bathe, I just want to . . .'

'Look,' he said, 'I couldn't care less if you want to give a formal bloody recitation. The cost's a penny.'

I paid him.

'Towels is extra.' He held his hand out.

'I don't want a towel.'

'Suit yourself.' He turned away, and I went in.

Eupolis, I knew, would not be in the hot-room, not with a book of poems. He would be waiting by the cold plunge, where the men gathered to oil and scrape themselves and talk after their bath. I carried on through.

I saw my teacher before he saw me.

He was sitting beside the pool, naked except for a towel round his waist. He looked scrawny and wrinkled as a plucked chicken, and almost as hairless. Beside him was a young man with thick dark hair, curled and shiny with oil. They were talking and laughing. Eupolis had one arm round the young man's shoulders. His other hand rested lightly on his partner's thigh.

Eupolis looked up and saw me. His face changed, his mouth opened to say something . . .

I ran. I ran as I had never run before, blinded by tears, colliding with walls, pillars, people. I had no idea where I was going. I simply wanted to get out, to run and keep running until I blotted the picture from my memory.

He did not mention it next day, or indeed ever. Nor did I. For both of us, it was better to pretend that it had never happened.

Milan (54–53 BC)

8

I put on my first adult mantle, as the custom is, on the morning of my fifteenth birthday.

Let me describe myself to you, as I was then: a simple pen-portrait in the third person, to allow objectivity.

Gentle Reader, I give you Virgil as he stands on the threshold of manhood.

He is well above middle height, with the build to match: a proper yokel fresh from the country such as you can see unloading vegetables any day in Cattle-Market Square, big-boned, dark-skinned, massively gauche as a young bull. His hair is dark, thick, naturally curly. He is regular of feature, and his face, touched that day for the first time by the razor, has that vulnerable, scraped look which hints of a nature at variance with his physical appearance. His eyes confirm this. They are large, lustrous and intelligent, but wary as a deer's. They slide away from your direct gaze, embarrassed by your scrutiny, as if unwilling to allow even a semblance of intimacy. His voice, were he to speak (he does not, very often, unless addressed) would be low, with a measured slowness which suggests dullness of wit, even imbecility; yet, if you have the patience to listen, you will find what he says to the point, although derivative and pedantic.

A nice enough lad, you say to yourself. Well set-up

physically but a bit, ah . . . (you frown, seeking a euphem-
ism, not finding one) strange. Not quite right in the head.
Still, it will be interesting to see what he makes of himself
in a year or two.

And so you go your way, and soon forget me.

9

Almost immediately after my sixteenth birthday I was sent to Milan, to study rhetoric.

This was, of course, my mother's doing, although my father was not as opposed to the idea as you might think, considering the expense involved: he was not the sort of man to turn back once he had put his hand to the plough, and I had shown myself an apt and able pupil over the last four years.

For Mother, naturally, it was the *cachet* of the thing that appealed.

'Publius? He's getting on terribly well, my dear – won't you have another of those delicious stuffed dates, by the way? He sends them to me specially every month from Milan, such a considerate boy, you can't get them here, the little man who sells them buys direct from Rome . . . where was I? Oh, yes, Publius. His teacher is very proud of him, says he'll make an absolutely splendid forensic orator, and then who knows? Rome, a political career, even a magistrate's purple stripe, if they give us the franchise. I mean that man Cicero managed it, they say he's very highly thought of . . . and how is your son Sextus getting on in the laundry business?'

It was worth the money to my mother, even had I spent the time playing dice.

While I was studying in Milan, I stayed with my father's brother and his family. Uncle Quintus was not in the least like my father: twenty years of soft living and self-indulgence had destroyed any resemblance completely.

My Uncle Quintus looked and behaved like a pig.

I am by nature abstemious. I eat little, and drink less, and the sight of people stuffing themselves disgusts me. Uncle Quintus and his wife, Aunt Gemella (who was even larger than he was), dined in the proper pukkah-Roman manner: formally (and continuously) between late afternoon and bedtime. They expected me to be present, at least for part of the time. It was not an elevating experience.

To make matters worse, Uncle Quintus had all the artistic sensibilities of a brick.

He traded (very successfully) in bronze and copper ware, everything from kitchen utensils to busts. You would have thought these last might have had some spiritual effect, but although he had certain facts at his finger-ends – the weight of metal, current selling price and marketability – on other matters, such as the mythological background to a piece or the name of the original Greek sculptor, he was totally ignorant. He had, he said, slaves whose business it was to know unimportant details like that. He could not be expected to remember everything.

His other main interest, after business and food, was politics. He wholeheartedly supported Julius Caesar, who (technically, at least) had been our governor for the past four years or so. I had my first taste of what was to be an almost nightly litany the second evening after I arrived.

'You mark my words, young Publius.' My uncle chewed on a handful of grapes, spat the pips into his palm, kneaded his huge swag-belly, belched. 'Caesar's the right sort. He's the boy for us. 'S far as most Romans're concerned we paint ourselves blue up here an' rub soap in our hair. Not Caesar. Our Gaius knows us better. He's got our interests at heart.'

Not realising that he preferred to deliver a monologue, I ventured a comment: 'Cisalpine Gaul is prime recruiting ground for the legions. Of course he has our interests at heart.'

Uncle Quintus stared at me pop-eyed above his wine-cup until I squirmed with embarrassment and looked down at my plate.

'That's as may be,' he said at last. 'But he'll come up trumps before long, you mark my words. You scratch my back, I'll scratch yours. We should've had full citizenship ten years since when Crassus was censor – would've had but for these snooty upper-class bastards in the Senate. The sooner Caesar's properly on top and sorts them out the better. Eh, Lucius?'

He turned to my cousin, the third member of the family. Lucius was three years older than me, a younger version of his father and already a partner in the business. At that precise moment he was doing terrible things to a pomegranate.

'Right, Dad,' he said, spitting out the pith.

'Soon as he's settled the hash of these painted savages across the Channel it'll be the Senate's turn,' Uncle Quintus said with gloomy satisfaction. 'Him and Pompey and Crassus, they've got Rome sewn up between them. They'll have the old-boy network farting dust, you wait and see.'

'*Quintus!*' said Aunt Gemella.

'Beg pardon. my dear,' Uncle Quintus said humbly, and reached for an apple. Lucius chuckled.

'And what about you, Publius?' My aunt turned to me. 'How was your first day at school?'

'Not bad,' I said.

'Load of nonsense, if you ask me,' said my uncle. 'What your father's thinking of putting you to a trade like that I just don't know. Filthy business, the law. He'd've done better setting you up on your own farm, or asking me to show you the ropes in our trading house.'

I got up.

'I've a bit of work to do for tomorrow,' I said. 'Excuse me, please.'

'Goodnight, Publius.' My aunt kissed me. Her cheek beneath the powder felt like a pig's bladder that boys blow up and use for a balloon.

'Night-night,' said my uncle. 'Sleep tight. Don't let the bedbug buggers bite.'

I shall say no more of these evenings. Take them as read.

I studied with the rhetor Afius Latro, a pleasant enough man, but hardly inspiring: the word *harmless* springs to mind. You could see why he had decided to teach oratory rather than to practise it. Technically, he was first-rate. He had all the techniques at his fingertips – a battery of styles, tricks of language and of voice, the full range of gestures. But he had no fire in his belly, and an orator without fire is like porridge without salt. You would watch him give a model speech, and you would say to yourself, 'That simile he took from Hortensius,' or 'Now he will stop and wipe his eyes with the hem of his mantle.'

Picture a slick but second-rate conjuror. The children watch entranced, while the adults, looking over their heads, think: The cloth is up his sleeve. He passed the coin to his left hand. That piece of rope is not the one he wants us to think he is cutting. And although they cannot see the precise act of fraud being perpetrated they know it is there, and watch the show with no more than amused tolerance.

That was Latro.

A year or so later, shortly after I arrived in Rome, I went to hear Cicero speak. I am not an unduly emotional person, apart from where poetry is concerned. I think with my head, not my heart, and I have an instinctive horror of being swayed by anyone against my better judgment. But of that speech I have no detailed memories. From the moment he stood up, he had me in the palm of his hand. To listen to him was like leaping into a mountain torrent: first the icy, numbing shock that paralyses the limbs and the brain, then the roaring, hammering fury of the current that drives you where it will, contemptuous of your struggles, to drown you or cast you up according to its whim; finally the moment of release, when you lie gasping and shivering, totally drained, feeling as if half the world has been used up around you and left only dross.

I doubt if I so much as drew breath the whole time he spoke. I certainly could not tell you what rhetorical tricks he used, or which gestures he employed.

Cicero had fire in his belly. He may have had his faults as a man, but by Hermes, he was an orator!

Latro was no mountain torrent, but at least he served as a sort of cold plunge after bathing.

I have heard it said that oratory and poetry are sisters. Like sisters, they share each other's clothes and jewellery, and there is no better training for a poet, to make him think about form and structure, than a stiff dose of rhetoric. Under Eupolis I had studied the fabric of poetry, but for me it was still poetry, and so special: the clothes and the jewellery flashed and glittered and dazzled me, try as I might to look at the mechanics of their making. With Latro, there was no danger of being dazzled by the outward show. For him, oratory wore her dresses inside out, and the stitches were plain for all to see.

I learned a lot from Latro.

Despite my mother's claims, however, it was clear from the first that I was no public speaker. I have already mentioned my voice. Although I had nothing like the problems of the Greek Demosthenes, who had to fill his mouth with pebbles to overcome a stammer, things were

bad enough. I had no volume. My throat would dry easily –
I have always been prone to diseases of the throat – and any
long period would invariably end in a croak. Then, as I have
already mentioned, there was the slowness of my speech.
Although this was not of great importance in delivering a
set oration, it did not allow for a great variation in pace;
while extempore speaking was out of the question.

All in all, as a school report would say, less than satisfactory.

I was less than satisfactory in other ways, too.

10

You will have noticed that so far I have made no mention of friends, or even (save in an instance or two) acquaintances. Even my parents have gone, as a writer would say, undeveloped.

This has been deliberate. I have mentioned no friends because I had none. I barely had acquaintances, or, for that matter (God help me!) parents.

That changed in Milan.

He was from Bergamo, the son of a local dignitary, and his name was Marcus. Marcus Acilius Simplex.

It was not just the name, of course: we are cursed with such a scarcity of first names that I must already have met dozens, if not hundreds, of Marcuses. But Marcus Simplex was different. He was exactly what my brother would have been, had he lived: my dead brother not only reincarnated but brought to his full potential.

Perhaps it was guilt that drove me, this once, to overcome my shyness. Remember, I was older now. I was able to look back with a more dispassionate eye and judge between my brother and my earlier self without a child's partisanship. Perhaps I merely wished to atone, and be forgiven.

Plato says that, in the beginning, human beings were created double. They had four eyes, two noses, two mouths, four legs, four arms. Then the gods split them down the middle, as you would an apple, and the two halves of each creature went their separate ways.

They have been trying to find each other ever since.

This may be relevant, too.

Marcus was studying with me under Latro. He was a year older than I was, and already a formidable speaker. Where I still laboured to master the basics, he had flashed through them and progressed to the thorniest of the rhetorical exercises: defending or attacking a particularly subtle or complex legal argument.

I had watched him, that all-important day, deliver one such speech. *Supposing*, the rubric went, *that the law offers a woman who has been seduced the right either to have her seducer marry her or to have him condemned to death. A man seduces two women on the same night. One woman asks that he be put to death, the other that he marry her. Defend either proposal.*

Marcus chose to defend the death penalty; but he argued it, not as the woman's lawyer, but as the seducer's.

When he had finished, my ribs, and the ribs of the rest of the class, were sore with laughing. Even Latro, who had sat through the opening stages with a brow black as thunder, had been stirred to a smile or two. At the end he had clapped Marcus on the back and said that it was 'quite well argued, my boy, if a little, ah, *unorthodox.*'

When class finished for the day, I went over to Marcus to offer my congratulations.

He grinned.

'I wasn't sure I'd get away with it,' he said. 'Old Barker was about a fingernail's breadth from apoplexy. Still, it went well enough in the end.'

'It went well because it was a brilliant speech brilliantly delivered.'

He laughed.

'Yes, it was, wasn't it?' Then, changing the subject as I knew he would: 'So how's the poetry coming?'

Marcus was one of the few people who knew of my ambition. I had begun a small collection of scribbles (I cannot dignify them by the name of poetry) in the Alexandrian style. I will not reproduce any of them here; and in any case they have been torn up long ago. Truth is one thing, self-flagellation another.

'Painfully,' I said.

'Buy me a drink and I'll let you read me some. Once I'm properly anaesthetised.'

The joke, typically Marcian, covered a serious offer. Marcus was not only a fine orator in the making, but also one of the best fledgling poets I have ever known. He could have been another Cicero, or . . . a Virgil.

Could have been. Six years later, he was lying gutted along with twenty thousand other could-have-beens on the field of Pharsalus. He was twenty-three.

I hate war.

We went round to one of the taverns off the Market Square and ordered a jug of their best wine. While he drank it, I read Marcus one of my poems – it was about a young she-goat, I remember – and he tore it to shreds. Justifiably.

'Don't forget, Publius,' he said when he had finished both the wine and the criticism. 'Everything must be integrated – feeling and metre, sound and form, language and allusions. Don't waste a word, a syllable. Starve your poems, give them the slimness and delicacy of . . . of . . .' He looked up, across the street. His eyes widened. 'Jupiter Best and Greatest!' he whispered. 'Look at those tits!'

I followed his eyes. Two women on the opposite pavement were examining the trinkets in a hawker's booth – or rather, pretending to: there was a studiedness about the way they held their heads, and the half glances they threw in our direction were unmistakable in their intent.

Their trade, too, was unmistakable, from the clothes they wore. They were prostitutes. What we called 'she-wolves'.

'How about it, Publius?' Marcus's eyes were still fixed on the two girls. The taller of the two looked directly at him and smiled.

Butterflies began to flutter in my stomach.

'No, I'd better be getting back,' I said. 'Uncle Quintus and Aunt Gemella will be expecting me.'

'Rubbish, it's still early,' he said. Then he looked at me, at my face, and grinned. 'Don't tell me it's your first time?' And when I blushed and said nothing: 'Priapus, it is your first time! That settles it. Don't worry, it's my treat.'

And before I could stop him he had called them over.

Why I didn't run, I do not know. I wish now that I had.

They were older, close up, than I had thought. Not much older than us, but certainly in their early twenties. The taller of the two – the one with big breasts – was Flora. She did most of the talking. The other was Lycisca.

'You students, then?' Flora had sat down on the bench next to Marcus, her thigh pressed against his. Marcus's right hand stroked it absently while he signalled to the waiter for more wine.

'That's right,' he said. 'Students of beauty, eager to learn under your tender tutelage and worship at your altar.'

His hand snaked beneath the table, between her legs.

Flora giggled, pressed her thighs together, trapping him.

'We've got a right one here,' she said to Lycisca. Then, to Marcus: 'Poet as well, are you?'

Marcus nodded at me.

'He's the poet,' he said. 'I'm just a simple rhymester.'

Lycisca snuggled up against me, ran her fingers through my hair.

'What's your name, love?' she said. 'You've got beautiful eyes. Make me go all funny.'

Her own eyes were chips of granite, ringed with black, the lids touched with green malachite. They cut me. I shuddered, and edged away.

'Oh, come on, beautiful!' She snuggled closer. 'Don't be shy. Read us a poem. I've never been with a real poet before.'

The waiter brought the wine and another two beakers. He winked at Marcus as he set them down and turned to leave. Flora poured for all of us.

'Come on, Publius, read her one,' said Marcus. He had transferred his right arm to Flora's shoulders, and the fingers of his hand were gently stroking the top of her breast where the dress left it exposed. *Go on*, his eyes said to me. *Don't leave me to do all the work.*

I flushed, muttered something about not having anything suitable for young ladies to hear.

Flora snorted.

'Hark at him!' she said. 'Young ladies, eh?'

'Well, I think it's nice.' Lycisca's mouth was at my ear now, her sharp little teeth nibbling the lobe. 'Least he's not all grab, like some of them. Never mind, love, you don't have to if you don't want to.'

I half rose.

'Marcus, I'm sorry, but I really ought to be going.'

Lycisca pulled me back down on to the bench. Her grip was steel-strong, quick as a clutching crab's.

'Maybe we'd all better, at that,' Flora said. 'It's only round the corner.' She turned to Marcus, suddenly businesslike. 'A silver piece. Each.'

Marcus whistled.

'That's a bit steep, isn't it?' he said.

'Oh, we're good. You'll get your money's worth.'

'We'd better.' He got up, his arm still round her shoulders, reached into his purse to pay for the wine.

'In advance,' said Flora.

Marcus grinned, handed her the money and dropped a few coins on the table.

We left.

They led us to a tenement building near the slaughterhouse. On the way we passed four farm-slaves pulling at an ox which stood stock-still in the middle of the road. Its eyes were white and rolling, its muzzle slick with foam and spittle, and it was bellowing in abject terror. I knew that the ox could smell the blood, foresee the hammer. As could I.

We climbed to the second storey, up two flights of stairs that reeked of urine and human faeces. Surprisingly, the room itself was clean, but completely bare of furniture except for a bed against each of the side walls. The space between had been divided by a curtain, but it had fallen down and lay in a loose bundle on the floor.

The two women began to undress as soon as the door was closed. They ignored us completely, the movements of their hands quick, economical. Practised. I stood just inside the room, my back to the wall, shaking as if with fever. Outside the window, the bellowing of the ox became more frantic. Then came the thud of the hammer, and the bellowing ceased.

Marcus had stripped off his tunic and under-drawers. He was already erect. He winked at me, lay down on the nearest bed. Flora, naked, climbed on top of him. Her hand reached down and guided him inside her.

'Come on, love.' Lycisca was naked too, and impatient.

Her breasts were smaller than Flora's, upturning, with purple nipples. I noticed, just above her pubic hair, a small ragged scar, pale silver against the brown skin. 'What you waiting for? Get your things off.'

Flora had begun to moan softly. I glanced over, then away again. Marcus had her left breast in his mouth and was sucking on it. The leather springs of the bed began to creak. I felt the sweat break out on my forehead.

Lycisca gave a *ttsch!* of annoyance. Before I could stop her, she had reached under my tunic and pulled down my drawers. Then, somehow, we were on the bed, with me on top and Flora underneath, legs wrapped round me. Her hand caught at my penis and squeezed.

I nearly threw up.

Lycisca squirmed. I felt the rasp of her pubic hair like wire against my leg. The squeezing turned to a gentle, persistent stroking. Her mouth was against my ear.

'Come on, love,' she whispered. 'First time, is it? Never mind, let me help. Let Lycisca help. Oh, that's better. Tha-a-a-t's better, just relax, let Lycisca do it for you, that's a clever boy . . .'

This was terrible. I felt sick, completely nauseated, as if her hand was some sort of animal moving against me: cold and clammy, a toad or a huge bloated slug, rubbing its skin against mine, coating me with its slime, polluting me . . .

The creaking from the other bed became louder, more rhythmical. In spite of myself, I glanced over. Marcus had changed position. He was on top now, his mouth still fastened like a leech to Flora's breast, his buttocks pumping up and down between her thighs. Her legs were around his waist, knees high, ankles crossed. She wriggled like an eel. The moans had changed to long shuddering gasps. As I watched, she bent her head and bit him in the hollow of the neck, just where it meets the shoulder. Marcus's head came up, arched back. He cried out – a strange, wavering cry like a wounded animal's – and straightened.

At the sound I felt myself stiffen in Lycisca's hand.

'That's better, love,' she said. 'I knew you could get it up if you tried. Now just let me . . .'

'*No!*'

I pulled myself away, fell heavily off the bed, crawled towards the door. I felt the bile rise in my throat, bent over, vomited; eyes stinging with sweat, rose, pulled up my drawers; vomited again, one arm against the door-jamb. Heard, behind me, Lycisca shouting, spitting like a wild-cat: 'Bastard! Filthy bastard! Get out of here! Call yourself a man? Bastard!'

I wrenched open the door, lurched outside, half staggered, half fell down the two flights of steps to the street; saw, through the stinging tears, faces thrust themselves at me: mocking, laughing, gaping, ugly faces . . .

I remembered Eupolis. How I had felt when I saw him with the young man in the bath-house. And I remembered Titus's words, thrown at me across an empty schoolroom: 'He's a queer! An arse-bandit! Understand?'

I leaned my head against a rough-stone wall, and wept.

12

I never told Marcus why I had run, nor did he ask, being too well bred to press for an explanation in the face of my reticence. I assume he thought it was nerves, and the situation never arose again. I was careful of that, for I no longer trusted myself.

That one experience, however, was enough, and although unpleasant it was, in retrospect, invaluable. Not only did it prove to me that I did not like women, but also that if I followed my own nature I would only end up despising myself and despised by others. Far better to suppress the urge or, if that was impossible, to learn to control it. This done, if I could not be happy, at least I would keep my pride and my self-respect.

I have never regretted my decision. Although my self-imposed celibacy has not been an easy burden to bear, it has saved me a great deal of pain.

Several years after this, while I was living near Naples, the local people (who are of course Greeks) gave me the nickname Parthenias – Virgin. In part this was a reference to one of my teachers, Parthenius, but it has far greater significance. First of all, it is a pun, being a Greek translation of the family name Virginius, which differs from mine only sightly. Secondly (at least so I like to think) it reflects the public *persona* which I have been at such pains to create. I regarded it as a compliment – still regard it as such, although it is . . . no longer true (I am not speaking sexually). The name shows at once the remarkable insight of our Greek masters and the complete impossibility of matching them in subtlety of language. We Italians can strive to emulate, but never surpass.

I stayed in Milan for a year. At the end of it, my mother wrote to me saying that she and Father had decided to send me to Rome.

Rome (53–49 BC)

13

Picture a plain stool, of the kind you might find in any farm kitchen: three-legged, rickety, much-repaired, eaten away in places by woodworm. A stool that was once an honest piece of furniture made by an honest craftsman, but has seen better days. Not beautiful, but still, after its fashion, serviceable.

That is Rome; or rather, that is the Roman state.

Examine the first leg of the stool. At first glance, it seems good, solid oak: well grained, seasoned, a little rough in places but basically sound. Look closer: the wood is rotten, split by cracks. A resolute man might pick it up, wrench it from its seating and break it across his knee like a dry twig.

That is Pompey.

The second leg is smooth and well polished: no everyday wood this, but costly cedar. Hold it to your nose. Sniff. It smells of expensive oils and unguents, conjures up argosies from Ind and Arabia. A leg out of place, you think, taken perhaps from the chair of an eastern king or a fat banker's dinner-table: tolerated, in its rustic setting, because of the role it plays, not for what it is.

That is Crassus.

The third leg is like the first, but more highly polished: flashier, less honest-seeming. Pick up the stool, examine the wood of this third leg. Scrape, with your fingernail, the paint from its surface. The third leg is not wood at all, but iron. An iron peg, jammed into the fabric of the Roman state.

That is Caesar.

Set the stool down. It stands – not straight (the legs are of unequal length) but well enough for practical purposes. Now pick it up again. Take a firm grip on it, and wrench from it its second leg.

That was Carrhae.

The news reached us in early summer. Crassus, eager to show himself the military equal of Pompey and Caesar, had invaded Persia with thirty-six thousand men. In May, the Persians met him at Carrhae and smashed his army. Sixteen thousand Romans and Italians slaughtered, ten thousand taken prisoner, seven sacred Eagles lost with the legions whose souls they housed. Crassus died later, murdered as he was conducting peace negotiations with the Persian general, his head and hands hacked off and sent as presents to the Persian king.

It was Rome's worst military disaster since Cannae.

How does the stool stand now?

14

The first thing I saw when I entered Rome was a corpse.

It lay sprawled on the pavement's edge, fifty yards inside the Flaminian Gate; not a man's body, but a woman's. Her throat had been cut, and she had been raped.

With hindsight, I can see that I was being given an omen. The gods may play cruel tricks, but in this, at least, they are merciful: they grant it to very few of us to foretell the future. To me she was only a corpse; but that was enough.

I had left the slaves to follow on more slowly with what little baggage I had with me. Carts and carriages are not allowed within the walls between sunrise and sunset, but there are always enough loungers around the gate willing to act as guides. The single attendant I had taken with me for appearance's sake looked askance at the woman's body, and made the sign against the evil eye. My guide, on the other hand, paid it no attention, stepping over the spread limbs as if they were branches cluttering his path.

'That's all right, sir,' he said when I asked him about it. 'We're early yet. They'll've cleaned her up in an hour or so.'

'But who was she?'

It was a stupid question, and he treated it as such: a long, slow stare, followed by a discreet expectoration into the gutter.

'Some slut caught in the rioting,' he said at last. 'Not a decent woman. Decent women don't go out at nights. Don't bother your head about her, she'll be seen to. The Esquiline you said you were bound for, wasn't it, sir?'

'What riots?' My brain must still have been numb with the shock.

The guide stopped, stared at me.

'Stranger, are you, sir?' he said. 'I mean, *real* stranger, like? Been going on for years, they have, off and on.' He spat again, continued walking. 'Mostly on. 'S these bastards in the Senate, brains in their arses, most of them, pardon my language. Want to cut back the corn dole and make us pay good money for the privilege of starving. We're not having that, we're freeborn citizens, same as them. Clodius, now, he's the lad, real gentleman is Clodius. Used to be one of the nobs but he couldn't stand their stink, came over to us instead. He keeps them in order.' He grinned like an old boot, leather face creasing. 'An' if a few bellies get slashed an' one or two heads broken, well, that's life, innit?' He nodded ahead of us. 'Market Square coming up, sir. You seen it before?'

'No, this is my first time in Rome.'

He expanded, nostrils widening, savouring the smell of a massive tip.

'First time, eh?' he said. 'Show you around, sir, 's my pleasure. Senate-house-on-the-left-there-Popular-'Sembly-building-thass-Speakers'-Platform-on-your-right-what-we-call-the-Beaks . . .'

'Thank you,' I said quickly. 'Thank you, but I'd sooner be left to myself.'

He snorted, dug a finger into his left nostril, pulled it out and inspected the result.

'Just tryin' to be helpful, sir. We turn left here. Up the Sacred Way. Mind your nice shoes in that pool of horse-piss.'

Rome stinks.

It stinks of rank Tiber mud thick with the decaying offal and human faeces carried into it by the Great Drain. It stinks of the dung and the refuse in the streets, and of the urine that stains its graffiti-scarred walls. It stinks of half a million sweating bodies crowded into too little space, squeezed into gimcrack tenement buildings that burn like torches at the first spark or crumble like punk-wood when the weight of humanity becomes too much for them. Its stench hangs above it like a miasma.

Rome is the perfect setting for Romans. I hate it.

I was staying with the family of Quintus Valerius Proculus, who did not stink.

Proculus was no relation, although I came to regard him as a second (or do I mean first?) father. He was a guest-friend of my mother's family – the Magii, as I think I mentioned, were well connected, despite my grandfather's trade – and very comfortably off, with a house on the slopes of the Esquiline not far from what were to become the Gardens of Maecenas . . .

Yes. The same house I now own, although Proculus had a son to follow him. The gods do play these nasty tricks, sometimes, especially gods in human guise. I will tell you how I came to own the house later, in its place.

Proculus was a middle-aged banker: solid, respectable, well known in the Market Square for both shrewdness and honesty – a remarkable combination in those times, or, I suspect, in any other. He was tall, distinguished, with iron-grey hair, pillar-straight and ice-eyed, quiet and precise in speech and dignified in bearing. On some men, respectability sits uneasily, like a borrowed cloak; others it wraps tight as a winding-sheet. Proculus wore it as simply and elegantly as he wore his own mantle.

His wife's name was Cornelia – not one of *the* Cornelii, but from a good branch of the family none the less: her father was of senatorial rank. More important, she was one of the most civilised, cultured women it has ever been my privilege to know; that, too, was a rare combination of qualities. She and Proculus had two children: a beautiful boy of eighteen months – Lucius – and a girl of fifteen . . .

I have shifted, it seems, from history to encomium. So be it. If I am to deliver a eulogy, then by all means let it be of Valeria Procula.

Take a handful of sparkling snow from the Riphaean heights: that is her skin. Take the blue-black sheen from a raven's wing: that is her hair; the softest of rose petals: the blush of her cheek; the wheeling Pleiads: her eyes . . .

I know. I know. It is poor, jobbing stuff. The stuff you expect from a hack poet who sells his rhymes at a penny a line to illiterates who want to impress their girl- or boyfriends. Not from me. Not from Virgil. But although poetry has been my life I have never been able to put into words what I felt for Valeria Procula.

I loved her. I, who have never physically loved a woman, who am incapable of physically loving a woman, I loved her.

Give me a moment. Give me a moment, please, of your charity. Give me a moment for memory.

15

I knew she was a poet almost as soon as I met her. No, I am not talking about physical signs: a frenzied rolling of the eye indicating divine possession; a tendency to walk into things while one's mind is elsewhere. These are burlesques, tricks of cheap Greek novelists. Nor do I mean anything more prosaic, such as ink-stains or a callus on the right middle finger. I cannot tell you *how* I knew her for a kindred spirit, but I did; and she recognised me just as quickly.

I was glad. It made our friendship inevitable.

We spent a lot of time together, mostly in the courtyard-garden at the back of the house. At first her parents were a little dubious of my intentions. Valeria was, as I have said, beautiful and moreover engaged to the son of a wealthy senator, and Proculus, although (because?) he was the most open-minded and civilised of men, had a sound knowledge of human nature. As time passed, however, they accepted our relationship without comment, understanding the harmlessness of it, and of myself. Perhaps there is a telepathy about those things, I do not know; whatever the reason, I was grateful for their tolerance, even if my gratitude was tinged a little with regret.

Picture the scene, then.

It is late summer. We are sitting in the colonnade which surrounds the garden. In front of us is a small fishpond with a marble fountain brought from Athens. On the fountain are two cupids riding on the back of a dolphin, its snout raised, spouting water which splashes into the pool. Overhanging the pool, a huge bush of rosemary, its scent filling the garden. A peacock struts through the rose-bed, trailing a tail like a tapestry, shimmering blue, green and gold. Valeria is sitting in a high-backed chair of cedar wood, like a throne, I on a low stool in front of her. She is wearing white. A sky-blue band around her forehead holds in her dark curls, two of which have escaped and lie soft against the peach-bloom of her cheek.

We have been reading Sappho.

She reads well. Her voice is light, the words feathers blown in the breeze, the Greek sweet on her tongue. I am lost in it, in the drowsy hum of the bees, and when the poem ends it has blended with the sunshine and the scent of the rosemary and pervades the garden like a golden mist.

She sets down the book.

'You read something now, Publius,' she says.

My mind is full of Sappho, but to read her, after Valeria, would be unseemly, like a frog contending with a nightingale. I compromise, change to Latin, to Catullus, most beautiful of our poets. Hesitate, begin:

> He seems to me the equal of a god—
> To surpass the gods, if it be right to say so—
> Who, sitting opposite you, watches and watches,
> Listens and listens to you
> Laughing sweetly.
> And I, poor wretch, am stripped of all my senses.
> For once I see you, Lesbia, I am nothing:
> A slow tongue, limbs burning with thin fire,
> Ears deafened by their own ringing, eyes wrapped in
>   darkness.

Valeria sits absolutely still, her face shut, unreadable. I have offended her. I wonder how I could have been so stupid, so insensitive, as to speak love-words I did not mean in a language that must convince by its very familiarity. Then, suddenly, she grins – a most unpoetic grin – and ruffles my hair.

'"Too much free time, my Publius,"' she says, capping my poem with its ending, substituting my own name for the poet's. '"That's your trouble. Idleness has been the ruin of you."'

I laugh, and the mood is broken. It is useless to contend with Valeria. The peacock spreads his tail and defecates on the marble slabs.

16

Perhaps I should introduce you at this point to another member of the Valerius family – or rather a prospective member – since he will appear again in my story: Valeria's fiancé, Marcus Cotta.

I did not much like Cotta. He resembled one of those plaster figurines that hucksters turn out from moulds by the thousand and sell as souvenirs outside the theatre or during the Games: the face is always the same, but the name inscribed on the base changes to fit whatever actor or charioteer or gladiator happens to be popular at the time. You can see any number of Cottas lounging about the Market Square of an evening, or exercising their thoroughbreds in Mars Field: smooth, dandyish young men with polished faces and polished voices, smelling of hair-oil, barber's powder and money. Cotta's only individuality – and his one redeeming feature, in my eyes – was his devotion to Valeria; and for that I could have forgiven him anything.

He didn't like me, either.

Oh, it was not a matter of jealousy; or rather, not of sexual jealousy. Cotta seemed to share Proculus's sixth sense regarding my harmlessness. It produced in him not an easy tolerance but a desire to dominate; I almost wrote, a desire to bully, but that is too strong a word: Cotta was no worse (and no better) than the average specimen of his class, which meant that he was sound enough judged by the standards of that class's slightly warped morality. His dislike of me was based on something less tangible than sexual jealousy. What he resented was that Valeria and I shared something which he could not comprehend, and yet which he realised was of vast importance: a common soul.

That sounds pretentious, I know, but I will let it stand, because it is the truth. How else can I put it? To say we were friends is too mild, and yet to use the phrase 'more than friends' is to beg the question; worse, to suggest a coy sexuality that was completely lacking on both sides. Nor can I say, 'We were like brother and sister.' That relationship is used too often, and too tritely, as a synonym for closeness: family ties are no guarantee of mutual sympathy, as I know to my cost. I could conjure with the name of Plato, in one of its forms; could say, for example, that 'our relationship partook of Plato's ideal', or that 'I loved her platonically.' Such an expression might convey my meaning admirably to a philosopher, but in everyday language it is far too cold – and far too negative – to serve my purpose.

You see the problem? Ignore, then, the pretentiousness of the phrase, and accept it in the spirit in which it is meant.

Valeria and I shared a common soul.

I offered you, in the preceding chapter, a double vignette, or diptych – idealised, perhaps, in the style of such things, but capturing the essence of my feelings for her. Let me give you another, now: a triptych this time, in stronger colours, of myself, Valeria and Cotta.

Again, it is summer; and again, we are in the garden behind the house. Climbing roses blaze red against the honey-dark stone of the columns. Cotta lies sprawled on the grass, his purple-edged tunic slightly stained with green, a jug of Proculus's best wine at his elbow. Valeria and I sit on chairs beneath the colonnade.

Cotta is in the worst of humours, for the worst of reasons.

He has just learned that a tenement block which he owns caught fire the previous night. Tenants on the first floor, above the shops, were evacuated safely. The rest burned.

'We got the bastard who caused it,' he is saying. 'He lit a brazier, would you believe – a bloody *brazier*, in this weather!'

Valeria is very still, her eyes wide and lustreless. I can see what she sees in her mind's eye: flames, livid-yellow in the darkness, gorging themselves on rotten, tinder-dry planking; hear with her the screams, smell the greasy black smoke, heavy with the sick-sweet stench of roasting flesh.

'How many?' she says.

Cotta looks up.

'How many what?'

'How many people died?'

He frowns.

'How should I know? These places are rabbit-warrens. Fifty . . . a hundred, maybe. It happened at night, so they'd be asleep.'

Valeria's face is drained of colour. I reach over, touch her hand. Her fingers clasp mine, briefly.

'It'll cost me millions,' Cotta is saying. 'It's not just the loss of the building. There's the rents. And you can't get good contractors now for love nor money. They charge you through the nose, and the work's not worth a damn.'

'Didn't anyone try to save them?' I am surprised to see that my hands are trembling.

'Couldn't get near the place.' Cotta scowls. 'It went up like a torch. And the nearest water supply was two streets away. Why the hell doesn't someone do something about the city's water?'

'Or about the city's buildings,' I say gently.

'What, the tenements?' He looks genuinely surprised. 'They're okay. And they're all the mob deserve. You want every sewer-rat in Rome to have his own town-house?

Marble floors, paintings on the walls, the way they live? The place'd be a slum inside a month.'

'No.' I sigh. 'I don't expect that. Only that the blocks be well built and well maintained, instead of the death-traps we have now.'

'Oh, sure! And where's the money going to come from?'

'From the rents, of course,' Valeria says. She still looks pale, but now it is with anger. 'How much did you charge a year for a room in your tenement, Marcus? One thousand? Two?'

'It was no more than the going rate.' Cotta sounds hurt. More, now he is faced with opposition from Valeria, he is definitely on the defensive. 'And senatorials have to make money somehow. We can't dirty our hands with trade like you narrow-stripers.'

I do not think he means it as an insult. For him it is a statement of fact, and it does not occur to him that we might take it otherwise. Valeria does not reply and, encouraged, Cotta presses on.

'Besides, the rents went to a good use.' He gestures with his wine-cup at the ring Valeria is wearing beside her iron betrothal ring. It is Alexandrian, inlaid with a love goddess and attendant cupids. 'They paid for that bit of jewellery I bought you on your birthday, for a start.'

'We don't mean you shouldn't make a profit, Marcus.' I keep my voice soft; I do not want a quarrel, for Valeria's sake. 'Only that you could've ploughed some of the money back in repairs. After all' – I search for words that he will understand – 'it's sound business sense to protect an investment, isn't it?'

'Or just think of it as conscience-money.' Valeria, it seems, doesn't particularly care whether they quarrel or not. I have never seen her so angry.

Cotta looks from one of us to the other. His expression is puzzled, and I realise that, quite genuinely, he cannot see what all the fuss is about. Suddenly I feel more sorry for him than angry. He is like a child who has been smacked for doing something he did not know was wrong. I glance at Valeria. She smiles, nods slightly; and says, 'I hear you've bought a new stallion, Marcus. Tell us about it.'

He does, at length, and the unnecessary quarrel is avoided. I touch Valeria's left arm in gratitude; and notice that, save for Cotta's betrothal ring, her hand is now bare of jewellery. The Alexandrian ring has gone, and I never see her wear it again.

I never . . .

Never again.

Close the picture, Virgil. Close it quickly!

Never again.

Never.

I have done with pictures of Valeria. They bring too much grief.

17

The rioting grew worse that autumn. Up on the Esquiline, we were above it for the most part, but the valley below, where the poorer classes lived, seethed like maggotty cheese. Elections were delayed for the second time in two years. Armed gangs – supporters of the aristocrat Milo, who was one of the candidates, and of the demagogue Clodius – roamed the streets and turned the city into a battleground. You did not go out at nights, if you valued your life, and in the morning it was not uncommon to see fresh blood glistening on the pavements or a huddle of what seemed like rags on a street corner. I found it best, when walking to and from the law courts in the Market Square, to close my eyes and ears to the world around me. I felt like a sane man walking through a city of madmen.

More and more, Proculus's house became for me an island of sanity, and I hurried back there as quickly as I could after classes. We dined late, as a rule – Proculus's business often occupied him well into the evening – and there was usually company. I enjoyed these dinners, if only because they contrasted so strongly with my Uncle Quintus's. I enjoyed their simplicity, their subordination of the act of eating and drinking to conversation. They were, in all senses of the word, civilised.

Also, it was through them that I made my first important contact as a budding poet.

It was a fine September evening. I was sitting in my room reading, taking advantage of the last of the sunlight, when Valeria put her head round the open door.

'So that's where you've got to,' she said.

I grinned and set the book down.

'Where else would I be?' I said. 'Some of us are here to study, after all. We can't all be rich dilettantes like you.'

She put out her tongue at me, walked over to the desk, picked up the book and examined its label.

'The *Phainomena*,' she sniffed. 'How boring.'

'I find it fascinating,' I said. 'But then women don't have the brains for scientific philosophy.'

'Prig,' she said. 'Anyway, I've read it in the original. This is a translation, and not a very good one at that.'

'It was all I could get! Anyway it doesn't matter much whether . . .'

She laughed, dropped the roll on to the desk.

'I wish you could see yourself,' she said. 'You've gone as red as a slice of sausage. Now put on your best mantle and come downstairs. It's dinnertime and I was sent to tell you.'

'Already? And my *best* mantle?'

'Father came home early and brought a guest with him.'

'Who?' I recovered Aratus, rolled him up and stuffed him into his case. 'Pompey himself? With Caesar to carry his slippers?'

She paused at the door.

'No, not quite,' she said. 'But put the mantle on anyway. Then at least he won't throw nuts at you in mistake for the performing bear.'

The first course had been served when I entered the dining-room. There was no sign of Valeria or her mother.

Not a family dinner, then, nor a literary or philosophical evening. Politics. I winced inwardly.

On the middle couch, in the place of honour, lay a man in his early twenties with sharp-cut features and an aristocratic nose. He looked up at me as I came in: a quick, assessing glance.

'Ah, Publius.' Proculus gestured towards the empty couch to the young man's left. 'So Valeria managed to roust you out. Pollio, this is the guest-friend from the north I mentioned, Vergilius Maro.'

'Asinius Pollio.' The young man leaned over and shook my hand as I lay down on the third couch. 'Pleased to meet you.'

My response of pleased surprise was genuine. I had heard of Pollio, of course, and I was glad Valeria had told me to put on my best mantle. He was the best of the up-and-coming young men at Rome: an all-rounder such as I knew I could never be and so regarded with awed admiration. Pollio had been a friend of Catullus, wrote excellent poetry and tragedy, composed orations in a pure Attic style and was thinking of trying his hand at history. He was also one of Caesar's most promising protégés, already earmarked for the magistrate's purple-edged mantle and the general's red cloak. All in all, a frighteningly accomplished character.

'We were just talking about the riots, Publius.' Proculus unshelled a quail's egg, dipped it in salt. 'I was asking Pollio here why Pompey doesn't do something.'

Pollio frowned.

'That's a job for the consuls, surely,' he said. 'Pompey has no power in Rome. He can't even enter the city so long as he has governor status.'

'It couldn't be that he simply wants things to fall apart completely, I suppose?'

Pollio paused in the act of reaching for an olive.

'Now why should he want that?' he asked.

'To force the Senate to appoint him dictator. Why else?'

'He'd be a fool to do any such thing.' That came out flat. 'To accept the dictatorship would be playing into the Senate's hands. It would set him on a collision course with Caesar and we'd have civil war within a month.'

'You think that's what the Senate want, sir?' I said. 'Another civil war?'

'It's not what they want, it's what they'll get, only they're too blind to see it. They've been trying to drive a wedge between Caesar and Pompey for years, and now Crassus is gone and Julia dead it looks like they're finally succeeding.'

Julia was Pompey's wife and Caesar's sister. She had died the year before, of complications after a miscarriage.

'Would that be such a bad thing?' Proculus smiled. 'Pompey is at least open to reason. And he's worked wonders these last few years stabilising the corn supply. Unlike your Caesar he does now seem to be aware of his responsibilities.'

Pollio laughed.

'I'm sorry, Proculus,' he said. 'You're talking like a senator, and I'm afraid the Senate keeps their collective brain in their collective rectum. Why should Pompey trust the Senate?' He held up his hands, fingers spread. 'First of all they snub Pompey, refusing to ratify his arrangements for the eastern provinces and the soldiers' land grants, both perfectly reasonable requests. Then they repeat the mistake with Caesar. They can't bar him from the consulship so they pass a dubious law giving him the forests and cattle-fords to govern after his term of office. Finally, they throw up their hands in horrified surprise when the two injured parties join forces. Now wouldn't you say that was just a little short-sighted?'

'All that's immaterial.' Proculus frowned. 'Both Pompey

and Caesar are subordinate to the laws of the state. They cannot be allowed to act out of self-interest.'

'And when those laws are themselves founded on self-interest, what then? Isn't it better to set them aside and do what we know to be right?'

Proculus set down his wine-cup with such force that the wine slopped on to the table and spread out over the polished wood.

'*No!*' he snapped. 'It is *not* better! The end does not justify the means. Oh, I'm not denying the Senate were partly to blame for the whole affair. But to get Caesar his Gallic provinces and Pompey land for his troops has cost us seven years of riots and bloodshed.'

'That was Clodius, not Caesar.'

'Clodius is Caesar's creature!'

'If the Senate hadn't been so pig-headed, my dear Proculus, Caesar wouldn't have needed to bypass them and use Clodius to push his legislation through the Popular Assembly.' Pollio selected another olive. 'And as a People's Magistrate Clodius has a perfect legal right to block any senatorial resolution that seems to him . . . misguided.'

'You mean that seems to Caesar . . . misguided.' Proculus beckoned the major-domo over, indicated the spilt wine. 'Mop that up, would you? And serve the main course.'

Pollio grinned.

'I suppose, then,' he said mischievously, 'you draw a distinction between Clodius and Milo?'

Proculus stiffened. I knew that he had mixed feelings about Annius Milo. Milo was a renegade aristocrat, a lover of violence for its own sake. Five years before, Pompey, with the Senate's blessing, had helped him form a gang to rival Clodius's. A pitched battle between the gangs had made a shambles of the Market Square and choked the Great Drain with corpses. Clodius's power had been severely shaken, if not completely broken. To many senators, including Proculus's beloved Cicero, Milo was a hero, the saviour of the state.

'The situation called for strong measures,' he said. 'I don't condone it, but it was necessary.'

Pollio pounced, laughing.

'So, after all, you *do* believe that the end justifies the means?' he said.

Proculus was saved from answering by the arrival of the main course, braised pork in an almond parsley sauce, with side dishes of leeks, cabbage and mushrooms. We ate for a while in silence.

Finally, Pollio dipped his fingers in the fingerbowl, dried them on his napkin and turned to face me.

'Proculus tells me you're a poet,' he said.

I blushed, my eyes on my plate.

'Nothing to be ashamed of. What do you write?'

'This and that. Epigrams, mostly. A little elegy.'

'Who's your favourite author?'

'Callimachus.'

He nodded approvingly.

'You couldn't do better. Latin authors?'

'Catullus and Calvus.'

'Not Cicero?' His eyes twinkled, and he cast a sidelong glance at Proculus.

'Not for poetry, no,' I said.

Pollio drew himself up, still looking slyly at Proculus, and intoned through his nose:

> O happy fate
> For the Roman state
> Born in my great
> Consulate.

I laughed. Proculus looked sour.

'That's hardly fair, Pollio,' he said. 'Cicero's written much better stuff than that.'

'But nothing so true to his own soul.' Pollio grinned again.

Proculus's sourness vanished, and he laughed.

'You're determined to bait me, aren't you, you young hound? Well, we all have our faults. Even you.'

Pollio leaned back to allow the slaves to remove the dirty dishes and replace them with bowls of fruit and nuts.

'For Cicero thwarting poor Catiline was the high point of the world's history,' he said. 'He's been dining out on it ever since.'

'Cicero is a great man.' Proculus selected a pear, began to peel it. 'Possibly one of the greatest Rome has ever produced.'

'So he keeps telling us. Great he may be, but he's a crashing bore all the same. And the quintessence of senatorial myopia.'

'Oh, come now!' Proculus laid down the knife. 'He's done more than any man alive to keep the state together these past ten years. If he's failed it's not his fault.'

'Then whose fault is it?' Pollio said. 'His so-called Good Men's Consensus was only an attempt to shore up the old, rotten forms of senatorial government, he put Pompey off by telling him in public and at great length how lucky he was to have Cicero as a friend and when Caesar offered him a place in the real government he turned it down flat. The man's purblind self-love never ceases to amaze me.'

'At least he's honest,' Proculus snapped. 'Even Caesar recognises that. It's why he's been at such pains to have him on his side. He needs Cicero's integrity to give his own underhand dealings a spurious respectability.'

'Rome needs strength before she needs respectability. Otherwise she'll go on wallowing like a ship stripped of its oars.'

'And you think Caesar is Plato's ideal pilot?' Proculus came as close as he ever could to a sneer. 'A fine pilot! Up to his ears in debt, private life a disgrace and two-faced as Janus!'

'Oh, he's no paragon.' Pollio smiled. 'He's out for himself all the way. But he's the best thing that could happen to Rome. They need each other, and if Caesar goes down then Rome goes down with him. Remember that.'

Proculus, realising perhaps that the conversation had strayed into areas too dangerous even perhaps for a dinner with friends, changed the subject at this point, and we discussed more abstract matters. When Pollio rose to go shortly afterwards, he paused at the door and turned back to me.

'Incidentally, Virgil,' he said. 'You mentioned Calvus. Call on me soon, and I'll introduce you. We poets must stick together.'

And so I met my first patron.

18

I do not want to tell the next part of my story.

I was in my room, reading over a speech of Hortensius, when Proculus came in without knocking. His face . . .

No, Virgil. Begin again. Tell it from the beginning.

It was the day after the end of the Winter Festival. Cotta's mother, Aemilia Rufina, had invited Valeria and her mother to a women's dinner. Cornelia had hesitated, as well she might: as I have said, people, especially women, did not go out much in the evenings for fear of the riots. Valeria, however, was insistent.

'Don't be ridiculous, Mother!' she said. 'We're practically neighbours! It's not as if we were taking a stroll through the Subura with no one but Publius to protect us.' And she grinned at me.

Cornelia refused to smile.

'Valeria,' she said, 'I do wish you'd take things more seriously, consider the dangers a little more.'

'But it's only a few hundred yards.' Valeria sat down on the arm of her mother's chair. Her voice was coaxing. 'And we'll have Cassio and Geta to protect us.' Cassio and his brother Geta were two of Proculus's slaves, big and strong as oxen, and totally devoted to the family.

Cornelia looked across at Proculus.

'What do you think, dear?' she said.

95 •

But Proculus was hardly listening. He was immersed in a letter he had just received from his agent in Damascus; evidently bad news, from his down-turned mouth. He raised his head momentarily.

'What?' he said. 'Oh, whatever you think best.' He stood up. 'Excuse me, I must answer this right away.'

And he disappeared in the direction of his study.

Valeria returned to the attack.

'Don't be such a stick-in-the-mud, Mother!' she said. 'We didn't go out at all over the Festival. Besides, you told me you wanted to show off your new brooch.'

This was clever. The brooch was a cameo in the latest style, with Cornelia's own profile between two leaping dolphins. Valeria and I had clubbed together to commission it as a Winter Festival present, and Cornelia had been delighted with it.

'Publius, what do you think?' Cornelia, almost beaten, fell back on her last line of defence. 'Should we go or not?'

'Oh, don't ask Publius!' Valeria laughed. 'He's bound to say no. He's an even bigger spoilsport than you are.'

I held up my hands, palm outwards.

'Don't involve me in your family squabbles,' I said. 'I've been mauled before, thank you. Besides, I've got a speech to read over for tomorrow and I don't have the time.'

Cornelia sighed.

'Valeria, you ought to be spanked,' she said. 'Very well, you can have your way. But we mustn't stay too late.'

Valeria hugged her, winking at me over her mother's shoulder.

I was busy all that afternoon and evening, after several days' enforced inactivity. Everything, of course, closes down during the Winter Festival, and then there is the inevitable domestic upheaval to contend with. I am at heart a traditionalist, and I suppose even slaves must have their holiday; but it does make things awkward when one has work to do.

It must have been about midnight, certainly long after I usually went to bed, because my eyes were hurting with the strain of several hours' reading by lamplight. I had been aware of noises downstairs – the bang of the front door, the low sound of voices – but I had paid them little attention, assuming that it was only Valeria and her mother returning. Then the door of my room opened and Proculus came in, carrying a lamp. His face was stiff and lifeless as a death-mask.

'Marcus Cotta is downstairs, Publius,' he said. 'He has some bad news. Cornelia and Valeria are . . .'

That was as far as he got. He gave a choking cough, turned and reeled from the room like a drunken man. The lamp fell from his hands, shattering on the inlaid wooden floor of the corridor outside. By the time I had dealt with the pool of burning oil, he had gone. I heard his study door slam.

Cotta was slumped on a stool in the living-room, his head in his hands. He looked up as I came in, his eyes empty.

'They're dead,' he said, without preamble. 'Murdered. Raped and murdered. Both of them.'

The room swam. I gripped the table and held it until the darkness had cleared from my eyes and the ringing from my ears. Then I sat down on a chair facing him.

'What happened?'

Cotta's round, boyish face (he was only a year older than me) was pale and drawn, devoid of expression.

'They left early,' he said. 'Cornelia wanted to get back. I offered to go with them, or send a few extra slaves, but she wouldn't hear of it. They'd be all right, she said, with Cassio and Geta and the two litter-bearers.'

He drew a deep breath. I signalled to one of the domestic slaves who were hovering just outside the living-room door to bring wine.

'Anyway,' Cotta went on, 'off they went and we thought no more about it. Some time later we heard someone banging on the street door. The porter opened up and found your Cassio slumped on the step with his guts hanging out.' He grinned suddenly, a twist of the mouth that had no humour in it. 'He's dead too, now, by the way. And Geta. They made a clean sweep.'

The slave came with the wine. He stood wide-eyed as I took the cup from him and held it out to Cotta. He ignored it, and me. I doubt if he even saw it.

'It was a gang of young roughs, so Cassio said. Not Clodius's. Well dressed, better class. Milo's, probably, out for a bit of fun.' Cotta closed his eyes, swayed. 'Pissed-drunk. Carried swords, not daggers. They went straight in, did for Geta then turned on Cassio. Left him for dead while they . . . were busy with the women.' He stretched his head back, clenched his teeth and spoke through them. 'The litter-bearers ran, of course. Couldn't see the cowardly bastards for dust.'

'Who was it? Did Cassio recognise any of them?' If the attackers had been upper-class young bloods, this was more than possible.

Cotta shook his head.

'No one he knew. Except' – his hand sketched a line on his cheek – 'the leader had a mark there. A scar. Maybe a birthmark.'

'Good family. Scar on his cheek. It should be easy enough to find him eventually.'

Cotta's eyes snapped open. He glared at me.

'Use your brains, Publius!' he said savagely. 'The bastard's halfway to Ostia by now! And if they do catch him, what'll he get? *Exile?*' He spat the word.

'For rape and murder? More than that, surely,' I said.

'You haven't been listening.' Cotta's voice was bitter. 'He's one of Milo's. They're the Senate's darlings. They're everyone's fucking darlings, so long as they keep the city mob down. You think they'll hand him over to the public executioner like he was some tuppeny-ha'penny villain?'

'For murdering and raping a knight's wife and daughter, yes, of course I think so.'

'Oh, you've got a lot to learn. You've got a hell of a lot to learn, Publius.' Cotta gave a wolf's grin. 'If we pukkah-Romans die before our time it's either because of war or politics. Nothing else even comes close.'

'Where are they now? Cornelia and . . . Valeria?'

'At home. We took them home. Go for them if you like.' He glanced towards the study door. 'But I'd go alone, if I were you.'

'What about you? Aren't you coming?'

'Oh, no.' He got up, his eyes glinting like a cat's in the lamplight. 'Oh, no. Not me, Publius. I've got business elsewhere. I've got things to do.'

When he had gone, I knocked gently on the door of the study; but there was no answer, and the door was locked. I set out for Cotta's house, taking half a dozen slaves with me, and two litters for the bodies.

Early next morning a young nobleman, Titus Lutatius Albinus, was found huddled against the wall of a brothel in an alley off the Sacred Way. He had a small strawberry birthmark on his right cheek, and his throat had been cut. Underneath the body lay Cornelia's cameo brooch.

19

We burned them four days later.

Proculus was in no fit state to make any of the necessary arrangements. I contacted his brother Sextus, who lived nearby, and he and his wife took charge of things quietly and with great efficiency. Proculus himself, with the baby Lucius and his nurse, were taken off to the country until the day of the funeral. I was invited, too, but I felt that it was better to stay where I was, and not burden them in their grief with the entertainment of a stranger. I put on mourning, and haunted the empty house like a ghost. If there had been any real spirits there, I would have welcomed them, if only to see her, hear her voice one last time. But there were none, and the place felt cold and hollow and hard as an old bone left for the wind to blow through.

They were burned on the same pyre. Proculus was present, of course, but he spoke to no one – his brother had delivered the funeral speech – and stood with his head wrapped in his mantle. When he stepped forwards with the torch as next of kin and turned from the dead towards me, his face was skull-like, eyes and cheeks sunken in, skin hanging in dull grey folds. His brother kept by his side throughout, guiding him unobtrusively with gentle touches as if he were manipulating a puppet, and led him to a waiting carriage as soon as it was done.

I watched the flames until they died. Not even the acrid smoke whipped up by the biting west wind could leach any more tears from my eyes. All I had had been shed long since, and there were no more to give her.

20

The day after the funeral, Cotta was charged with the murder of Lutatius Albinus.

I think, perhaps, under different circumstances the affair would have been hushed up, in the best interests of all concerned. After all, the evidence linking Albinus with the deaths was overwhelming: both the description given by Cassio before he died and the presence of the brooch pointed to him unmistakably. Also against him was his character – he was, as Cotta had guessed, a noted follower of Milo and frequently involved in brawls and running fights with Clodius's thugs. Furthermore, he lived on the Esquiline, only a hundred yards from where the incident had taken place.

That it was not hushed up was due to Albinus's father. Blind to his son's faults, he refused to accept that the young man would involve himself in rape and murder. Street-fighting, yes: after all, if the consuls were too weak, or too irresponsible, to keep the peace then the better elements must take it upon themselves to do so. But not rape. And not murder. The boy came from good stock. There must be some mistake, he must have been mistaken for someone else, his killer must be punished and the family honour vindicated . . . and so on. Although his senatorial friends tactfully tried to dissuade him from pressing the case, he was insistent that prosecution should go ahead.

There was no question, of course, of Cotta's being refused bail. He was a senator's son, and as such a subscriber to the unwritten code of *noblesse oblige*. Together with everyone else I assumed that, in accordance with the usual practice of someone threatened with a prosecution against which he can offer no defence, he would take the opportunity to slip quietly away from Rome and allow the case to go by default, thus saving time, money and embarrassment for all concerned. He did not. He chose to remain in the city and stand trial. But I was even more surprised when, returning home after my day at the courts several days after his arraignment, I found him waiting to talk with me.

He was sitting in Cornelia's chair, toying with a cup of wine which the slave had brought him. He got up when I came in. My surprise must have shown in my face, because he grinned.

'Yes, it's me, Publius,' he said. 'Not off to Africa yet awhile, as you can see.'

'How are you, Marcus?'

'Reasonably fit and blooming.' He frowned into his wine-cup. 'How's Proculus?'

'Still taking it hard.' I sat down on the stool. 'His brother's looking after him for a few weeks yet. And of course there's the baby to consider.'

The slave came in to take charge of my mantle, and I told him to bring me a cup of water and some more wine for Cotta.

'No, no more for me, thanks.' Cotta set the cup down on the table. 'I won't stay long. I only came to ask a favour.'

'What sort of favour?'

Cotta looked up. His face was grave, but his eyes twinkled.

'I want you to defend me in this murder trial,' he said. 'I want you to be my lawyer.'

I believe I must have gaped like a fool, because he laughed.

'I'm serious, Publius,' he said. 'Oh, only as seconder, of course. My father's got Caesennius Philo to lead.'

'You're out of your mind!' The slave re-entered, and I waved him away. 'I've never spoken before a jury in my life, let alone as defending counsel in a murder trial!'

'Now's as good a time as any to start, then,' he said. 'And it'll do you no harm as far as your career's concerned, I can promise you that.'

'Whose idea was this, for heaven's sake?'

Cotta shrugged.

'Mine, I suppose,' he said. 'But I've cleared it with my father, so don't worry, the appointment's official.'

'But why me? I mean, there are dozens of far more experienced speakers around. And Philo's a top-ranker. What's he going to think about having me for a junior?'

'Publius, you underestimate yourself.' Cotta sat back down in the chair. 'In any case, I'd rather have you than someone with more experience but who's not personally concerned.' He frowned. 'Valeria thought a lot of you. She'd've liked to know that someone ... that one of the family was involved. And I believed that you'd want that too.'

'Of course I do! That's not the point. A murder trial's no game. What'll happen to you if I make a mess of it?'

'You won't make a mess of it.'

'It's a distinct possibility.' I got up and began to pace the room. 'Who's prosecuting?'

'Marcellus.'

I stopped, turned to face him, appalled.

'*Marcellus?* He's one of the best lawyers in the city! Marcus, you're out of your mind!'

Cotta regarded me levelly.

'It's my decision,' he said. 'My responsibility. Completely. Will you do it? For Valeria?'

I hesitated. Perhaps it might not be so bad after all. A seconder played a relatively minor part in a trial. He was the footsoldier to his leader's general, doing as he was told, keeping to the plains of the argument while his more experienced colleague roamed the heights. Writing the speech would pose few problems – in composition I knew that I was reasonably competent – and, so long as Philo kept the cross-examinations for himself, as I knew he would, I could manage my delivery without wholly disgracing myself. And Cotta was right. I owed it to Valeria to help her fiancé all I could.

That thought reminded me of the one thing I must be sure of before I agreed.

'All right,' I said. 'I'll do it. So long as you tell me one thing first.'

'Of course.' He grinned. 'Anything you like.'

'Was it you, Marcus? Did you kill him?'

The smile vanished.

'What does that matter?' he said.

'It matters to me. If you didn't, then fine. If you did, then I have to know. I'll still defend you, believe me, to the best of my ability. But I won't go into my first case believing a lie.'

'Finicky about the first time, are you, Publius?' he said. 'See yourself as a virgin, do you?'

'Yes, if you like.'

He was silent for a long time. Then he said, 'Most lawyers don't ask that question. It complicates matters.'

'I'm not a lawyer. And I'm asking you as a friend, not as a client. Did you do it, Marcus? Yes or no?'

He turned away.

'No, of course not!' he said irritably. 'Oh, I looked for him all right. But I never found him. He must've come across one of Clodius's gang.'

'You swear you had nothing to do with it?'

'Look, Virgil!' He turned back to face me. 'I've said so, haven't I? Isn't that good enough for you? Now stop asking bloody silly questions.'

'Swear it. Please. For Valeria.'

He took a deep breath, let it out slowly.

'All right,' he said. 'All right, if that's the way you want it.' He raised his right hand above his head. 'I swear by Jupiter Best and Greatest and the powers of Hell that I was in no way responsible for that fucker Lutatius's death. Much though I may wish otherwise.' He lowered his arm. 'Does that satisfy you?'

'Yes. Thank you.'

'You're welcome,' he said sourly, getting to his feet. 'I'd best be going. I've taken up too much of your valuable time already.'

'Marcus?' I said.

He turned at the door.

'Yes?'

'Thank you. For the chance. I appreciate it. Really.'

He scowled. Then his face broke into a grin.

'That's all right,' he said. 'Just be sure and get me off.'

'I'll try my best. I can't promise more.'

He nodded, turned again to go.

'Oh, by the way,' I said, following him to the front door. 'When's the trial?'

The porter opened the door for him. He paused on the step.

'Not for two or three months, I shouldn't think,' he said. 'You've got plenty of time. But you'd better talk to Philo before you're much older, all the same.'

'I'll do that,' I said. The butterflies were already beginning to stir in my stomach. 'See you later, Marcus. And thanks again.'

He waved, and was gone. I returned to my law books with a new sense of urgency.

21

Before the date of the trial was fixed, however, something else happened; an event that almost split the state in two. To explain it, I must go back a little, and enter the realm of politics.

The riots, if you remember, were a result of the struggle between the two faction leaders: Clodius, supported by the urban mob, and Milo by the right-wing elements in the Senate. Between them, they had effectively paralysed political life at Rome. Elections had been delayed to such a degree that the consuls for the year had not been appointed until July, halfway through their term, and the consular elections for the following year were facing similar disruptions. The only man with the power to change this state of affairs was Pompey. At present, he was outside Rome, debarred from entering the city boundaries by his governorial status (technically he commanded the legions in Spain as that province's governor, but he had left them to his deputies while he dealt with the far more important – and popular – task of securing Rome's corn supplies).

Pompey's opponents declared that his reluctance to intervene was deliberate policy. By allowing things to slide into anarchy, they said, he was forcing his own appointment as dictator. If so, then he was well on the way to success. Milo had put himself forward as a consular candidate for the following year. Clodius, not to be outdone, was seeking election to the office of City Judge: a position which would give him great influence over the courts. The election campaigns sparked off a fresh wave of violence between the two factions that prevented any appointments being made at all and lasted into the new year. On 18 January Milo and Clodius, each with a gang of their supporters, met outside Rome, on the Appian Way. Whether this meeting was accidental, or Milo, learning that his opponent would be travelling that day, had gone out intent on murder, is uncertain; but the two gangs clashed, and in the resulting skirmish Clodius was killed. His followers took the body back to Rome and burned down the Senate House as his pyre.

The news shook the city. It was not that many tears were shed for Clodius. With his record he had had little chance of dying in his bed. But he was a People's Magistrate, and as such his person was sacrosanct. In killing him Milo had broken not only human but divine law, and struck at the very roots of the Roman constitution. On the other hand, the destruction of the Senate House was a challenge to constituted authority which could not be ignored. The Senate met outside Rome and passed their Emergency Decree. Pompey was empowered to levy troops in Italy and use them to restore order in the city. Later, at the instigation of the more right-wing elements, he was appointed sole consul. This avoided the use of the ominous title 'dictator', but the result was the same.

Rome had become a monarchy.

'Pollio was right,' Proculus said, shifting his weight on the dining-couch. 'Caesar can't just sit back and watch Pompey take over Rome. There'll be war. It's only a matter of time.'

He looked terrible: hollow-eyed, gaunt-cheeked, more like an eighty-year-old than a man in the prime of life. I could almost count the bones in the hand which held the wine-cup.

'Not necessarily, sir.' I sipped my wine and water. 'The troops are only being used to restore order. They're no threat to Caesar. And Pompey is consul, not dictator. There's no reason why he shouldn't have a colleague when things settle down a bit.'

'Oh, I don't mind.' Proculus gave a ghastly smile. 'Not personally. The whole lot can go to perdition as far as I'm concerned.'

'At least the riots have been stopped,' I said, trying to lighten his mood. 'And they say Pompey has introduced stricter laws against bribery in the courts. That shows a certain concern for order.'

'Then the state really will collapse,' Proculus said with a shade of his old dryness. 'Make bribery impossible and you deprive a large percentage of our fellow-citizens of their main source of income. Pompey will have worse riots on his hands soon, if he's not careful.'

'He wants to make sure that Milo has a proper trial.'

Proculus nodded.

'Declaring his impartiality,' he said. 'Very wise, especially if he intends to keep in with Caesar, although it'll lose him a few friends in the Senate. But he'll have to be careful, all the same.'

Someone was knocking on the street door.

'Were you expecting anyone?' Proculus said.

'No.'

It was Cotta. Seeing Proculus, he paused on the threshold of the dining-room.

'I'm sorry, sir,' he said. 'I didn't know you were back.' He looked at me. 'If it's inconvenient I'll . . .'

'Not at all, Marcus.' Proculus got up, slowly, like an old man. 'You're welcome, of course.'

'I came to see Publius on business. But perhaps another time would be better.'

Proculus smiled.

'Don't worry, my boy,' he said. 'You're always welcome here. Stay. Have some wine. But if you'll excuse me,' he turned, 'I'll retire to my study.'

We watched him go, heard the study door shut behind him.

'How long has he been home?' Cotta said.

'Only a couple of days.'

'He looks terrible.'

'At least he can talk about it now.' I gestured towards the couch. 'Sit down. Have you eaten?'

'Yes, thanks. But some wine wouldn't go amiss.' He nodded to the slave, who filled a cup and handed it to him. 'I came to give you some news about the case.'

'Oh, yes? Good news or bad?'

'Good.' He drank. 'We're having it brought forward a month.'

I sat back.

'But that's in three weeks' time!' I said. 'Why, for heaven's sake?'

'Can you do it?'

'Does Philo know?' Philo, if you remember, was my leader.

'Of course. He suggested it. If we can force this through we catch the opposition properly on the hop.'

'In what way?'

Cotta grinned.

'Word's just come through about the Milo trial. It's to be in two months' time, in April. Cicero's defending, of course – you know he's always supported Milo – and guess who the seconder is?'

'Not Marcellus?'

Cotta's grin broadened.

'Right. Our prosecutor Marcus Claudius Marcellus. He's had to withdraw from the case to work on the new brief. As from today, the opposition's in a shambles. You see now why Philo wants to press ahead?'

'But they'll never agree! They'll ask for a postponement!'

'Of course they will, but they won't get it.' Cotta helped himself to a bunch of grapes from the bowl on the table. 'We've got friends who'll see to that.'

'Who's prosecuting now? Do you know yet?'

'Oh, yes. Furius Barbatus.'

'He's good.'

'Of course he's good!' Cotta grinned. 'I never said this would be easy.'

I went to bed that night in a better frame of mind than I had been for weeks. Bringing the case forward would certainly give us the advantage, but it was not altogether an unfair one. Just as in battle if one's opponent slips it would be the act of a fool or a madman to step back and wait for him to regain his feet, in law it is an advocate's duty to exploit any opening given by the other side. Cotta's reasons for advancing the date of the trial were valid ones, and I did not look beyond them.

I should have done. Of course I should. But then, I always was naïve.

22

The trial took place on 1 March.

I felt as if I was going to my own execution, and must have looked it. I think I have mentioned my aversion even to appearing in public, let alone delivering a speech. Poetry recitals are just tolerable, so long as they are before a small group of sympathetic friends: like a carpenter shaping a beam, habitude has, if not smoothed down my self-consciousness, at least lopped off its more prominent excrescences. Also, of course, there is no question of improvisation in reciting poetry, nor does one have to think in terms of gesture or visual effect, as is necessary in court. The lawyer, in addition to being a superb speaker, must be a consummate actor: and I have never been able to act.

I went down to the Market Square that morning like a rich patron surrounded by his clients: Proculus accompanied me, with his brother Sextus and a dozen other relatives, friends and well wishers. Everything felt unreal, as if I were taking part in a play. Even the familiar city streets had become painted stage-curtains, the jostling press of people mere extras, paid to lend reality to my progress. I could imagine them, when I was out of sight, leave off their haggling, roll up the canvas buildings and stow them away for another performance; or, if the cast and properties were limited, run silently ahead of me and repeat the charade a street or two further on.

I was, I am ashamed to admit it, slightly drunk. Before we had left, Proculus had insisted that I swallow a cupful of neat wine; which, coming on top of a sleepless night and no breakfast, had combined with my usual abstemiousness with predictable effect. If he hoped that it would loosen my speech then I am afraid he was disappointed. The colours of the morning seemed brighter, certainly – in that there are any colours in dingy Rome – and the day, as I have said, had taken on a muzzy unreality; but the wine sat heavy on my tongue, and the words either did not come or tripped over each other in their haste to be quit of me.

The Market Square was packed; but then it always was. The whole legal and commercial machinery of an empire squeezed into six hundred by two hundred yards does not tend to create an impression of space.

We pushed through the crowds and entered the hall assigned to us. It was comparatively quieter here, although still full of people, and despite the fact that I knew it well, alien: there is a vast difference between being one of the audience and one of the principal players, and I was very much aware of it. Everyone, I felt, was watching me. Conversations stopped, whispers – none of them, I was sure, complimentary to me – took their place. I was weighed, found wanting, dismissed. Beneath my heavy woollen mantle, although it was a cold day, I felt the sweat break out all over my body, and my mouth became as dry as if I had eaten a handful of sand.

I wished fervently that I were elsewhere. Or, better still, dead and buried.

Philo was chatting with an elderly man at the other end of the hall. He looked up as we came in, broke off his conversation and made his leisurely way towards us. He seemed completely at his ease, was smiling, even, as he laid his hand on my arm.

'All set, Virgil?' he said.

I could not trust my voice. I nodded, and clutched the rolls on which my speech was written as if I felt someone would rush up and steal them, leaving me wordless to face the jurymen.

'Good. Don't look so anxious, boy, they won't eat you, we're going to win.' He turned to Proculus. I saw his eyes narrow, take in the gaunt face, the haunted gaze, the mantle that sat like a scarecrow's wrappings. 'How are you, Quintus?'

'Well, thank you.' Proculus tried a smile. The effect was ghastly.

'We're going to win,' Philo repeated, in a different tone, like someone talking to a child. 'Now go over there and sit down with your brother while I talk to young Virgil here.'

Proculus did as he was told, puppetlike. Philo watched him go with a frown.

'He still hasn't got over it, then?' he said to me in a low voice.

'No, not yet. I doubt if he ever will.'

'Jupiter!' Philo turned away. 'The bastard's dead, that's one consolation. But it won't bring them back.'

'No,' I said. 'It won't.'

The narrowed eyes examined me closely, then he slapped me on the shoulder.

'Come on, man,' he said. 'That's enough of that! Let's get on with it.'

I liked Philo. He was a small man in his early forties, barely the height of my shoulder, thin and wiry as a terrier and just as snappish. He was also an excellent forensic lawyer – not in Cicero's class, of course, but then no one was – and a man of considerable learning and culture. I could not have asked for a better – or a more sympathetic – leader.

'Cotta hasn't arrived yet,' he said, 'but then it's still early. Nor has Favonius.' Favonius was the judge.

'You think he'll turn up?' The butterflies had started in earnest, and I was clutching at straws.

He smiled.

'Cotta? Of course he will. Saw him myself last night. Don't worry, lad, everything's going according to plan. I told you, we're going to win.'

'You can't be sure of that.' Some demon had taken control of my tongue. This was not how lawyers were supposed to speak on the morning of the trial.

He looked at me strangely, seemed about to say something, then changed his mind.

'No, I can't. Nothing is certain in an uncertain world. But we can do our best, can't we?'

'Of course we can.' I smiled.

Philo's attention was caught by a movement at the door behind me.

'Here's Cotta now,' he said.

I turned. Cotta, surrounded by friends of his own, had just come in. He saw us, waved, came towards us. He was looking fresh and unconcerned – happy, even – as if the whole proceedings were a party arranged for his benefit. Not like a man, I thought, about to be tried for murder.

I should have had my suspicions then. If I had not been so preoccupied, perhaps I would have.

'Virgil. Philo.' He nodded to us. 'Okay. Let's get it over with.'

Philo laughed.

'Don't be in such a hurry,' he said. 'We can't start without the judge, and we've only got half the jury in yet.'

'Everything's all right, isn't it? I mean, you managed to . . .'

'Of course, of course,' Philo said hastily.

Cotta breathed a sigh of relief.

'Fine,' he said, then turned to me. 'So how about it, Publius? All set for the big day?'

'Not really.' I smiled. The butterflies brushed at my insides with their wings.

'You'll do marvels, I'm sure. Don't worry about it.' He looked round the rapidly filling courtroom. 'Has the opposition arrived yet?'

'Albinus is over there in the far corner, talking to Barbatus.'

I glanced across. Barbatus I knew. Our principal opponent – the dead man's father – was the image of a Roman aristocrat, tall, straight-nosed, with the air of a superior camel. He was talking to (or rather at) a much older man, grey-haired, a little stooped, in a senator's purple-edged mantle.

The crowd stirred, fell silent. Again, Philo looked towards the door.

'Here's Favonius,' he said. 'Let the comedy begin.'

It was a strange thing to say. Even at the time, I noticed that – although not so strange in retrospect. We made our way to the front of the court and stood in silence for the judge, preceded by his six ceremonial guards carrying the rods and axes. Then the crowd closed in behind him and the trial began.

Barbatus's opening speech was first rate. I should, of course, have been taking notes, but I could only sit like the simplest of country yokels, listening and occasionally staring at the people around me. Faced with the hard evidence of the dead Albinus's guilt, he made no attempt to excuse his crime. Instead, he played for sympathy. Albinus, he said, had been a young man of good family possessed of too high spirits. Who among the jury who was a father himself could find overmuch fault with that? Especially since his wildness was directed to a constructive end (I noticed that Barbatus did not labour this point. Feelings against Milo and his gang were still running high). Then, young men have a fondness for wine. Where is the harm in some innocent spree, a combination of youthful high spirits and the gift of Bacchus? And if in the course of such an innocent spree the youth – unused, perhaps, to drink – should be prompted to an action which, in his sober condition, would be abhorrent to him and which he would bitterly regret afterwards, should he, because of that one foolish, tragic mistake be deprived of life, and not only that, but deprived of life in such a disgraceful, arbitrary fashion as if there were no law in Rome, no law, gentlemen of the jury, such as is administered by such upstanding, impartial, responsible citizens as yourselves . . .

You know the sort of thing. Barbatus did it superbly, as I have said, but I was watching the jury as he spoke, and I saw their faces.

The jury were bored.

I could not understand it. Here was one of Rome's best lawyers giving one of his most sterling speeches, and the jury could not care less! Startled, I looked at the judge. Favonius was examining his fingernails. He even yawned.

Barbatus, although he must have been aware, as any orator is, of the impression he was creating, showed no concern at all. He turned now, as I had expected he would, from a panegyric of Albinus to a vilification of Cotta. But – again to my surprise – it was milk-and-water stuff. Cotta was no blue-eyed boy. Had I been arguing for the other side, I could have brought in twice the evidence Barbatus used, and struck far more telling blows in the process, without resorting even to exaggeration. Barbatus did nothing of the kind. His attack on Cotta's character was perfunctory and, in tone, almost apologetic; and when he suddenly wound up with a carefully balanced sentence, thanked the jury and retired to his place beside his client I felt almost cheated.

But I had no time, then, to think about all this. Philo

had given me a nod, and I knew that I had my cue to speak.

We had agreed, Philo and I, that this would be the way we would do it. It is not uncommon for the more experienced lawyer to speak last, especially if he is defending, since his is the last voice the jury will hear. Human nature being what it is, under these circumstances a good orator can sway the vote even counter to the run of the evidence. This, however, was little consolation to me. I got to my feet, prepared to address the jury, took in the circle of interested, anonymous faces . . . and promptly went to pieces.

I will spare you a full account. Think of your own most embarrassing experience, and then imagine it watched by a hundred strangers, each intent on missing not the slightest detail. I was fortunate to be only providing the rough sketch of the case for Philo to fill in later, and not required to make any telling points of my own. In any event, if I had had the least conceit of myself as a practising lawyer, that speech was enough to destroy it utterly. I blushed, I stuttered, I lost my place, contradicted myself, dropped my notes: did everything but throw myself on the mercy of the court as if I were the accused. It was an appalling performance.

I was perhaps halfway through the speech when I noticed a strange thing – and, as you can appreciate, it would have to be very noticeable to register with me in my condition. The jury, who had sat listless and bored throughout Barbatus's address, were listening to me with rapt attention. Had I been Cicero himself, I could not have asked for a better response. When I made a point, heads would nod sagely in agreement. If I tried a piece of irony or sarcasm, instead of falling flat as it deserved it would be greeted with a ripple of appreciative laughter, even applause. Favonius himself had suddenly come awake, and was smiling at me in an almost avuncular fashion. When I finally stammered my way to a halt, and, cheeks burning, slunk back to my seat beside Philo, it was to a respectful and approving murmur.

Philo laid a hand on my arm and smiled.

'Well done, lad!' he whispered. 'Very well done!'

I was shaking so much with embarrassment and self-loathing that I could not answer. I appreciated his kindness – appreciated the kindness of the whole court in the face of what was probably the worst exhibition of forensic oratory ever seen at Rome – but I knew that if ever lawyer failed his client through his own stupidity that lawyer was myself. I could have crawled into a hole and begged them to heap the earth on top of me.

23

We won the case by a substantial majority verdict.

I could not believe it when the votes were counted. I simply sat there as if someone had struck me between the eyes with a hammer like a calf being slaughtered.

It was not that Philo had been exceptionally brilliant. His speeches were capable enough, his cross-examinations competent but hardly telling. Nor did Barbatus make any serious errors: if anything, his had been the better technical performance, and his seconder (whose name I cannot now recall), although he was no first-ranker, had done a very workmanlike job. There must have been another reason. When the court rose and the backslapping and congratulations began, I found that I could take no part in them. I felt drained and lost, and just a little unclean.

'Well, Publius.' Cotta broke out of a group of smiling, laughing admirers and put an arm round my shoulders. 'You've been blooded now, and no mistake. I knew you could do it.'

'Then you knew more than I did,' I said. 'More than I do. The question is, how did you know?'

He stiffened. His arm fell away and he looked at me sideways.

'What do you mean?'

'We ought to have lost. Or at best scraped through. We

were completely outclassed, thanks to me, and you must have known we would be. Yet you knew from the first that it didn't matter, that we would win. That's my question, Marcus. How did you know? How could you?'

He smiled, a little nervously, looked round for support, but Philo was deep in conversation with Favonius. Barbatus and Albinus had already left, Albinus, stiff-backed and empty-eyed, as if he had lost his son a second time, this time irrevocably. As he had quitted the courtroom, he had looked, briefly, towards where Cotta was sitting. Although he had not spoken, his look had screamed, 'Murderer!'; and I was to take it with me, that night, knowing what I then knew, into my dreams.

'These things happen, Publius,' Cotta said. 'Juries are funny animals, they don't always follow the rules. Perhaps they liked the look of my face. Perhaps they felt sorry for me. Perhaps you weren't as bad as you thought.'

'Perhaps they were bribed,' I said brutally.

The nervous smile increased in breadth, stayed fixed.

'Now why should anyone do that?' he said.

'I should think the reason was obvious. If we'd lost the case you'd be on your way out of Rome by now, at best, and not likely to be back for some time.'

'But you didn't lose.' The smile disappeared, and he looked petulant. 'You won, and I'm grateful. I don't deserve this, Publius.'

'Why did you bring the case forward?'

I could see that he had not expected that. His eyes shifted.

'I told you. Marcellus had given up the brief.'

'And left it to Barbatus. Who did pretty well in the short time allowed, didn't he? Or did he? Speaking of Barbatus, I thought he pulled his punches fairly obviously, wouldn't you agree?'

Cotta shrugged. He was looking sullen now, and casting

glances over his shoulder as if seeking an excuse to break off the conversation. But I would not let him go.

'You'd have to take that up with the man himself,' he said. 'Now really, Virgil, I have quite a few things to see to and . . .'

'Bringing the trial forward wouldn't have had anything to do with Pompey's up-and-coming law on court bribery, I suppose?'

He did not need to answer. His eyes told me I had hit the centre of the mark. There was a silence.

'All right,' he said at last. 'All right, we bribed the jury. So what? It's done all the time. And you did pretty well out of it yourself, didn't you? A fledgling lawyer up against a top-notcher like Barbatus and still winning his case? You're a made man, Virgil, and it's thanks to me. Or rather to Valeria.'

'You keep her out of this!'

'Why should I? You think I'd've had you otherwise?' Cotta sneered. 'Oh, yes, we'd've won whatever you did, but if we'd got someone else the reason wouldn't've been so bloody obvious, would it? You be grateful, Virgil, you just be grateful. And keep your mouth shut!'

'If you hadn't sworn that you didn't kill the man . . .' I began.

I got no further, because I saw his eyes change, saw the truth in them. Suddenly, I felt sick to my stomach. I give you my word that that was the first time the thought had crossed my mind. In my innocence, I had imagined that bribery was the worst of his crimes.

'You swore!' I said. 'You gave your solemn oath to me that you didn't kill him, and you did, didn't you, Cotta?'

He glanced nervously over his shoulder, but there was no one standing near us, and Philo and Favonius were still locked in heated debate about (I think) the interpretation of an obscure property law.

'Keep your voice down!' Cotta said. 'Of course I killed him! He deserved to die ten times over for what he did to Valeria!'

'But you swore to me that you had nothing to do with it.' Even then the enormity of the situation had not sunk in, and I could only repeat the obvious, like a drowning man clutching at a twig. 'Marcus, you swore!'

'Of course I swore!' He was showing signs of losing his temper. 'You wouldn't've done it otherwise, and I owed it to Valeria to give you a hand up the ladder.'

'I said I'd defend you even if you had murdered him.'

'Oh, you said sure enough!' He waved this aside. 'What does it matter, anyway? It was only an oath.'

'It matters to me,' I said. And without another word I turned my back on him and walked from the courtroom.

I never spoke to Cotta again.

Oh, yes, it mattered. I had lost my virginity that day. I had lost my virginity as a lawyer, in my first case: lost it to rape, like Valeria. I went straight to the nearest bath-house and had them scrub me until my skin was red-raw and bleeding, and at the end of it I still felt filthy. Philo had known, I was sure. He had known everything, and yet he could still carry on with the charade. I had respected Philo, looked up to him. Now . . .

Philo was a whore. And if Philo was a whore, then so was the oratory he practised.

It was my first time in court, and my last. Once virginity has been lost it cannot be regained. I decided, whatever my parents might say, that I would give up law and concentrate on poetry and philosophy. There, I was a virgin still, and would be more careful with my virginity.

I told you I was naïve.

24

I have made no mention of poetry for some time. Nor have I said more about Pollio. To tell the truth, I had had little leisure to read or write anything over these months, and at that point I felt drawn more to philosophy than poetry. Philosophers answer questions, poets only ask them, and I had had enough, then, of answerless questions.

None the less, I had done my duty. I had called on Pollio, walked with him to the Market Square, discussed poetry as far as my feeble abilities would allow. I had noticed him at the back of the courtroom during Cotta's trial, and his presence there caused me extra blushes. But he had not, yet, made good his promise to introduce me to the poet Calvus.

That was remedied towards the end of March. Pollio had avoided a formal dinner-party, for which I was grateful: in that setting the exalted company would have tied my tongue completely and made the evening a torture. Instead, I was simply invited to 'drop round for a chat with some friends' – a prospect (for I knew who these friends would be) which was alarming enough.

Pollio's house was on the slopes of the Palatine, not far from Cicero's; that is, in one of the most exclusive parts of the city. The slave who answered my knock listened gravely to my mumbled explanations (from his appearance, he could have been a professor of rhetoric) and led me through an expensively decorated lobby to the dining-room. He pushed apart the polished cypress wood doors and announced me.

The table had been cleared apart from some vases of spring flowers and a beautiful Greek silver wine-bowl with matching goblets. On the couches lay Pollio himself, two older men and a youngster of about my own age or less.

'Virgil! Glad you could make it!' Pollio looked up and smiled as I hovered, uncertain, on the threshold. 'Come in, lie down by Gallus there' – he indicated the young man on the left-hand couch – 'and I'll introduce you to everyone.'

He was speaking Greek, and I realised that this was in deference to the eldest member of the party. Parthenius was in his late forties, neat and dapper with a carefully trimmed beard in the Greek style and a rather oily skin. He was, I knew, the greatest living expert on Callimachus.

'You haven't met Calvus either, have you?' Pollio said when I had greeted Parthenius respectfully. 'Gaius, this is young Vergilius Maro, who expressed such admiration for your poetry.'

Calvus held out his hand.

'Delighted to meet you, Virgil. Always glad to meet a man of taste.'

I smiled. It was difficult not to smile at Calvus when he decided to be charming. He was the perfect example of the triumph of character over appearance. Short, almost completely bald (although he had just turned thirty) and irregular of feature, he still managed to be one of the most exciting men in Rome, especially to women.

That left the young man on my immediate right. On closer view he was younger than I had thought – perhaps only sixteen or seventeen – but he had an aliveness and a sense of quiet confidence far beyond his years that I envied.

'Cornelius Gallus.' Pollio completed the introductions.

'The son of a friend of mine from Fréjus, studying in Rome.'

Fréjus is in Gaul Proper, beyond the Alps. That explained the red hair and greenish eyes.

We shook hands.

'Pleased to meet you,' I said. 'Have you been here long?'

'Only a few days. I'm still settling in.' His Greek accent was better than mine. Marseilles, of course, is full of Greeks, but he must have had a special tutor. A rich family, then, even though they were provincials.

'Some wine, Virgil.' Pollio signalled to the slave who stepped forwards immediately with an extra goblet.

'A little, please. But mostly water.'

'It's not strong.' Pollio laughed. 'Don't worry, you haven't been asked to a drinking party.'

'A water-drinker.' Parthenius nodded in approval. 'Good for you.'

'If you ask me,' Calvus grunted, 'it's nothing short of sacrilegious. Especially with the wine you serve, Pollio.' He turned to me. 'By the bye, I saw you in court not long ago, didn't I? The Albinus case?'

I reddened and muttered something about not having made much of a showing. He waved my apologies aside.

'Just a touch of nerves. It can happen to anyone the first time.' He winked at Parthenius. 'Even water-drinkers like Demosthenes, eh? And if he could get over it, Virgil, then so can you.'

'I don't intend to try,' I said. 'I'm not cut out for law. Or for politics.'

'Oh, but you should try.' Calvus frowned. 'Aristotle was right. Man is a political animal. Poetry's all very well, but a complete man should take an interest in public affairs, too. Don't you agree, Pollio?'

'Absolutely.' Pollio held up his cup to be filled. 'If a

man doesn't involve himself with politics then like it or not they'll involve themselves with him. Besides, it's his civic duty.'

'There speaks the Stoic.' Parthenius smiled. 'But if our young friend inclines rather towards Epicureanism then I applaud his choice. It's better for the philosopher – or the poet – to keep clear of politics. Too much politics and too little philosophy has been the ruination of Rome.'

'Whereas the opposite has been the ruination of Greece?' That was Calvus, and it brought a general laugh. 'Philosophy's one thing, but if Virgil wants to be a poet as well he'll get precious little encouragement from your Epicurean friends.'

'Come, now, that's hardly fair,' Parthenius murmured. 'We're not totally opposed to poetry, except in the fields of philosophy and science, where simple prose is far more suitable.'

'You'd call Lucretius a prose writer, then?' Calvus said mischievously. Lucretius's poem 'On Things As They Are' was both a first-class exposition of Epicurean philosophy and breathtaking poetry.

Parthenius frowned.

'It has its points,' he said. 'But the poet himself admitted that he was only sugaring the pill. And he died mad. Scarcely a man to be imitated.'

Pollio turned to Gallus.

'What do you think?' he said. 'Should a poet involve himself with politics or not?'

In Gallus's position, I would have blushed and stuttered and contradicted myself a dozen times in my eagerness not to offend; but he took the matter coolly and with due pause for thought.

'I think you yourself, sir, and Asinius Pollio here, are all the proof needed of that.'

Calvus gave a bark of laughter.

'He turns a pretty compliment, too!' he said.

'I think we may distinguish between the man and his art,' Parthenius said. 'Poetry as such can have no place in politics, since it persuades through emotion, not through reason.'

'Yet you yourself, sir, said that Lucretius merely sugared the philosophical pill.' Gallus smiled. 'How many converts has he brought to Epicureanism through his poem? A patient will go more readily to a doctor who sweetens his medicine with honey than to one who doesn't.'

'Only if the medicine is effective!'

'Ah,' Pollio said. 'That's the nub of it. For the poet to have the right to preach, what he preaches must itself be right. And who decides that?'

'Precisely,' Parthenius said. 'In general, poets wield too dangerous a power to be allowed to meddle either with philosophy or politics. A poet who preaches a creed indefensible by reason, or shores up a corrupt regime and persuades men with his poetry that it is a paradise on earth has sold his own soul and deserves to be damned.'

Gallus laughed, and turned to me.

'A poor look-out for us young poets, Virgil,' he said. 'It seems you're right to steer clear of politics. The temptation to sell your services might be too great.'

The conversation shifted then to other matters; but I have never forgotten it. Perhaps if Gallus and I had followed Parthenius's advice and stayed away from politics the ending of this story would be different. For both of us.

25

If the case against Cotta had demonstrated to me the basic venality of forensic oratory, Milo's trial in early April that year showed how helpless it was against brute force.

Pompey, for once, had acted with a nice combination of inflexibility and tact. Armed with his commission from the Senate, he had raised troops and used them to police the city. His methods were direct, brutal and effective; and in a matter of days the rioting and street-fights which had troubled the city for years were over.

If he had played the game and used his position to root out only the remnants of the Clodian faction, the Senate would have been satisfied: he was their man after all, and they could continue to pretend to themselves that they still held the reins. But Pompey had little choice. Milo's feud with Clodius had provided a safe, even useful outlet for his violent, energetic nature. Now that Clodius was dead, Milo would be looking for other ways to power: a fact which would not escape the notice of Pompey's rival Caesar, still away on campaign in Gaul. Milo had to be removed, and removed permanently. Pompey proceeded to arrange a trial that would virtually assure his condemnation. To make certain that the point was not lost, he attended the trial himself, surrounded by his bodyguard, while a strong detachment of troops ringed the Market Square. If any doubt remained of where the real power lay, and of what the future held, the conduct of Milo's trial effectively stifled it.

I was there, of course. Everyone was. On the final day of the trial, when Cicero was due to deliver his main speech for the defence, I was standing on the steps of the Temple of Concord, between an unshaven Syrian and a thin-faced aristocrat with a petulant mouth. Beneath and facing us, at the edge of the square itself, stood a line of soldiers with drawn swords. The principals had not yet appeared.

Someone shouted my name, and I turned.

It was Gallus. He pushed his way through the crowd and squeezed, grinning, between me and the Syrian.

'I thought I recognised you,' he said. 'Not given up on politics altogether, then?'

'I came to see Cicero.'

'So did I. Can't we get any closer?'

'It would seem not.'

We were wedged so tightly that I could hardly move my arms, let alone shift my position.

'You think there'll be any more trouble?'

'I doubt it,' I said bitterly. 'Pompey's shown he won't stand for any nonsense.'

The previous day, a gang of Clodius's supporters had tried to break through the cordon. Pompey's troops had responded immediately. What few killings were necessary had been performed with ruthless, machine-like efficiency. I had seen it all from the other side of the square, and it had sickened me.

'You don't sound as if you approve.'

'I approve of the results. Not of the methods.'

'They're the only ones that work.'

A trumpet sounded. The soldiers raised their shields.

'Here we go,' Gallus whispered, as the crowd fell silent. '"Those about to die salute you."'

It was a travesty.

You will have read, of course, Cicero's published speech. Admittedly, these literary productions are always to some degree a product of wishful thinking: they represent, not what was actually said, but an idealised version of it, rewritten with hindsight and polished in the quiet of the study for the benefit of leisured readers and inky-fingered students. On the demerit side – and this is especially true of Cicero – they cannot convey the power of the living voice, or the charged atmosphere of the courtroom. I have read with pleasure many of Cicero's speeches, but where I was actually present at the time of delivery the written words ring flat as lead coins against my memories and I cannot give them the attention they deserve.

The speech for Milo is an exception. The Cicero who delivered it was a jerking puppet stumbling about the stage, mouthing words with no meaning. His voice that could burn the flesh from your bones and send the blood singing through your veins shook like an old man's, was as weak as a third-rate actor's; not that I heard much of what he actually said, for the Clodians in the crowd were in full cry, and no attempt was made to quieten them. Shouted insults, it seemed, did not concern the authorities: they merely served to intimidate the defence, which bothered no one, or at least no one of importance. At one point, when the shouting had become orchestrated into a terrifying, wolf-like ululation, Cicero stopped altogether. He raised his head and stared straight at Pompey who sat expressionless as a statue within his ring of iron. The two faced each other for the space of perhaps two minutes across the breadth of the Market Square, while the wolves howled around them. Then Cicero turned again towards where I stood, and I saw his face. His eyes were empty and lost-looking, as if some night-walking demon had sucked the soul from his body and left the empty carcass.

Apart from the catcalls of the mob, there was total silence when he finished speaking; not the stunned silence to which he was well accustomed, but the silence of indifference.

To a man like Cicero, that must have been worse than the jeers.

Milo was condemned, of course, and went into exile at Marseilles. They say that, when Cicero sent him the written version of the speech, Milo thanked him, remarking sarcastically that he was glad it had not been delivered, since in that case he would have missed the excellent Massilian red mullet. That was unfair. If Cicero failed, it was not through want of trying – or even through cowardice. The art in which he was pre-eminent was simply no longer relevant.

The future sat there, surrounded by its iron ring of soldiers, and presided over the first death-throes of the Republic.

26

I saw Gallus frequently after the Milo speech. In fact, we soon discovered that we shared a teacher in the rhetorician Epidius.

I have not said much about my studies at Rome, nor will I, largely because other events far outweighed them in importance; but perhaps I should say a little now, for the sake of completeness. My parents had sent me to Rome, as you know, to study oratory. I had not enrolled under any particular teacher before my arrival; however, once I was properly settled in and had had a chance to watch the teachers at first hand, I had chosen Epidius.

Partly, I chose him because he was Greek: Greece, to me, was everything that was civilised, in contrast to the barbarism of Rome. Unlike most Greek rhetoricians, however, he taught the plain Attic style of oratory, which is based on reasoned argument rather than emotional impact. This I found suited both my nature and my abilities.

It would seem that I was not in the minority. Epidius was a popular teacher – even a fashionable one; in fact, had I come to Rome a few years later I might have found myself studying alongside the future ruler of the Roman world.

Yes. I also shared Epidius with Octavian, and with his friend Marcus Agrippa. However, they were after my time, and we did not meet until he already held half the earth in his cupped hands and needed a poet to stop it slipping through his fingers. In a way, I regret not having known Octavian as a very young man. Not because it would have advanced me politically, as it did Gallus (and what good did it do him?) but because I would have had an earlier form with which to compare the later figure.

I saw, once, at Thebes, a wooden statue of Proserpina. The face of the goddess was black and stern with age, seamed with cracks and wrinkles like an old woman's; yet her smile was that of a young girl. The priest told me she was the queen of Hell, but I saw only the child gathering flowers, whom Death had caught and ground beneath his heel. Which of us was right: I, or the priest? Could one have taken sand and pumice and scoured away the blackness and the wrinkles from the child's face? Or did the darkness go too deep, and time merely make visible what was already there? I do not know. I will never know.

Perhaps, if I had met Octavian then, I might understand him a little better now.

I continued to study with Epidius even after I had privately given up all thoughts of a legal career. To a certain extent, this was for my parents' benefit: they had sent me to Rome to study public speaking, and I owed it to them to make no sudden decisions. Besides, as I have said, the study of rhetoric is, if not essential for a poet, at least of great practical value; and Epidius was an excellent teacher. From him I learned the importance of simplicity and euphony, and how properly used they can be more effective than high-flown bombast.

My other teacher, albeit an unofficial one, was Parthenius. What he saw in me I do not know, for it was long enough before I could bring myself to show him even the best of my poor scribblings; but it was he who sought me out, not the other way round. He came to call on me a few days after we met at Pollio's, ostensibly to bring me a copy of a book I had mentioned wanting to read. We talked at great length about poetry (after I had got over my shyness) and he invited me to his house for supper that evening, when I met – by, I later discovered, prior arrangement – the last of my future mentors, his friend Siro the Epicurean. I will say nothing more of either Parthenius or Siro at present, except that I was fortunate enough to enjoy their friendship and teaching for many years thereafter.

I was walking along Pullian Street about a month after Milo's trial when I met Gallus coming towards me. He had a flower tucked behind his ear – it was the third day of the Festival of Blossoms – and he had obviously been drinking.

'Where are you off to, Virgil?' he said.

I showed him the book I was carrying. One of the end-horns had become detached from the roller.

'I took this down to Caninus's to have it repaired' – Caninus was a bookseller in the Argiletum – 'but he's closed for the holiday.'

'Of course he's closed, you fool!' Gallus grinned. 'Anybody but you would've known that. What's the book? Anything interesting?'

'Not to you. He's an Epicurean. I borrowed him from Parthenius.'

He examined the title and frowned.

'Philodemus, eh? Virgil, that's no stuff for holiday reading. Shove it under your mantle and come into town with me. Have a bit of fun for a change.'

'Really, Gallus, I don't think . . .'

'Yes you do. Too much and too often.' He took me by the arm and turned me round, back the way I had come. 'An hour or two away from your books won't do you any harm. Besides, there's someone I want you to meet.'

'Who's that?'

'Wait and see!'

I found myself trotting along beside him like a school-boy.

'Well, at least tell me where we're going,' I said.

'To a theatrical performance.' He removed the flower from behind his ear and stuck it behind mine. It promptly fell off. 'After that . . . well, that depends.'

We turned left down the Corneta towards the fishmarket. The streets were crowded, even more so than usual, and most people were as pleasantly drunk as Gallus. Up ahead of us two she-wolves, arms linked, wove in and out of the crowd, singing an Alexandrian love song at the tops of their rough young-old voices, and I remembered Milan; but the Festival of Blossoms belongs to the prostitutes' patron goddess, so perhaps they had the right. Certainly no one seemed to mind.

'What sort of theatrical performance?' I asked.

'If I told you that you wouldn't come.' Gallus steered me round a street-porter, asleep with his back to the wall hugging a wine-flask. 'It's not in Pompey's theatre, anyway, that much I will tell you.'

That came as a mixed blessing. Pompey's theatre was on the far side of the Capitol, in the Plain of Mars – a fair way off. On the other hand, being the only stone-built theatre in the city it tended to host the most reputable performances. Anything held elsewhere was likely to be dubious.

We crossed the Market Square and turned down the Velabrum towards Cattle-Market Square and the Tiber. Now most of the crowd seemed to be travelling in our direction, and its composition confirmed my fears. Very few mantles were in evidence, and of these most could have done with a visit to the cleaners. Most of the men wore simple tunics, and the women were shrill-voiced and raucous.

'They're set up near the Flumentan Gate,' Gallus said. 'And it won't cost a penny, I know one of the cast.'

'Intimately?'

He grinned.

'Intimately.'

I put two and two together.

'It's a mime, isn't it?' I said. 'Gallus, for God's sake, let me get back to my Philodemus! I won't enjoy this, I promise you.'

'Have you ever seen a mime?'

'Well, no, but . . .'

'Then consider it as an educational experience.'

We walked on in silence.

'Whose is it?' I said at last.

'Laberius's. It's called *Mars and Venus*.'

'Oh, for heaven's sake . . . !'

Laberius was a Roman knight, quite well connected but with a taste for low life and gutter humour. He was a bitter opponent of Caesar, and his productions – one could hardly dignify them with the name of plays – often had a scurrilous political content, basic enough to appeal to his working-class audience. They also (although Laberius was not alone in this) contained off-colour crowd-pullers such as performing animals, female strippers and live sex. Thinking of this, I shuddered. I could imagine what kind of performance *Mars and Venus* would be.

'Who's your friend?'

'Her stage name's Cytheris,' he said.

We turned the corner and I saw our destination ahead. Most theatres, even although they are temporary structures, look solid enough, and some are extensively (and expensively) decorated with portable marble columns and bronzes. This one, however, being designed for a mime, was merely a stage with a semi-circular auditorium of raised tiers. The canvas awning that served to keep off the rain had been drawn back to let in the light.

'We're at the front.' Gallus nodded familiarly to the man

on the gate, who looked like an ex-prize-fighter. The man grinned and waved us through.

I was interested despite myself: as Gallus had said, it was an educational experience. A small orchestra – double flute, hand-drum and finger-cymbals – was warming up to one side as the audience took their seats and got out their oranges and nuts. A few more middle-class spectators joined us in the first rows – I noticed several narrow-striped mantles, although as yet no broad-striped senatorials. Most of them were young, and Gallus greeted some by their first names. There were even a few women.

Then the curtain went down, and the performance began.

27

It was everything I had feared.

You know the story of Mars and Venus, of course. The red-faced, blustering war god and the voluptuous goddess of love are lovers; clandestine lovers, since Venus is married to Vulcan, the ugly, lame blacksmith god (I retain the Latin forms of the names, although the original story is Greek). One day, Vulcan announces his intention to visit his island of Lemnos. Off he sets; and no sooner has he gone than Mars arrives, by prearrangement, and is welcomed by Venus. The two lovers hurry upstairs to bed.

But Vulcan, although a cuckold, is no fool. He knows perfectly well what has been going on behind his back. His trip to Lemnos is a ruse. He has made an unbreakable net; and returning unexpectedly he catches Mars and Venus in bed, throws the net over them and locks them tight together *in flagrante delicto*.

Then he invites the other gods to come and look.

You can imagine how the story would translate into Roman comedy: Mars the handsome, swaggering soldier, Venus the beautiful wife and cuckold Vulcan, the old buffoon who none the less gets the better of them in the end. A standard comic plot, with enough juice in it to adapt well to the coarseness of mime.

Except that was not at all how Laberius played it.

So much was obvious from the first scene, a domestic quarrel between Venus and her husband. Vulcan came as no surprise. He was the stock comic figure of fun, the lecherous old fool with his padded phallus trailing the ground in front of him. The surprise was Venus.

She was no beauty, but a whore past her prime, with rouged cheeks (actors in the mime wear no masks) and green-lidded eyes ringed with black. Her character, too, had more of the shrew in it than the siren: she beat her husband about the stage with a slapstick, screaming like a fishwife and using language that I had never expected to hear on a public stage.

The audience loved it. Gallus was doubled over laughing, holding his side. I am afraid I simply sat, straight-faced and rigid with embarrassment. If our seats had not been in the middle of the row I would have walked out.

'Oh, come on, Virgil!' Gallus had at last noticed my disapproval. 'It's all in fun! Don't be such a prude!'

'I see nothing funny in representing one of the principal goddesses of the Roman state as a foul-mouthed harpy.'

'Nonsense! No one believes in her anyway these days. Not seriously.'

'That's beside the point.' There was a *crack!* from the stage as the goddess caught her husband a double-handed blow on his rump. Vulcan leapt into the air with a howl, clutching his bared buttocks, and the audience roared. 'I suppose Venus is your friend Cytheris.'

Gallus's mouth dropped open in astonishment. Then he grinned.

'Give me some credit for taste,' he said. 'You mean you haven't noticed?'

'Noticed what?'

The grin broadened.

'Oh, nothing,' he said. 'No, that's not Cytheris. She's on later.'

He turned back to watch the performance. Venus had grabbed Vulcan – she was at least a hand-span taller than he was – and was shaking him like a rag doll. All at once, he reached up, grasped her long golden hair, and pulled.

The hair came away in his hand, revealing a man's gleaming scalp. The audience erupted.

I doubt if I could have been more surprised if the head had come off with the wig. Venus mimed consternation, covered 'her' baldness with a patched napkin and rushed headlong from the stage, followed by Vulcan, waving the slapstick. The applause was terrific.

'She's a man.' In my shock I stated the obvious.

Gallus was applauding with the rest.

'Of course she is,' he said. 'The point'd be lost otherwise, wouldn't it?'

It took me a minute to realise what he meant. Then the whole thing became obvious, and I cursed myself for a fool.

Venus was Caesar.

I must have been the only person in the theatre who had not known it from the start. Laberius, as I said, was a political satirist who appealed to all classes from the lowest to the highest – witness that day's audience. And he had his knife into Caesar. His Venus was as perfect a bit of character assassination as I have ever seen. To Caesar's notorious sexual ambiguity was added the extra fillip that Venus was the ancestress of the Julian clan. The burlesque ending to the scene ought to have told me, if nothing else: Caesar's sensitivity over his baldness was almost legendary.

'Laberius will never get away with this, surely?' I turned back to Gallus. 'I mean, satire's one thing, but this stuff . . .' Words failed me.

'Oh, he'll burn his fingers sooner or later. Not that Caesar minds much so long as he keeps away from straight politics.'

'You mean this *isn't* straight politics?'

Gallus laughed and did not answer.

The orchestra had struck up a rollicking dance tune, and on to the stage bounced – there is no other word for it – one of the most beautiful girls I have ever seen.

'Now *this* is Cytheris,' Gallus said.

She was dark-haired and lithe as a willow sapling. The bells on her girdle – and she wore nothing else – jingled as she sprang on to her hands and walked across the stage, clapping her feet in time to the music. Another girl, wearing, if anything, rather less, came on behind her and tossed a ball in the air, which Cytheris caught neatly with her feet and began to juggle, while the audience beat time. Then she tossed the ball back to her assistant and flipped herself right-way-up. The audience cheered.

Two more girls came on, dressed as minimally as Cytheris's assistant. They held short coloured batons. Forming a tri-angle with Cytheris at its centre, the three began to toss the batons back and forth to each other in time to the music, weaving a complex pattern of red, yellow and blue in the midst of which Cytheris performed the bump-and-grind of the Greek cordax-dance.

I could almost feel the waves of lust from the audience around and behind me. Gallus, in contrast, sat smiling quietly, with an occasional sideways glance at my face.

The hand-drum beat a quick tattoo and the music cut off abruptly just as the last hand snatched the last baton from the air. All four girls faced the audience, bowed, and left the stage to riotous applause.

'Well, what do you think of her?' Gallus turned to me.

'She's certainly . . . talented,' I said, rather stiffly.

He shot me a sly grin.

'Oh, she's talented all right,' he said. 'You take my word for it.'

I was saved from replying by the resumption of the

performance. Venus re-entered, again wearing her wig, and delivered a soliloquy. Laberius had stood the plot on its head. Venus, it seemed, may have been desperate to get Mars into bed with her, but her feelings were no longer reciprocated: Mars, she told us, had found someone else.

Now that I understood the play's political nature, I knew what to expect, even before Mars made his entrance. Where they had got the actor from I do not know, but with his faintly protruberant eyes and fish-like expression he was the exact image of Pompey: he had only to stop and look straight-faced and pop-eyed at the audience to bring the house down. He was dressed in the caricature of a soldier's uniform, with a long scabbarded sword that kept mixing itself up, to the audience's delight, with the huge phallus that drooped from beneath his tunic – a fact which the two actors made much use of, since it was Venus who had the job of untangling it while complaining of her lover's unfaithfulness. The dialogue was explicit both sexually and politically; and, although I cannot say that I enjoyed it much, extremely witty.

I will not try to describe the whole play – you can probably imagine it, if you have not actually read it: the usual mixture of knockabout comedy and smutty jokes grafted on to an emaciated plot, but with the political aspect to pad it out and give it substance. Cytheris did not appear again until the last act. She played Mars's new mistress Potentia – that is, Power.

Mars entered pushing her on an immense bed, decorated with matrimonial wreaths; and although she had not a single line her short white dress with its broad purple senator's stripe made the playwright's intentions clear enough for even the least politically minded of his audience. Having placed the bed centre-stage, the war god raised his monstrous phallus, spoke a few solemn words in the true Pompeian manner on the burdens of office and of doing one's duty by the state, and jumped on top of her. Cytheris parted her legs, and the audience roared. Beside me, Gallus was almost crying with laughter. I sat immobile, writhing with embarrassment and wishing the thing would end.

But Laberius was not done with us yet. As the bed heaved up and down under Mars's divine efforts, Venus entered, spied the pair and gave vent to a tirade against both. Hitching up her skirts, she revealed a stuffed property phallus even bigger than her lover's. Holding it upright, she dived on to the bed which, either by accident or design, promptly collapsed; at which point Vulcan reappeared and cast his net over the three struggling figures.

That signalled the end of the play – not that I think the audience could have taken much more without damaging itself physically. It only remained for Vulcan to step forward and deliver the epilogue:

> You see, my friends, our farce is play'd
> With all its actors duly laid.
> POTENTIA has got her oats
> From P*** and C***, the rutting stoats.
> Great VENUS, skewer'd and skewering, sighs
> At every glance from MARS's eyes.
> He now to me must make amends—
> So put your hands together, friends!

And they did. I was surprised that the theatre did not come down about our ears with the mere noise of the cheering, let alone with the stamping of feet.

'Come on, Virgil.' Gallus was applauding with the best of them. 'Admit you enjoyed it.'

'It was . . . *different*,' I said. 'But I still don't see how Laberius gets away with it. Caesar's one thing, he's in Gaul. But Pompey's at Rome. And he must know what's going on.'

'Laberius has powerful friends,' Gallus said. 'Besides, ridicule's a dangerous weapon to counter. Taking it seriously only makes you look more ridiculous.' He got up. 'Now come and I'll introduce you to Cytheris.'

Octavian would, I am sure, have written splendid mimes, although his talent for propaganda took a blacker turn; and when I think of what he did to Gallus I cannot help comparing Caesar's treatment of poor Laberius.

Laberius did go too far. He cracked one joke too many, and Caesar took the subtle revenge of ordering him to appear as an actor in one of his own plays, which of course meant automatic loss of citizenship. Laberius complied, but the dignified prologue in which he conveyed his apologies moved Caesar to pardon him and restore his rank. The humiliation was warning enough, and Laberius never penned another joke, blue or otherwise.

Octavian would never have exercised such effective yet kindly poetic justice. He might pardon outspokenness (so long as it was a substitute for action), he might even pardon outright treason (so long as the traitor's teeth were drawn, and pardon was expedient); but he would never pardon an attack on his self-love. Self-love is the very centre of Octavian's being. Touch that, and you touch Octavian on the quick, and set yourself beyond all hope of mercy. As Gallus found to his cost.

Gods – especially self-created gods – do not laugh at themselves, nor do they allow others to laugh at them. To do so would be to admit that they fall short of perfection.

28

I was pleasantly surprised by Cytheris.

You will forgive me, I am sure, my preconceptions. When one sees a girl stripped almost naked dancing on her hands to please the crowd at a mime, one naturally makes certain assumptions as to her character and intellectual capability. In Cytheris's case, such assumptions would be completely unfounded.

Not that Gallus wanted her for her mind: that was obvious from the way his fingers stroked her hip as he introduced us. But he was clearly prepared to treat her as an intellectual equal, and this impressed me.

'Cytheris is almost a neighbour of yours, Virgil,' he said. 'She's from Ravenna.'

'Hardly a neighbour, then,' I smiled. 'But I wouldn't have thought that there would be many Greeks in that part of Italy.'

Cytheris laughed.

'That's only my stage name,' she said. 'Really, I'm ordinary Volumnia.'

'Hardly ordinary,' I said, and she smiled a dazzling smile.

'I thought you said your friend didn't like women,' she said to Gallus; then, turning back to me as he reddened and began to stutter: 'How did you enjoy the show?'

'Oh, Virgil's a serious scholar,' Gallus recovered himself. 'He doesn't believe in enjoying himself. *I* thought you were magnificent.'

'Come on, now,' I said. 'I'm not so prim as all that. I liked it very much.'

'Nonsense. I was watching you. You sat through it as if you had a poker up your rectum.'

Cytheris laughed at my embarrassment, and placed a hand on my arm.

'Never mind,' she said. 'It's not to everyone's taste. I'm not so keen on it myself, but I have to eat. Speaking of which . . .' She smiled up at Gallus.

'Join us, Publius?' Gallus said.

'Of course he will,' Cytheris said before I could make the excuse I had ready. She gathered my right arm up in her left and put her right round Gallus's waist. 'Even serious scholars must eat. Where are we going?'

'I thought we'd slum it at Rufio's. That's not too far.'

'All right.'

The wineshop had a small, private garden at the back. Gallus was obviously expected – a table had been laid and the dinner arrived so promptly that it must have been ordered in advance. I looked around with interest: even this, to me, was an adventure. Like most people who can afford it I preferred to eat at home or with friends. Cookshops, like wayside inns on a journey, are chancy things at best, and best avoided.

This particular cookshop, however, proved to be an exception. The food was simple and fresh – no dubious sauces to disguise the taste of the meat, but cold country ham, cheese, salad, and the most delicious olives I had ever tasted. The wine, too, was far above the ordinary.

'Rufio's a freedman of my father's,' Gallus explained when I asked him about it. 'He knows what he'd get if he poisoned his ex-master's son and heir.'

And he winked at the owner himself as he bustled about with the wine. The man – he looked like a Spaniard – broke into a broad smile and nodded.

'So you didn't like the mime, Virgil,' Cytheris said.

'It was a little . . . near the bone for me,' I admitted.

Gallus laughed.

'Near the bone!' he said. 'If Laberius had shaved Caesar any closer he'd've made a eunuch of him.'

'Yet when you consider Laberius as a dramatist there's little difference between him and Aristophanes,' Cytheris said.

I must admit I was surprised. Mimic actresses do not usually profess a knowledge of classical Greek drama. Nor are they quite so articulate.

'Except in quality,' I said.

'Oh, yes, naturally.' She took a bird-like sip at her wine. 'But at least he serves the same basic purpose.'

'Which is?'

'To mention the unmentionable. To drag dark things into the light and set them in perspective. To question the rightness of political actions. All of that's necessary in a healthy society.'

'Don't you think you're dignifying it just a little?'

She looked at me directly: a thing I find disconcerting in a woman.

'No, I don't think so. Isn't what we do better – and more useful – than trotting out the stale domestic comedies of boring old Menander? You don't think it's significant that Greek theatre lost its cutting edge when Philip of Macedon destroyed the city states? Or that Aristophanes wrote his best plays before free speech died in Athens?'

I was becoming interested.

'Then you consider politics essential to drama?'

'Of course. Politics and morality. What other subjects are there? Look at Sophocles. And not only drama. Take any of the arts, especially poetry . . .'

Gallus had been listening to us with a smile on his face. Now he held up his hand.

'This is not,' he said firmly, 'the time for intellectual discussion. Now shut up, the pair of you, and eat your dinners.'

Cytheris kicked him lightly on the shin.

'Barbarian,' she said. 'A typical Gaul, isn't he, Virgil?'

I found myself smiling.

'You don't write poetry as well, I suppose?' I said.

Cytheris, her mouth full of sausage, shook her head, swallowed.

'Too difficult. I've enough trouble with other people's words. What I'd really like to do' – she selected a piece of lettuce – 'is act in proper plays instead of throwing my boobs around and ending up on my back nine times out of ten.'

'Only nine?' Gallus said. 'Anyway, whoever heard of a female actor? A proper one, I mean.'

'Why not? You think I couldn't play Hecuba as well as any man?'

'You'd be bored stiff inside a month.'

'I'm bored stiff enough as it is.' She grinned. 'As you should know.'

Gallus gave a bark of laughter.

'Careful,' he said. 'Virgil's blushing again.'

'How much of that was true?' I said quickly, to cover my embarrassment. 'About Pompey and the Senate, I mean?'

'The alliance?' Gallus pitted an olive. 'Poetic licence at the moment, but it's not far outside the truth. The Senate need a strong man on their side to counter Caesar, Pompey needs respectability. Oh, they'll circle each other for a while yet like two dogs sniffing each other up, but that's what it'll come to in the end.'

'And Caesar?'

'He's got his hands full with the Gallic revolt, but that

won't last for ever. When he puts it down – which he will – he'll want a triumph and a consulate. *That* will be when things get interesting.'

'He'll have deserved them, surely.'

Gallus poured himself another cup of wine.

'Try telling that to some of these knotheads in the Senate,' he said. 'They'd sooner give the consulate to the slave who mucks out the senatorial privy than to Caesar.'

'The Senate can't prevent it, surely. Consular elections are by open vote.'

'They don't have to. Caesar's caught in a cleft stick. To run for consul, he must come to Rome, only he can't because of his governor's status.'

'He can run in absentia, then,' I said. 'There're precedents. All it takes is . . .' I stopped.

Gallus nodded.

'That's right,' he said. 'All it takes is a dispensation from the Senate. You see how it works? The bastards only have to wait until his command runs out in two years' time and they've got him cold as a private citizen.'

'Caesar can do a lot in two years.'

'Only if Pompey decides to play ball and further his interests from the inside. If he sticks with the Senate then that's another matter. The door's shut in his face. The constitutional door, anyway.'

'All right. So supposing he doesn't feel like handing back his armies when his time runs out? Supposing he decides to stay on?'

'Then he's in open rebellion, and isolated.' Gallus shrugged. 'You see why the Senate need Pompey so badly? With him on their side Caesar's stymied constitutionally.'

'And militarily?'

'That too. He may have an edge, but it's not one to gamble on. He won't go that way if he can avoid it.'

'You've heard Caesar's latest *bon mot*, of course?' Cytheris put in.

Gallus grinned at her.

'No,' he said. 'Tell us.'

Cytheris poured wine into her cup.

'It seems that he was' – she smiled demurely – 'letting his hair down at a party, and someone asked him about his plans. "Once I'm finished in Gaul," he said, "I'm going to dance on the members of the Senate."'

Gallus hooted.

'He has style, I'll say that.' He raised his cup in silent salute.

'You think he means it?' I said.

'Caesar's always at his most serious when he makes a joke. Of course he means it.'

'Then there'll be trouble?'

'If the Senate don't wake up to the real world, yes. And if Pompey doesn't come off the fence, or makes the wrong choice.'

'You think it'll come to fighting?'

'Not if Caesar can help it. He doesn't want war, can't afford it. But if the Senate are stupid enough to back him into a corner then he'll turn. And then they'll find that the wolf has teeth.'

It was two and a half years before the wolf finally turned. When it did, it was to tear Rome's throat out.

29

They were busy years for me, as far as my poetry was concerned. Not that I wrote much, or at least much of any worth – a few short poems, a longer piece, nothing very memorable. However, I was studying hard under Epidius, Parthenius and Siro and, with Pollio's help, building up a circle of friends. My rhetorical studies gradually but inexorably fell by the wayside: even my parents were compelled to admit, both from my own letters and those sent by Proculus and others, that I was not cut out to be a lawyer. It was a great disappointment to them.

Proculus was almost his old self again, after months of bitter struggle. When he had returned to the house on the Esquiline he had been nothing but a mumbling bag of bones, an old man with a face all pits and hollows like a nursery demon. He still carried the burden of the two deaths – it had bent his back and turned his hair completely white – but time had made it bearable, and it did not gall his shoulders as it had once done. He even talked of them, sometimes, Cornelia and Valeria. It was more than I could bring myself to do, and I admired his courage.

The winter after the events I have described brought fresh grief, although, I am ashamed to say it, not more poignant. A letter from my mother mentioned in passing that she was suffering from intermittent stomach pains: she had tried various remedies and even gone the length of consulting a Greek doctor in Cremona, with no better result. Because the bearer had himself fallen ill on the way, the letter, dated late October, did not arrive until just before the Winter Festival. Two days later I received a second message (I cannot call it a letter), this time from my father and dated 30 November, to say that my mother was dead.

The news came as a shock, of course, being completely unexpected; but I cannot honestly say it touched me very deeply. I had been home only twice since coming to Rome, and on both occasions our relationship had been, not strained, exactly, but distant. I grew my beard and put on mourning, but I did not return to Cremona. There was little point: Mother was long buried, winter had made the roads difficult for travel, and besides, my father specifically forbade it. He had his true son Gaius, now rising ten, beside him and had no need of strangers.

Gaius I have not mentioned, I know, since his birth. This is not to say I had anything against him – far from it: he was a fine lad, as good as Marcus whose place he had filled in my parents' affections. Yet I doubt if I had spoken to him – really spoken, I do not count pleasantries – more than two or three times. In constitution, he was far more delicate than I am: although I occasionally cough blood, with him the malady took a more severe form which was later to kill him. Yet he was his father's son, stronger in spirit than in body, a natural farmer with a feel for the land. If he had lived to proper manhood, my father would have been proud of him.

Shortly before my mother's death, my father had sold the farm near Cremona and bought a larger property just outside Mantua. He did this partly out of duty: the farm had belonged to one of his many brothers who had died suddenly the year before, leaving only a widow and three daughters, and he wished to ensure that the girls were provided with a proper dowry. Altruism, however, was not his only motive: it was fine land, and even after paying a fair price (which the women would not have got had they sold it on the open market) he reckoned he had made a good bargain.

Events at Rome were proving Gallus right. Caesar had put down the Gallic revolt and turned his attention to securing the consulship, which the Senate were determined not to let him have, and with it his future. Pompey was becoming more and more jealous of his colleague's military reputation, while Caesar himself was becoming increasingly disillusioned with Pompey's efforts at Rome on his behalf. To the Senate's mind, if the wedge could be driven deeper between the two their alliance could be split apart like a rotten log. As the time for Caesar to give up his command drew nearer and Pompey still made no move to help him, the Senate grew bolder. Representatives tactfully sounded Pompey out as to his likely reaction should Caesar fail to meet the deadline. He was non-committal, but many people suspected that he was waiting for Caesar to strike a secret bargain.

If so, then he was disappointed. A politician of Caesar's calibre had no need for bargains – at least, not with Pompey. Shortly before the deadline was due to expire, one of his foremost opponents, the People's Magistrate Curio, suddenly changed sides. With a tame People's Magistrate in his pocket, Caesar could now block the legislation which the Senate needed to destroy him. The Senate howled, but there was nothing they could do until Curio's term of office came to an end. The anti-Caesar lobby was effectively hamstrung for the next twelve months. All it could do was wait, and plan, and hope.

The crisis came with the results of the magisterial elections for the following year. Curio, of course, was debarred from serving a second term; but his replacement was Antony, and Antony was Caesar's man. Faced with the prospect of yet another year's deadlock, the Senate pressed for war. On 7 January, in a stormy meeting of the House, Antony and his colleague Cassius, both supporters of Caesar, were advised to leave Rome for their own safety. Pompey, forced off the fence at last, was elected dictator and given command of the senatorial armies.

It took Antony and Cassius three days to reach Caesar on the Italian border. On being informed of the situation, he gave the order for his troops to cross the Rubicon, the small stream that separates Italy from the Gallic provinces; and by doing so placed himself for the first time irrevocably outside the law.

The civil war had begun.

Campania (January 49 BC–September 40 BC)

30

Rome was in chaos.

Imagine a hive that has been kicked over and smashed. The bees fly about wildly, aimlessly: some are angry, spoiling for a fight and, finding none, grow angrier still. Others, their world suddenly overturned and made alien, busy themselves with the familiar but now futile task of gathering the spilt honey and repairing the shattered comb. Some few turn on their fellows, perhaps settling old scores. But most do nothing, for there is nothing to be done. Lost and confused, they fly around the wrecked hive simply because to move is to do, and movement, where constructive action is not possible, makes them feel that they are achieving something.

Within hours of the Senate's passing their Emergency Decree, the Appian Way, leading south to Naples, was a solid mass of vehicles. Most of those who fled were aristocrats who had cried for war and, now they had it, found that they did not want it after all. Pompey's troops were everywhere, but those I saw looked as nervous and unhappy as the civilians: Caesar's military skills were already legendary, and to be on the receiving end of them was the common soldiers' nightmare.

They were right to be worried. The senatorial forces were outgeneralled from the start. Almost before they realised that they had an enemy to fight, Caesar had marched south and taken the Etruscan passes, giving him a clear route across the Apennines to Rome. The army sent against him promptly defected, without putting up even a token resistance. When the news reached the city, the Senate and senior magistrates packed their bags and fled. Pompey, rightly counting the war in Italy as lost, embarked his troops at Brindisi and crossed over to Greece.

I remember, years later, talking to a soldier who had lost an arm at Gergovia. It was, he said, a strange experience. He was fighting against a huge Gaul armed with a broadsword when he had slipped in a pool of blood. Immediately he had felt a light blow upon his swordarm, halfway between elbow and wrist. He straightened, drew back his sword to stab his opponent – and discovered that both the sword and the hand that held it were missing. There was no pain, he said (although that of course came later); only a feeling of vast surprise when he looked down and saw his forearm, hand still clutching the hilt of the sword, lying at his feet.

That was how most people felt in Rome during that latter period. With the Senate and magistrates gone, and the city emptied of troops, one would have expected riots, looting, the general breakdown of law and order – a return to the violence of a few years previously; yet there was very little disturbance of any kind. People simply waited, stunned. It was eerie.

Both Pollio and Gallus went early, to join Caesar. Pollio had always supported him, I knew, and Gallus's father was a personal friend of his. Not that this last was necessary: I have yet to meet anyone from beyond the Po who is not, at heart, a Caesarian. Of my other friends, some went east to Caesar, some south to Pompey. Few stayed where they were. Proculus, it is true, decided to remain, although he was the Senate's man through and through and made no secret of it; but then I do not believe that Proculus cared much what happened to him personally one way or the other.

I left Rome in mid-February for Campania, on the invitation of my teacher Siro, who had a villa on the coast just outside Naples. Parthenius, too, was invited, which would have decided me had I been wavering. I was not. Rome without friends was a lonely place. Without my teachers, it would have been unbearable.

I should perhaps say more about this invitation, since it has governed the course of my life ever since. I have told you that Parthenius and Siro were Epicureans, and that Epicureans abstain from politics. Even without their influence, I suspect that such a philosophy would have appealed to me at the time. I found what I had seen of self-serving (and, after all, what else is politics?) both frightening and disgusting. It had raped and killed Valeria and her mother, corrupted Philo, my principal in Cotta's trial, subordinated Roman justice to the military force of Pompey. To pursue it was to ask for the gift of Midas which, once acquired, steals the life from everything it touches even as it turns it to gold. Politics was evil, and I wanted no part in it, even as a bystander.

Siro and Parthenius shared my feelings. The Campanian villa was to be our philosophical refuge; the gathering-point for people like ourselves, who wished to withdraw from a world gone mad and shut the door upon it – either to live together in community or, if they were forced by circumstances to be in the world, to use when the world allowed for their own spiritual re-creation. In this it succeeded admirably. The years I spent there were, except when the world intruded on them, the happiest of my life.

It was a society which lent itself naturally to organisation, which suited me very well. I have always preferred, where possible, the stability of a daily routine: only when one follows a well-marked and unvarying path can one's mind relax its grip on the body's reins and stray down avenues of its own. I rose at dawn, or slightly before, bathed, and ate sparingly. Then, depending on the weather, or what I had in hand, I would walk on the beach for an hour or so, turning ideas over in my mind, or sit with a book in the sun-lounge overlooking the sea. If I had a poem to write, I would work on it throughout the day, beginning with the rough, inchoate mass and licking it gradually into shape, as a she-bear does her cubs. If not, then I would divide the day between philosophy and poetry – philosophy first, as being the more serious subject.

In the evening, we would talk. That was the best time of all.

I studied far more than I wrote. Siro had an excellent library. Most of the books dealt with philosophy, of course – Epicureans regard poetry as frivolous – but Parthenius had brought the larger part of his own library from Rome, which remedied the deficiency admirably. There were also other friends – temporary guests at the villa or like-minded residents living nearby – whose tastes and interests added to the store.

Good books, good friends, and the leisure to enjoy them. Can you wonder that I was happy, these years?

I am no historian, save when necessary. The events of the first five years did not affect me except in their broadest sense, so a brief résumé will suffice. If you wish a full account you must read Pollio, who fought through them as one of Caesar's commanders.

It took Caesar eighteen months to bring Pompey to bay and smash his main army at Pharsalus. Twenty thousand died on both sides.

Twenty thousand. Twenty thousand hearts stopped by the touch of Midas's finger that transformed their living flesh into the stuff of power. Twenty thousand fratricides marked down to 'political necessity'.

Pompey himself escaped to Egypt, only to be murdered as he stepped ashore. His embalmed head and signet ring were presented to Caesar as an earnest of goodwill by the young King Ptolemy and his sister Cleopatra. The manner of his death did more to stiffen resistance than he could have done alive. Caesar took a year and a half to break Pompeian resistance in Africa at Thapsus, and a further eleven months to finish the job at Munda in southern Spain.

The Spanish campaign threw up two hostages to time, both of whom will be important later. First was Pompey's son Sextus, who was the only one of the leaders to survive the battle and slip through Caesar's net. The second was Caesar's seventeen-year-old grand-nephew who, despite illness, had insisted on joining him. Undeterred by rough roads and even by the experience of shipwreck, this sterling young man played a hero's part in the campaign, making the best of impressions by the fortitude with which he faced danger and hardship . . .

Yes. I am talking of Octavian. The man who stands accused by Virgil of cowardice and physical and moral turpitude. You did not recognise him? Ah, but wait. There were other factors.

Caesar's current will, drawn up before the civil war, named Pompey as his principal heir. That will, obviously, would have to be changed – but who was Caesar to put in Pompey's place? He had no obvious heir, no legitimate son to inherit his mantle automatically when he finally laid it aside. And devotion, fortitude and courage were qualities Caesar admired above all others. Especially in good-looking young men who were also his blood-relatives.

How could Octavian afford *not* to show them, with the prospect of a new will in the offing? Or do you think he was too young to realise what he was doing, or how much was at stake? The result was a foregone conclusion. After Munda, it was the young Octavian's name which replaced Pompey's at the head of the newly redrafted will, and Rome had a new crown prince almost before she knew she had a king.

The campaign which led to Munda was the true beginning of the Augustan principate. And I do not refer to Caesar's campaign against the Pompeians.

Hail Augustus.

31

It was late summer, September, I think, or possibly October, some four years after I came to Naples. I had been walking by the seashore, trying out a poem. The day was unseasonably hot and dry, the lines refused to shape themselves. Under these circumstances, I knew, the best thing I could do was to leave them to come or not in their own good time. Feeling overwarm and slightly irritated, I returned to the villa.

As soon as I entered, I could hear voices from the courtyard-garden – Siro's and another, which I did not recognise. Had the poem worked, I would have gone straight to my room to write it down. As it was, I was looking for a distraction. I went through.

Siro was standing by the pear tree. He was in his seventies by then, small and bent and white, like a twig stripped of its bark. You could almost count his bones, thin and brittle as a bird's. He was talking to a much younger man, with a thin face and petulant mouth – an aristocrat, from the looks of him, dressed with expensive, self-conscious simplicity.

'Ah, Virgil,' Siro said. 'You're back early.'

'A poem that refuses to co-operate,' I said.

'You know Junius Brutus?'

The man's eyes gave the lie to the softness of his face. They had the hard, uncompromising gaze of the fanatic.

Brutus could have stared the sun out of countenance, if he thought it stood in the way of his principles.

'No.' We clasped hands. 'Pleased to meet you.'

'The pleasure's mine.' His voice was low, almost deprecatory. 'But, if you will forgive me, we have met before.'

I frowned.

'Milo's trial,' he said. 'You were with Cornelius Gallus.'

I remembered him now. We had been standing next to each other, on the steps of the Temple of Concord. He must have had a phenomenal memory for faces. To my recollection, on that occasion we had not exchanged a single word, or even a glance.

'What did you think of it?' I asked. 'The trial.'

'A travesty and a crime. Milo deserved thanks, not exile.'

The two short sentences had all the quality of an inscription. You could hear the crash of mallet on chisel.

'He got death, in the end,' I said. 'He should have left well alone.'

Brutus stared at me. I felt uncomfortable, as if by arguing I had committed a solecism. After the outbreak of war, Milo had returned to Italy in an attempt to raise the south against Caesar. His skull had been smashed by a slinger's bolt beneath the walls of Compsa.

'To die fighting tyranny is glorious, and to preserve the state our greatest duty,' Brutus said.

'Oh, quite.' I kept my face straight. Out of the corner of my eye, I noticed that Siro was looking at him with disapproval.

'Milo thought he was opposing a tyrant,' Brutus continued. Suddenly, with no warning at all, he bared his teeth in a hard smile. His eyes remained cold and sharp as a winter's frost. 'He was mistaken, of course.'

'Of course,' I said drily. Brutus's devotion to Caesar was well known. Also the reason for it.

'The roses have made a fine showing this year, have they not?' Siro remarked.

Brutus gave him a sharp look.

'Meaning I must avoid politics?' he said. 'They offend your Epicurean sensibilities, Siro? Well, I'm sorry, but—'

'Meaning that the roses have made a fine showing,' Siro broke in calmly.

Brutus's lips puckered, as if he had bitten on a lemon; but he shifted the talk to other matters. It was like making conversation with a tiger who has more than half a mind to have you for supper, and I was not sorry when he left us, saying he had business elsewhere. I did not see him again.

I was reading in my room later that afternoon when one of the slaves informed me that Pollio had arrived and was waiting below.

I came down at a rush. I had known that he was back in Rome – he held one of the senior magistracies for that year – but not that he had had any plans to visit Naples. He was sitting in the sun-lounge, looking out over the sea. As he turned to greet me, I saw that he had aged . . . hardened is a better word. Four years previously, he had been the soft-skinned aesthete. Now everything about him shouted soldier.

'You're looking well, Virgil,' he said as we shook hands.

'And you.' I sent the slave, who had followed me in, for wine. 'It's not often we have two such important visitors on the same day.'

His head came up.

'Two?' he said.

'Junius Brutus. You've just missed him. Count yourself lucky.'

'Brutus?' Pollio's eyes widened. 'What was he doing here?'

'Wrangling, mostly. Arguing philosophy with Siro, like the good Stoic he is. And he has business in Naples.'

'Did he actually say that?'

Pollio's tone puzzled me. There was an urgency to it beyond mere curiosity.

'No,' I said. 'He mentioned having some business to attend to. I only assumed it was in town. Maybe I'm wrong.'

'Cicero's in Naples,' Pollio said. 'Staying with friends for a few days. Thinking of buying yet another villa.'

'Perhaps Brutus's business is with Cicero, then. They know each other very well, don't they?'

'Yes,' said Pollio. 'They do. Although I suspect that even Cicero finds the acquaintanceship a little trying.'

At that moment the slave came with the wine, and the question that was on my lips went unasked. Pollio drank, staring out of the window, westward across the sea.

'Caesar's given me three legions and Further Spain,' he said. 'Pompey's son Sextus is still free. We'll have no peace until he's dead.'

'Then he's not taking command himself? Caesar, I mean.'

'I wish he was!' Pollio turned to face me. His voice was savage. 'At least he'd be safely out of Rome.'

That surprised me.

'He's not still in Spain?' I said.

Pollio set the empty cup down on the table and began to pace the room.

'No, he's back. Taking the reins into his own hands, he says. In a way he's right, there's a lot to be done and Rome needs a firm grip. But he's making fresh enemies right, left and centre.'

'Surely that's nothing new.' I poured a little wine for myself, and added water.

'Fresh enemies, I said.' Pollio frowned. 'The old ones he can cope with. He knows about them. These are friends, or used to be. And he doesn't seem to be aware of it, or even worse doesn't care.'

'Brutus?' I said.

'Brutus is one of them. His brother Decimus. Gaius Trebonius and Gaius Cassius. Half a dozen others, with more every day. All good friends who have reason to be grateful for past and present kindnesses.' He smiled bitterly. 'Who needs enemies, eh?'

'Why?' I asked the simple question.

'Oh, the usual mixture of reasons. For some, the more . . . upright ones like our friend Brutus' – his mouth twisted – 'it's a crisis of conscience. Caesar, they think, is becoming too much the autocrat.'

'And is he?'

Pollio's eyes opened wide and he stared at me as if I had suddenly grown an extra head.

'Of course he is, man!' he said. 'He can't avoid it. Spend half a day at Rome and you'd realise that. He has to, if he's to get things done. I told you, the city needs a strong hand. And he is dictator, after all.'

'The dictatorship's a temporary office. It's only valid in times of national emergency.'

Pollio's hand slapped the table. The pent-up violence of the blow shocked me, and for the first time I realised how much strain he was under.

'Don't you start, Virgil!' he snapped. 'The old system was rotten as a piece of maggoty meat. Caesar's the only man who can hold the state together, and with him gone these good old boys with their good old names would wreck it in a year. Caesar has to take sole control and keep it.'

'You want him king?' I said. 'You want us to go back to the Tarquins? You know what happened to them.'

'Yes, and so does Brutus. I think he sees himself in the shoes of his famous ancestor. You know what Caesar says of him? "What Brutus wants, he wants with a vengeance." The gods save us from self-righteous patriots!'

I was positively alarmed now. I had no love for Caesar,

but he had at least brought stability. Now it seemed that that stability was under serious threat.

'But Brutus has always supported Caesar,' I said. 'He's one of his right-hand men, as well as being . . . well . . .' I stopped.

'As well as being Caesar's natural son,' Pollio finished for me. 'So the rumour goes, anyway. But we're not talking parricide. Not yet.' He stopped his pacing and poured himself another cup of wine. 'Not yet. As for the kingship, there are faults on both sides. Caesar's vain, he likes external show, that's his weak spot. His enemies are playing on it, voting him all sorts of extravagant honours they know he'll accept, feeding his vanity in the hopes that it'll goad staunch traditionalists like Brutus to do their dirty work for them. And they will, you mark my words, before much longer, if Caesar stays at Rome.'

'He's not aiming at the kingship, surely,' I said. 'He wouldn't be so stupid.'

It would, I knew, be unbelievable stupidity. The title of king has been anathema to Romans since the earlier Brutus drove out Tarquin the Proud four and a half centuries ago. If Caesar were to assume the crown he would need all his armies to help him hold it.

Pollio shook his head.

'Of course not,' he said. 'But he's allowing himself to be voted the trappings, and that's just as bad. It's his blind spot, I told you, and it'll be the death of him.' He caught himself, forced a smile. 'I shouldn't have said that. Make the sign.'

I smiled and made the sign to avert bad luck. Pollio took a deep breath and sat down.

'Leave it,' he said. 'Politics isn't why I came, and it's a dirty business. How's the poetry coming along?'

'Slowly,' I said.

'Anything particular on at the moment?'

'Not really. A few bits and pieces.' I suspected that there

was a reason behind the question, but could not see what it was. 'Nothing of much importance.'

'Good.' Pollio frowned, reached into a fold in his mantle, brought out a book and handed it over. 'You've read this, I suppose?'

I examined the title. Theocritus's *Idylls*.

'Yes, of course,' I said. 'Theocritus is one of my favourites.'

'Anyone ever turned him into Latin? I don't mean translated. An adaptation.'

'Not that I know of.'

'Care to have a shot at it?' And when I did not answer: 'I'd arrange publication, naturally.'

I sat down, my head whirling. Despite Pollio's offhand manner, it was a momentous offer; what amounted to a major commission – my first – by one of the most respected men in Rome. It could make me as a poet. If I did it well.

If I did it well.

'I don't know what to say,' I managed at last.

'Say yes.'

'But Theocritus . . . I'm not nearly good enough.'

'You are. The last poems you sent me showed that.' We had kept up a correspondence, naturally, while he had been out of Italy: disjointed, by necessity, but as regular as we could make it. I had sent him copies of whatever poor stuff I happened to be working on, and his criticism had helped me enormously.

'Why don't you do it yourself?'

He shrugged.

'I don't have the time,' he said. 'And anyway, you're by far the better poet.'

'That's nonsense.'

'Not at all. I've produced the best I'm capable of. I may write more – I will when I've more leisure – but I'll never write better. You're different, Virgil. You'll keep on improving, however long you write. You can't help it.'

I blushed, but my brain was beginning to seethe with ideas. Few poets are amenable to adaptation, just as only certain plants may be dug from their native soil and transferred successfully to grow elsewhere; but I had always felt that Theocritus was one of them. He was, in a way, already acclimatised, for he had lived the first part of his life at Syracuse, and his poetry breathes the Sicilian countryside. The *Idylls* are pastoral vignettes, simple stories of shepherds and shepherdesses and their rustic concerns; yet the simplicity is deceptive, for Theocritus is a master-craftsman, and each poem is an exquisite miniature perfectly executed in painstaking detail. Such poetry could well transfer its setting from the Sicilian to the Italian countryside – to Campania, even to Cremona and Mantua . . .

'Let me think it over,' I said.

Pollio grinned.

'Fair enough,' he said. 'I'm not asking you to have the thing finished in six months, I know how slowly you work. Don't start until you're ready and take as long as you want.'

'It may take me years. If it ever gets done at all.'

'It'll get done.' Pollio took the wine-cup from my hand and filled it to the brim. 'And however long it takes it'll be worth the wait, I'm sure of that. Now sit down and drink this. You'll need proper fortification if I'm to bore you with my African reminiscences.'

I laughed and drank.

It was to be two years before I completed the first of the *Pastorals* to my satisfaction, and a further eight before all of them were published. By that time, the world had changed again and both I and my poetry had changed with it. The *Pastorals* made me, certainly, but in a way, as you will see, they were also my undoing.

Pollio stayed with us for two days, then, the following February, a further three or four before setting out for Spain. We did not discuss the political situation to any great extent on that occasion, but I could see that he was sick with worry.

'Caesar's planning to invade Persia,' he said. 'If he'd take himself off east now and leave Rome to settle down I'd breathe a lot easier. He's like a child with a stick poking a hornets' nest to see the insects flying about.'

'You think they'll sting him?' I asked.

He turned a haggard face towards me.

'I think they'll kill him,' he said.

Six weeks later the news arrived from Rome. The hornets had swarmed in earnest, and Caesar was dead.

32

Do you know the story of Oedipus?

Oedipus was the son of Laius, king of Thebes, and of his queen Jocasta. For years they had been childless. Laius goes to the oracle of Apollo at Delphi to ask help of the god.

'I have no heir,' he says. 'Tell me, Apollo, how I may get myself a son.'

'Count yourself fortunate, Laius,' Apollo tells him. 'Your son will kill his father and marry his mother.'

Laius is horrified. He returns to Thebes and without giving her a reason puts his wife aside. Jocasta in her fury makes him drunk and slips into his bed. She conceives, and nine months later bears his child.

Laius is no murderer, yet he knows the child cannot be allowed to live. He takes the baby from its nurse, pierces its feet with a nail, and leaves it to die on Mount Cithaeron. Oedipus is found by a shepherd and taken to Corinth, where he is adopted by the king, Polybus, and his wife Periboea.

Oedipus grows to young manhood thinking that Polybus and Periboea are his true parents. Taunted over his lack of resemblance to them, he goes to Delphi seeking an answer from the god.

'Father-murderer!' the god screams. 'Mother-copulator!

You pollute the ground you walk on, you make filthy the air you breathe! Leave my shrine!'

Oedipus, sick with disgust, flees from Delphi, not towards Corinth – for he loves his parents dearly – but to Thebes. He meets an old man in a chariot, who orders him roughly out of his path. Oedipus in his anger pulls the old man to the ground and kills him, not knowing that the stranger is Laius, his father.

He travels on, and meets with the Sphinx, a monster with the head of a woman, the body of a lion, a serpent's tail and eagle's wings.

'You cannot pass me,' says the Sphinx, 'unless you answer my riddle.'

'Ask on,' says Oedipus.

'What creature walks on four legs and on two and on three, and is weaker the more legs it has?'

'Man,' says Oedipus. 'For he crawls when a baby, walks erect in his prime and leans upon a stick when age takes him.'

The Sphinx, knowing itself answered, leaps from the crag on which it perches and is dashed to pieces on the rocks below.

Oedipus comes to Thebes and is welcomed as the slayer of the Sphinx. The Thebans take him as their king, he marries the widowed Jocasta and gets children on her.

Time passes. Oedipus's crime begins to stink. Plague wraps the city. Flies breed. People die and are left unburied in the streets, or burned in heaps on greasily smoking pyres. Oedipus sends to Delphi to ask how the god's anger may be turned.

'Drive out the murderer of Laius,' says the god.

Easy to say, thinks Oedipus. But who is Laius's murderer? The old man was killed by an unknown assailant, and there were no witnesses. Yet Oedipus cannot rest until the problem is solved. He pokes and pries, asks questions, digs into the past as a farmer digs into a dung-heap, turning it over and over until the stench rises and fills his world. Jocasta, realising the truth, begs him to let things be, but in his pride he will not, until he has laid bare the whole, rotten, stinking mess and stands naked amid the ruin he himself has caused. His mother-wife hangs herself, and in his new-found knowledge and self-loathing he takes the brooch from her breast and puts out his own eyes.

Hubris. The Greek word is untranslatable: a gnawing, destructive canker of overweening pride and self-love. In his pride, Oedipus dared to tamper with the universal order, and his tampering destroyed him.

Hubris destroyed Caesar as thoroughly as it did Oedipus. What were the events of the Festival of Wolves, if not a product of Caesar's hubris?

The day is dark with black clouds and hail. The priests of Pan, their foreheads smeared with the blood of dogs, run screaming through the streets of Rome, hairy as goats, lashing any woman they meet with their rawhide thongs to make her fertile. One of them – Antony – carries a crown. He approaches the dais where upon a gilded throne Caesar sits stiff-faced, immobile, robed in purple, red-booted to the calf like the ancient Alban kings, watching the rites. Three times priest-Antony offers Caesar the crown, three times Caesar puts it from him, while the mob howls about them, demanding that he take it; until Caesar's gesture of refusal becomes mere stylised pretence . . .

Hubris.

He died a month later.

He had ample warning, so they say. Ghosts walked the Market Square, owls were seen in broad daylight and crows roosted in the temples. Lightning struck his statue, obliterating the first letter of his name. The night before the murder, his wife Calpurnia dreamt of it in her sleep, and begged him not to attend the Senate. On his way to the meeting, a certain Artemidorus handed him a note on which the details of the plot were given in full, down to the names of the conspirators. All this he ignored. Fate could not touch him, no, not him, not Caesar. Other men, perhaps. But not Caesar.

Hubris.

They stabbed him at the base of Pompey's statue; and when he fell they stabbed him again and again, until they were sure of him. After he was dead, his son Brutus raised the bloody dagger aloft above his father's head and cried: 'Cicero!'

What Brutus wanted, he wanted with a vengeance. No matter who it hurt.

33

We felt the shock of Caesar's death even at Naples, where politics was held in low regard as a topic of conversation. Most of our community approved of the assassins' motives, and even of their methods: tyrannicide has an honourable place in Greek as well as Roman history. I did not (although I didn't say so very loudly); first of all because I had met and talked with Brutus, and if the others were anything like him then they were far less sympathetic figures than the man they had killed; secondly because, like Pollio, I was for order over chaos, and as far as I could see order had received a setback. Like all fanatics, Brutus and his friends had concentrated on sweeping away the system they opposed, without thinking of what to put in its place or of the realities of power. To my mind that is as criminal as consciously to set up an unjust and tyrannical regime – worse, for when no one is in control the very fabric of society falls apart and evil prospers at every level just as surely as scum rises to the surface of a stagnant pond.

We were well supplied with news over the next month, mainly because it was grist to the Epicurean mill: the deviousness of professional politicians overcoming the ideals of (Stoic) philosophers who foolishly believed that philosophy and politics could ever mix. Antony's speech, and the reading of Caesar's will which left his gardens across the river to the people and three hundred silver pieces to each adult male citizen, stirred up the mob against the killers, and they were forced to flee from Rome. Reasoned argument cuts no ice with the Roman mob where their purses are concerned. Anyone could have told Brutus that, but he would not have listened. He had to learn the hard way.

Nor was the august Roman Senate of any use. Many of them were Caesar's appointees; and once Antony had pointed out that if they cancelled Caesar's legislation they would be out on their senatorial ears they were quick to shelve their principles and temper their support for his murderers. Cicero, too, kept quiet. Above all, he was a realist, and must have found Brutus's much-publicised cry over Caesar's corpse extremely embarrassing. Slowly but surely, Antony, standing in Caesar's shadow, was gathering the reins of power into his own hands, and the Republicans could only watch helplessly and grind their teeth in rage.

Early in May, however, news came that was to change the situation completely, although neither we nor anyone else realised it. Caesar's heir Octavian landed in Italy, at a small fishing village called Lupiae, not far from Brindisi.

It is difficult to talk about Octavian without hindsight. To you, my reader, I know that it is as if the leading actor has finally stepped on to the stage, and that the others will at once stand back and allow him his natural pre-eminence, or try to upstage him and, inevitably, fail. Ghostly Augustus already looms behind his shoulder, bathing him in divine radiance. Whatever Octavian does will be, somehow, *right*, his final victory god-ordained, only a matter of time.

Disabuse yourself of that view, if you can. See him for what he was, not for what he was to become. Judge him as if he were simply one racehorse among many. Weigh his chances in the power stakes against such experienced runners as Antony, Cassius, Cicero and the rest of the field. It is only by doing so that you will appreciate both his greatness and the less savoury aspects of his character.

He is nineteen years old, hardly more than a boy, thin-chested, spindly-legged, of poor constitution and delicate health. He has little experience of warfare, none of command. His education has been academic, albeit the best that money could buy (although his spelling and orthography are appalling). His natural father's family, although wealthy and highly respectable, are political lightweights – provincials, outwith the tenuous, iron-strong network of influence which ensures, even as he lies in his cradle, that a boy will rise to high political rank.

Against this, set three things: his friends, Agrippa and Maecenas (I will come to them later); his standing as Caesar's adopted son; and, last but not least, his single-minded ruthlessness. Others may have discounted Octavian's chances of success. Octavian himself never did, not for one moment. Armoured in his perfect egoism, he searched out his opponents' weaknesses one by one, pulled his adversaries down, and trod upon their naked backs.

Towards the end of April, Octavian entered Rome. He was hailed by the people and by Caesar's veterans as the dead dictator's son and avenger. Significantly, he was careful to accept his role publicly, and by implication to cast doubts both on Antony's position as Caesar's legitimate successor and on his willingness to avenge a murdered friend: over the past month Antony had been building up a fragile *modus vivendi* with the Tyrannicides and the Senate. The appearance of a nimbus around the sun was also, somehow, linked with his arrival and interpreted as a divine imprimatur of his claims . . .

You see how it works? Nothing you could put your finger on. No threats, no demands beyond the reasonable, no out-and-out challenge to the status quo. And yet somehow the balance is shifted in Octavian's favour. He becomes the champion of right, the people's darling, and the light that shines on him casts shadows that are both inevitable and opportune. He is like a wrestler who, without obvious exertion, moves his body *so* and causes his heavier opponent to use his own strength against himself. The balance shifts, slips, and the surprised opponent is pulled off his feet and crashes to the ground.

Most wrestlers learn from their first fall not to underestimate their adversary, or to trust him. Antony did not.

These two things were the nails in Antony's coffin.

Underestimation and trust.

34 ∫

It must have been July, or perhaps August, the year of
Caesar's death. I had spent the day in Naples, and had
just turned into Demetrius's bookshop near Potters' Row
when I collided heavily with a dark-haired boy on his way
out, his arms full of books. I apologised profusely.

'That's all right, sir,' the boy said. 'My fault. In too much
of a hurry as usual. Dad says I'll meet myself coming back
one of these days.'

I picked up a book that had fallen to the pavement and
glanced at the title: Gaius Lucilius's *Satires*.

'An interesting choice,' I said, handing it back. Lucilius
was not a fashionable author. His *Satires* – written about
a century previously – were a miscellaneous collection of
Latin hexameter verses; lively, romping poetry in the old
rustic tradition, but shaggy and raw-boned as a porter's
mule. I was surprised that Demetrius had them in stock.

The boy smiled.

'I like him,' he said. 'He has a voice of his own. Roman,
not Greek. I'd like to polish him up some time.'

He was not boasting, merely stating a fact. I found myself
smiling in return.

'You're a poet, then?' I said.

'Not yet.'

'At school here?'

He laughed.

'No,' he said. 'At Rome. Or was, anyway, up to last year.'

I noticed then that he was older than I had thought, seventeen or eighteen at least, but very short for his age. I apologised again.

'That's all right,' he said. 'A lot of people make that mistake. I'm used to it.'

We had gradually drifted back into the shop. Demetrius, a fat, balding Greek with one eye, was talking to the chief copy-slave. He made to come over, but I waved him back.

'You're staying in Naples?' I said.

'Only for a few days, visiting my uncle. I'm on my way to Athens to study.'

This interested me still more. Athens was – is – the place where young men of good family (and long purse) go to finish their education. This young man hardly seemed of that class. His dress, although respectable, was not expensive, and by his speech I would have placed him no higher than middle-class provincial. He noticed my ill-concealed surprise (he was clearly an observant lad) and laughed again.

'Oh, I'm no aristocrat,' he said. 'Uncle's got a potter's shop a few doors down. And Dad's an ex-slave.'

I flushed, feeling that perhaps I had offended him, but he did not seem to mind. I doubt if I have ever met anyone quite so self-possessed.

'My grandfather was a potter, too,' I found myself saying.

'Really? Here in Naples?'

'No, in Mantua. I used to play in his shop when I was a child.'

'I still do, in Uncle Titus's. It drives him mad.'

It was my turn to laugh. His naïve directness, after the rarefied conversation of Siro and Parthenius, was refreshing. It reminded me a little of Valeria's.

The young man had rearranged the books under his arm into a more manageable bundle.

'I'd best be off. Uncle will be wondering where I've got to.' A thought seemed to strike him. 'Look, why not come round for a cup of wine? If you're not too busy, that is.'

I hesitated. I do not make friends readily, certainly not on casual acquaintance. On the other hand, my business was finished – I had only dropped in to Demetrius's to browse – it was hot, and I was free for the rest of the day. Also I was curious.

The young man noticed my hesitation.

'But of course you have other things to do,' he said politely. 'It's my turn to apologise.'

That decided me.

'Not at all,' I said. 'I'd be delighted.' I held out my hand. 'Publius Vergilius Maro.'

He took it in a firm grip.

'Quintus Horatius Flaccus,' he said.

It was like stepping back into my childhood world with its dun colours, its rich, earthy smells. In the front part of the shop two slaves were working. They looked up as we entered. Horace waved to them, and they smiled back. The slap of wet clay on the mixing-board, the click and hum of the wheel greeted me like old friends, whispered to me like gentle ghosts. My fingers tingled, remembering the feel of the clay spinning between them and my grandfather's hands pressed against mine. It sounds illogical, I know, but I experienced for an instant an almost unbearable sense of loss, of lost simplicity, that brought the tears to my eyes. If it had been my grandfather who pushed aside the rough curtain at the back of the shop and stepped out to meet us, wiping the clay from his hands, I would not have been surprised, only grateful, as if somehow (do not ask me how, or why) I had been forgiven.

'This is Virgil, Uncle Titus,' Horace said. 'His grandfather was a potter in Mantua.'

The introduction, too, was right, and in perfect character. Not, *We bumped into each other in Demetrius's bookshop*, but, *His grandfather was a potter*. I shook the old man's hand.

'Pleased to meet you, sir,' I said.

'He's a bit deaf,' said Horace.

'Rubbish!' His uncle pulled up a stool. 'Sit down and take the weight off your feet, sir. I'll get you some wine.'

I was glad to sit down. I felt like a clumsy giant beside these two. The old man was hardly taller than his nephew, big-bellied as one of his own oil-jars, with a scalp totally devoid of hair that gleamed as if it had been polished. He disappeared back through the curtain.

I watched as one of the slaves – a northern Greek, from the looks of him, and as old as his master – threw a lump of clay on the wheel and brought up a cooking-pot like those I remembered from my grandfather's shop. The curtain parted again and the old man reappeared. He was carrying a tray loaded with a wine-jug and cups, bread, olives in their own oil and a goat's-milk cheese, which he set down on the ground beside me.

'Nothing fancy,' he said, 'but the cheese is good. Eat up.'

I tried a piece. It was sharp and tangy, an honest country cheese like the ones we used to make on the farm.

'You dig in too, Quintus,' the old man said to Horace. 'You won't find cheese like that in Athens.'

'How soon do you leave?' I said.

'Before the end of the month.' Horace poured the wine and took a long swallow from his cup.

'Who are you studying with?'

'Theomnestes and Cratippus.'

I was impressed. Theomnestes was a leading light of the Academy. Cratippus was one of the better Peripatetics.

'You'll excuse me, sir, I've got work to do,' the old man said; and when I made to rise: 'No, don't get up. Stay as long as you like, you're in no one's way. A pleasure to meet you.'

And he left.

'Have you been to Athens?' Horace asked.

'I'm afraid not. My parents sent me to Rome.'

'They live in Mantua?'

'My father has a farm there.'

He nodded.

'Dad has one too, now. A small one, near Venusia. He loves it.'

'And your mother?'

'She's dead.'

It was strange, but I had almost known that that would be the answer; as if I were looking into a mirror, seeing myself not as I was but as I might have been. My next question came unbidden, almost involuntarily. It hurt me even as I asked it, as if I were ripping the scab from a wound.

'You get on well with your father?'

Horace paused. Then, deliberately, he set down his wine-cup.

'He's the best man in the world,' he said. 'If I'm worth anything now, I owe it all to him. If I ever amount to anything more in the future, the credit's all his.'

I felt pain sharp as a knife twist in my gut.

'Dad showed me how to live,' Horace went on. 'Not taught me. *Showed* me. "Look at that man," he'd say. "He has money, but inside he's dead. No one respects him. No one loves him. Don't be like that man, Quintus." Or, "Look at that one. He keeps his word, deals fairly, stands by his friends. You do the same, and you won't go far wrong, my boy."' He picked up the cup and drank. 'That's what I call an education. The rest's nothing beside it.'

I thought of my own father. Sometimes it had seemed that he could not so much as remember my name.

Horace tore a piece of bread from the loaf, dipped it in olive oil and bit into it.

'Dad scrimped and saved from his freedman's wages,' he said. 'God knows how. Did I tell you he was an auctioneer's assistant? He took me to Rome, gave me a rich boy's schooling.' He laughed suddenly. 'I've still got the scars on my backside to prove it. We couldn't afford a slave to carry the books, of course, so he did it himself. The other boys laughed, but he couldn't care less, and nor could I.'

'Your father must be a marvellous man,' I said. I felt curiously hollow inside. My chest was as empty as a bronze statue's.

'No more than yours, I'm sure,' he said politely. 'He farms near Mantua, you said?'

But I did not want to talk about my father. What could I say? *I'm nothing to him. Never have been. We don't even write any more.* I took a sip of wine, and pretended I had not heard.

'You have somewhere to stay in Athens?'

He shrugged.

'The friend of a friend of a friend's,' he said. 'It's hard, though, to be leaving Rome just when things are finally happening.'

'Things?'

'The killing of the tyrant. The fight for freedom. The shaking-off of chains.'

He spoke naturally, without self-consciousness and without, I think, noticing the melodrama inherent in the phrases he had used. I thought of Brutus; of his hard eyes and tight, thin lips. He might have used these words. But when he had spoken of tyrants, and freedom, and chains the words had hissed in the air like slingers' bolts. You could hear, in their wake, the thud of stricken flesh and the crunch of shattered bone. This boy was different. Tyrannicide for him was a nursery tale, black and white, hero against villain, untrammelled by the messy realities of human nature. He was, perhaps, only four or five years younger than me; yet in the face of his honest idealism I felt ancient and cynical, and not a little soiled.

I envied him. I still do. His opinions have changed over the years, but his character has not.

We talked a little more – about philosophy, and about poetry. I did not realise at the time, of course – and after this one meeting I lost sight of him for almost five years – but Horace was to become one of my closest friends. In addition to being an excellent poet he is the most truly humane man I have ever known, and the least affected by vanity and self-seeking. Horace has been good enough to call me half of his soul. I know this is undeserved; yet he is half of mine, and by far the better half. If I could choose to be anyone else in the world, I would choose him. Failing that I am proud to call him my friend.

35

The events of the next eighteen months were a lesson in the politics of power, taught by a young man barely twenty years old. They brought him, if not yet ultimate power, then at least the position his adoptive father had held thirteen years before, but legitimised by formal vote of the Senate; and they brought me . . . well, you will see what they brought me.

Since Octavian's entry into Rome, his relationship with Antony had become increasingly strained. This was intentional on Octavian's part: if he was to create space for himself, then he must first detach Caesar's troops from Antony, and then Antony from his claims to legitimate authority.

He succeeded admirably. If that word is not inappropriate.

In early October he left Rome for the south and began to work on the soldiers' sympathies: if Antony really wished to avenge Caesar, then why were the killers still at large? Was there some secret agreement? Why, if Antony valued Caesar's men as highly as he said he did, had he been so stingy over their bounties? He, on the other hand, had been more than generous. Surely they would do better to transfer their loyalty to a general who showed more appreciation . . . ?

And so on. You have the idea. So did Antony. Cursing his own stupidity in having allowed Octavian access to his troops in the first place he hurried to Brindisi, knocked a few heads together and prepared, before any more harm was done, to lead the army north in a show of force. Which was, of course, what Octavian had hoped he would do. The target was Brutus's brother Decimus, who held the town of Modeno.

Octavian then embarked on the second stage of his plan. 'Here I am,' he told the Senate. 'Use me as you will.' He made no mention now of avenging Caesar, nor of the sin of fraternising with his killers, of whom Decimus Brutus was one. Octavian's sense of filial duty was nothing if not elastic.

The Senate had no choice. Believing that once the crisis was past and Modeno relieved young Octavian could be brushed aside or swatted like an overbothersome wasp, they gave him the joint command together with the newly elected consuls Hirtius and Pansa.

I do not intend to describe the Modeno campaign, which was a confused and messy business and cost the state both her consuls – Hirtius killed outright, Pansa dead of wounds. In April, the town was relieved and Antony retreated northwards. Once the danger was over, the Senate tried to rid themselves of Octavian . . .

The Arab nomads tell of a particularly unpleasant character called the Old Man of the Sea. This monster in human shape waits by the side of a stream, begging travellers to carry him over to the other bank. No sooner has he sat himself on the traveller's shoulders than he wraps his legs about his victim's throat, so that the man must choose between being strangled or taking his unwelcome guest wherever he wants to go. In fact, the choice is no choice at all, and the end result is the same: the Old Man will not give up his steed, so long as it has a spark of life left in it.

The Senate faced a similar problem with Octavian. The more they tried to shake him off, the tighter he clung. They ordered him to lay down his command; he refused. They appealed to the legions themselves; the legions mutinied. They instructed Lepidus, their commander in Gaul, to intervene; Lepidus defected to Antony, taking his seven legions with him. Finally, in July, Octavian himself took the offensive. A party of army sergeants entered the Senate House and, on his behalf, demanded the consulship. When an indignant senator asked what gave a twenty-year-old boy the right to the state's highest office, the leader drew his sword and held it out, point towards the man's throat.

'This,' he said.

As an argument, it was unanswerable. On 19 August Octavian became consul.

At the installation ceremony, twelve vultures flew above the Capitol – the same sign as had greeted Romulus at Rome's founding. The priests, of course, declared them to be an omen that the new consul would prove a second Romulus; that his consulate would inaugurate a new era for Rome. Perhaps they were right. Perhaps the gods really do talk to us in these hieroglyphs of the air. I have my suspicions.

Call me cynical if you will; but any birdcatcher worth his salt can perform *that* kind of miracle. And those vultures reeked of Octavian.

36

I had better, before I go any further, say a little about Antony.

This part of my story is difficult for me. I am too close to events, and it would be easy to portray him through Octavian's eyes: a dangerous, drunken, lecherous sot who deserted his own kind and would have sold Rome for a kiss from his Egyptian whore. On the other hand, I must beware of allowing my antipathy towards Octavian to drive me to the other extreme, and paint him in glowing colours like the hero of an eastern legend. Antony was neither hero nor villain. He was only a man, with a man's failings, and he died because he could not rise above himself, or sink lower.

When I was a child, we had a neighbour by the name of Pomptinus. Pomptinus owned a prize bull called Ajax which was the envy of the countryside. Any cow he covered (and he would cover any that lifted her tail to him) was sure to calve at the first attempt, and Ajax's sons and daughters were famous further afield than Cremona.

Pomptinus was very proud of Ajax. I remember my father saying sourly that he treated the bull better than his own children, feeding him corn with his own hand, sitting up with him when he fell sick, talking to him for hours on end when he should have been plaiting hurdles or sharpening stakes. And Ajax, in his turn, loved his master. He would follow Pomptinus around the farm like a dog, even allowing him to ride on his back (although no one else would have dared, for to all but Pomptinus Ajax had a wicked temper).

One day in early spring Pomptinus went missing. He had told his sons that morning that he had a ditch to dig on the boundary of his farm and had not returned by evening. When it was properly dark, the sons became worried. They roused the farm-slaves, mounted a search, and discovered Pomptinus lying beside the half-dug ditch. He was alive but badly mauled. Over him stood Ajax, his horns bloody; and scattered around the clearing were the gutted bodies of five wolves.

When he recovered consciousness Pomptinus told his sons what had happened. He had been digging the ditch, with Ajax, as usual, grazing a few yards away. Suddenly he had looked up and seen the wolves coming towards him; it had been a hard winter, and the shortage of game had driven them to seek easier pickings on the farms near the river. He had dropped his mattock and run, but before he could reach the safety of the trees the whole pack were on him.

The next thing Pomptinus knew, Ajax was standing over him. Time and again the wolves rushed in, only to come up against those terrible horns. Ajax scattered the pack like chaff, tossing them as a farmer tosses bales of straw. Pomptinus saw three disembowelled before he fainted from the pain of his wounds.

That is not the end of the story. After the incident of the wolves, nothing was too good for the bull. If Pomptinus could have afforded it, Ajax would have eaten gilded corn from a golden manger and washed it down with the finest of wines. As it was, he was granted honourable retirement. Nothing heavier was set on his neck than a garland of flowers at the Spring Festival, and Pomptinus bought a stretch of prime grazing land from his nearest neighbour so that Ajax should have the sweetest grass to eat throughout the summer.

Now, Pomptinus had an enemy, a small farmer named Cluvius whom he had worsted in a land suit some years before. Cluvius had been looking ever since for an opportunity to get his revenge, and the purchase of the grazing land brought him his chance. The land lay beside the river, and beyond it – guarded, of course, by hurdles – was a deep and treacherous bog. One day when the river was full and he knew that Pomptinus was elsewhere, Cluvius removed the hurdles. Then he took a sack of corn; and little by little, by throwing handfuls of corn further and further into the bog, he enticed the bull into the mud where he stuck, sank and eventually drowned.

That, if you like, was the story of Antony and Octavian. Antony's virtues were Ajax's: he was brave, honourable and completely faithful to his master Caesar, whom he would cheerfully have died to protect or to avenge. Yet his subservience to gross appetites proved his downfall: like Cluvius, Octavian used it to entice his enemy further into the mud, then stood on the bank and watched him wallow and drown.

As a Roman, I can see that Antony brought ruin on himself, and that his death was the best thing for Rome. Yet, as a man, I pity him as I pitied the bull. In the last analysis, he was a far better man than his adversary, and Octavian's motives were no more worthy of honour than Cluvius's.

37

In late November of that year I went to Rome on business for Siro. I had arranged as usual to stay with Proculus, in the house on the Esquiline which had been my second home even after Valeria's death.

We had had news in Naples, of course, of recent political developments. Octavian had gone north a few weeks before, and met Antony and Lepidus at Bononia. Now, so rumour had it, they were marching south with the army at their backs.

By the time I had reached Alba, traffic on the Appian Way had become a constant stream: wagons, for the most part, piled high with crates, expensive carriages pulled by bloodstock horses; even the occasional litter. All signs that many of Rome's wealthier citizens had tested the wind and decided to move south to healthier climes. Just outside the Capenan Gate, where the road enters the city, an overladen wagon had collapsed, blocking the carriageway. Sweating slaves were labouring to empty it of its packing-cases while the drivers behind cursed and shouted. Beside it, unregarded, lay what I took at first to be a corpse wrapped in bandages. Remembering my first visit to Rome ten years before I shivered and made the sign against bad luck; but the body was only a bronze statue unloaded from one of the damaged crates.

It was late when I arrived at Proculus's house. Everything was in darkness, a circumstance I found strange since a torch was usually kept burning in the wall-cresset. Telling the litter-men to wait, I went up to the door and knocked. For a long time there was no answer. I had almost decided that Proculus, too, had gone and was wondering what to do next when a voice behind the door said, 'Who's there?'

The voice belonged to Helenus, Proculus's chief slave. He sounded frightened.

'Helenus! It's me, Virgil!' I shouted. 'Come on, man, open up! It's perishing out here!'

The door opened,

'Virgil!' Helenus's face was drawn. 'We'd given you up, sir!'

He held the door open – but not, I noticed, very far. I dismissed the litter and entered. Helenus closed the door behind me and barred it.

'The master's in his study,' he said. 'Go straight through.'

'How are you, Helenus?'

He gave me a ghastly smile. His face was grey.

'Oh, *I'm* all right, sir,' he said; and would have said more, but Proculus was already crossing the hall.

'Virgil! Welcome home, my boy!'

He had changed since I had last seen him, and mostly for the better. There was a brightness to his eyes and a straightness to his back that belonged to a man years younger; but his face was grave.

'You're looking well, sir,' I said as we shook hands.

'No better than you.' He smiled, held me at arm's length. 'Good to have you back. You had a good journey?'

'Tolerable enough,' I said. 'How's Lucius?'

Lucius, if you remember, was his son. He would be rising twelve now.

'Fine, thank God.' Proculus signalled Helenus to bring wine. 'I've sent him to my cousin in Rhodes, away from the troubles. Now come in and sit down. You must be tired.'

'Not especially,' I said. 'What troubles in particular?'

Proculus laughed as he led the way into the sitting-room.

'I was forgetting,' he said. 'You're pretty much out of the world these days.'

I smiled.

'We're not as out of touch as all that. But you haven't answered my question.'

We lay down on the couches. Helenus reappeared with a loaded tray: wine and a bowl of fruit. As he lifted the jug to pour his hand twitched. Wine slopped over the rim of the cup and splashed on to the table.

'I'm sorry, sir,' Helenus said. He dabbed at the spilt liquid with a napkin, head down.

Proculus took the jug and poured the wine himself.

'Some plain water for our guest, Helenus,' he said. 'Had you forgotten?'

Helenus straightened. For a moment, his mouth worked as if he were about to say something. Then he turned and left the room. I looked enquiringly at Proculus, but he seemed not to have noticed anything unusual.

'You know they've reached Rome?' he said. I did not have to ask who he meant.

'No. When?'

'Two days ago. The Senate have ratified what was agreed at Bononia. Spain and Old Gaul for Lepidus. Africa, Sicily and Sardinia for Octavian.' Proculus carefully divided an apple. 'Italy and the rest of Gaul for Antony.'

'I suppose it was only to be expected,' I said.

Helenus reappeared and set the jug of water down beside me. His face was wooden, expressionless.

Proculus frowned.

'Oh, they'll fall out eventually,' he said, 'like the greedy children they are. Each will want it all. And when the squabbling starts we'll be there to pick up the pieces.'

My hand paused above the water-jug.

'We?'

An expression I could not place flitted across Proculus's face.

'Perhaps I shouldn't say "we". I mean what Cicero calls the Good Element. Properly constituted authority and its supporters.'

I felt a twinge of unease.

'But surely,' I said, 'Octavian *is* the properly constituted authority. He is consul, after all, whether you like it or not.'

'Not any more. He's resigned in favour of Bassus.'

I simply stared at him. He nodded.

'That's right. He, Antony and Lepidus are now extraordinary magistrates for the reconstruction of the state. The post lasts for five years.' Proculus sipped his wine. 'A good trade for a run-of-the-mill consulate, wouldn't you say?'

'Is it legal?'

'You think that matters?' Proculus set his wine-cup down. 'The Senate have confirmed it, at any rate. They had no choice, they know where the real power lies. For the moment.'

'Only for the moment?'

'There's still the east.'

'Brutus and Cassius?' I could not keep the scorn from my voice.

Proculus regarded me carefully, and I felt myself flushing.

'We're not fools, Virgil,' he said at last. 'Brutus left Italy to avoid a civil war, not through cowardice or lack of support. He's spent the last fifteen months gathering men and money in north Greece. And Cassius has over a dozen legions in Syria.'

'You think they count for much against Caesar's Gallic veterans?'

Helenus, standing against the wall behind his master's right shoulder, shifted position slightly. He was frowning at me.

'Perhaps not, man for man,' Proculus said. 'But Brutus and Cassius have time on their side. The longer they wait the better. Antony and his friends will come to blows sooner or later, and that'll be the end of that. In the meantime, young Sextus Pompey's got enough ships to discourage a seaborne attack. And a blockade of Italy combined with Antony's land requisitions could produce enough unrest to tip the balance.'

'What land requisitions?'

Proculus stopped.

'You hadn't heard?' he said; and then: 'No, of course you hadn't. Antony is requisitioning land from the eighteen richest towns to pay off the troops. He . . .'

'Where?' Somehow, I already knew the answer. My throat felt dry.

'Beneventum. Capua,' Proculus said unwillingly. 'Cremona in the north . . .'

'Mantua?'

He nodded.

'Mantua too,' he said. 'Your father still farms near there?'

Before I could answer, we were interrupted by a loud knocking at the front door. Helenus stiffened. The knocking was repeated, louder this time, as if someone were pounding the panels with a hammer or the hilt of a sword.

'See who it is, Helenus,' Proculus said.

Helenus did not move.

'Helenus,' Proculus's voice was surprisingly mild. 'Do your job. Answer the door, please.'

I looked from one to the other in amazement. Helenus

had been Proculus's slave from birth, but I had never before seen him take such a liberty. And Proculus, although he treated slaves with great consideration, had no time for disobedience.

Helenus was still standing like a marble statue behind his master's couch. Proculus rose.

'Very well,' he said. 'I'll do it myself. Excuse me, Virgil.'

He got up and left the room. I could hear the sound of bolts being drawn, the clatter of the door and the murmur of voices.

'What's going on?' I asked Helenus . . . and then I realised that the man was crying. He stood stiff and straight while the tears gouged channels down the rigid wood of his cheeks.

The front door closed. In the hall, metal clinked and voices growled. Proculus said something in answer; and a moment later rejoined us. He did not look at Helenus.

'I'm sorry,' he said to me. 'I had hoped I might spare you this.'

'Who is it? Who's out there?'

'Five soldiers and an officer, a Marcus Vibius. I've known him since he was a child. Hence' – his mouth twisted –' this small indulgence.'

'I don't understand.'

'A list of . . . enemies of the state was posted in the Market Square this morning. By order of Antony and Octavian. My name was included.'

'You're being arrested?' I could not believe this was happening.

'Not exactly,' Proculus said gently.

'You should have run, sir,' Helenus burst out. 'You had time. You could still do it.'

'Where would I run to?' Proculus said.

'They're going to kill him.' Helenus turned to me. 'It was a death-list was put up. Tell him to run!'

'Virgil will tell me nothing of the kind,' Proculus said

sharply. 'He's a good Epicurean as well as a good friend. He knows that death is meaningless. Especially to me.' He grasped my hand, shook it firmly. 'Goodbye, my boy. Remember me to your father next time you see him.'

I felt as a man does who suffers some sudden accident. My brain was completely numb. I could only think, looking at the table: They might at least give him time to finish his wine.

Proculus turned to Helenus.

'Vibius has kindly allowed me to make my own arrangements,' he said. 'See that he and his men are offered refreshments while they wait. Instructions for my funeral are in the top left-hand bureau drawer. My will, of course, is superfluous under the circumstances but you will find it in the same place. Thank you for your service over the years.'

That was all. He nodded, once to me, once to Helenus. Then he went out. The study door opened and closed.

I saw his body after it was all over. He had not slit his wrists as I had expected but stabbed himself. Whether he intended by this to spare both himself and us the ravages of a lingering death, or wished simply to avoid undue mess, I do not know. I suspect the latter: Proculus was always fastidious. There was certainly very little blood, since the dagger stayed in the wound until Helenus drew it out.

38

Proculus's death was civilised compared to the carnage that followed.

Imagine a fox who has slipped into a crowded hen-run. He kills indiscriminately, seizing the chickens one by one as they fly around in panic, snapping their necks, tearing them limb from limb, tossing the mangled bodies aside. The air about him as he runs is thick with feathers, and the dust under his paws is churned into a sodden red porridge.

That was Rome, under the triumvirs' 'reconstruction'. In the space of ten days, three hundred senators and two thousand knights died; murdered by Antony and Octavian either because of their politics or, more often, simply for the sake of their wealth. Others, more fortunate, escaped to the coast where Sextus Pompey, himself under sentence of death, arranged for them to be picked up and taken to Sicily. Cicero, Antony's bitterest opponent, was not of their number. At the start of the proscriptions, he had been at his villa near Formiae. He made a half-hearted attempt to join Pompey, but was intercepted and killed. His head and hands were hacked off, and Antony had them nailed to the speakers' platform in the Market Square for the mob to gape at.

I was not there to see them. I had left Rome the day after Proculus died, bound for Mantua. What Proculus had said about land confiscations had worried me deeply, and I was greatly concerned about my father. It was not an easy journey. Patrols had been stationed at the city gates to check for fugitives, and the roads beyond them were full of soldiers eager to swell their army pay by a little extortion. Nevertheless, a northern route was a hundred times safer than the road to Capua would have been. No fugitive in his right mind would go north, where the triumvirs' main armies lay.

The journey took me eight days, travelling on horseback with two slaves. Even without the added dangers it would have been unpleasant in the extreme. The weather, bad enough at Rome, deteriorated as we went north. A bitingly cold wind drove rain into our eyes, half blinding us and slowing the horses' pace at times to a walk. Many of the inns were closed through fear of the soldiers; those which remained open were fleapits of the worst kind. I slept all seven nights wrapped in my cloak, and even so woke scratching.

I did not recognise my father, nor he me.

He opened the door himself. At first, I took him for one of his own slaves, and not a house-slave at that. He had crumbled away like a clod of dry earth; his skin, dull, mud-brown and desiccated, hung from him in dry folds and pouches. When he put out a hand like a claw to brush my chest, and I looked into his eyes, I realised that he was almost blind.

'It's me, Father,' I said. 'Publius.'

His brow furrowed.

'Publius? Which Publius?'

'Your son. I've come from Rome.'

He stepped back to allow me in. The farmhouse, although not the one of my childhood, was instantly familiar, built to the same plan. I would have taken his arm to lead him into the living-room, but he shook me off.

'I can see well enough,' he said. 'I don't need your help.'

The place was a mess, and stank. Scraps of food – stale bread, rotten apples, some spilt bean stew – lay scattered on the floor. The table was piled with dirty dishes, some of them broken. I stood on the threshold and stared.

'Where are the slaves?' I said.

'Run off.' My father was standing beside me. I caught his sour-sweet smell, the same as that of the room but with overtones of urine. His tunic was so filthy I could not tell its colour.

'And Gaius? My brother Gaius?'

'Dead these two months,' he said.

I moved to the table, began mechanically to pile the dishes one on the other.

'You never told me. You never wrote,' I said.

'Why should I?'

I closed my eyes, feeling the bitterness build up inside me.

'I'm your son.'

'Are you?' he shot back. 'I had two sons. Both of them are dead, Marcus and Gaius both. I had a farm, once, too. Everything's gone now.'

So I had been right. The farm had been confiscated.

'We'll talk about it later,' I said wearily. 'First of all let's get this place cleaned up.'

I went back outside and called in my slaves from the barn, where they had gone to sleep with the horses.

'He came five days ago,' my father said. 'A smooth-faced young bastard of an officer with a letter I couldn't read. Said he'd orders from Caesar.'

The name would be Caesar, of course. As soon as he had arrived at Rome, Octavian had had his adoption legalised. Now he was officially Gaius Julius Caesar. Only his enemies still called him Octavian.

The room was clean and tidy now, and the slaves had lit two charcoal braziers to take off the December chill. My father had washed and changed his tunic. He sat opposite me sipping at the wine I had warmed and mixed with barley and honey. It was almost homely. A domestic scene, featuring the loving father and the dutiful son.

'I told him he was a liar.' The old man smiled, and I noticed that his teeth were brown and broken. 'Caesar would never give an order like that. We supported him. He'd never throw us off our land, take our farms. Besides, he's dead. Murdered by those senatorial bastards at Rome.'

I explained. Or tried to.

'Did he mention any other names? The messenger, I mean?'

'Someone called Pollio. And a Cornelius Gallus.'

I sat back. Of course. Pollio would be a logical choice for deputy. He had commanded the Spanish legions which had formed part of the triumvirs' army and was a proven administrator. But Gallus? Had he risen so fast in Octavian's estimation?

'You're sure?'

'There's nothing wrong with my ears, boy.'

The thing was beginning to look more hopeful. If Pollio and Gallus were in charge of land requisitions in the north then they would at least give me a fair hearing.

'Where are they now? Cremona?'

'Milan.' He had caught the excitement in my voice. 'You know them?'

'Very well. Pollio commissioned some poems from me.'

'Is that so?' my father said sourly. 'Then you may be worth something after all. Surprise surprise.'

As praise it was not much, but it was better than nothing. A beggar must be thankful for what he is given.

I set off next day for Milan, alone, since I had thought it best to leave the slaves with my father. Pollio had gone to Rome several days before – I realised with some chagrin that I had probably passed him on the road – but Gallus was in residence at the provincial governor's mansion. When I entered, he was dictating a letter to a Greek secretary. He looked up, stared as if he had seen a ghost, then came over and embraced me warmly.

'Virgil! What brings you here?'

I told him, and he looked grave.

'There's not much I can do,' he said. 'The papers have been signed and the ownership transferred. But leave it with me, I'll work something out even if I have to appeal to Caesar himself.'

'I'd rather you didn't do that,' I said.

'Why not?' He dismissed the secretary and sat on the edge of the desk.

I felt uncomfortable. It had been years since I had seen Gallus. He had changed very little physically, except for a general broadening and thickening. But he was Octavian's man now, and I did not know how our past friendship would measure up against that.

'Let's just say I'd prefer not to be obligated.'

'Rubbish!' Gallus grinned. 'He's no ogre. He'd be delighted to help, I'm sure.'

'I've seen examples of his helpfulness at Rome,' I said before I could stop myself. 'I left before I had to stomach any more of them.'

The grin faded.

'That was necessary. Is necessary. There can be no half measures, Virgil. He's only doing what he has to. For peace.'

'A graveyard's peaceful. That's because it's full of corpses.' I knew I was being melodramatic, and probably foolish – even fatally so; but I could not stop myself.

'Listen!' Gallus gripped my arm so hard that it hurt. 'You can't make an omelette without breaking eggs. It's necessary, Publius. Caesar – Julius Caesar – tried half measures and got himself killed. His son can't afford to repeat the mistake. He has too much to lose.'

'He killed Proculus. Was that particular egg "necessary"?'

I could see that Gallus was shaken. He had liked and respected Proculus almost as much as I had.

'*Proculus?*' he whispered. 'Proculus is dead?'

'He committed suicide ten days ago. On your master's orders.'

Gallus shook his head.

'Not Caesar's orders. Not his. Antony's, perhaps.'

I shrugged wearily and turned aside.

'Does it matter? He's dead, anyway. Whoever gave the order.'

Gallus was silent for a long time. Then he said, in a low voice, 'I'm sorry, Publius. Really I am. But it doesn't change anything. Octavian – Caesar, I mean . . .'

'Why not call him Octavian?'

'Caesar,' he stressed the word, 'is doing everything for the best. Strong measures are necessary if we're to save the state. It's like cutting off a diseased arm.'

'Perhaps we should have a second opinion.'

'We haven't the time!' Gallus's hand slammed down on the desk. 'You must understand this! Antony and Caesar can't afford to ignore any viable opposition. And they can't work without men and money. It's terrible, I know, but it has to be done. Publius, it is necessary!'

'If I hear that word again I'll throw up.'

Gallus flushed.

'Look,' he said. 'I don't want to argue. Not when we haven't seen each other for so long. I know I'm right, and I hope you'll realise it too in time. But let's leave it for now. Please.'

I took a deep breath and tried to calm myself. Gallus was

right. He was my best friend, we had not seen each other for years, and yet all I could do was shout at him.

'Very well,' I said.

'How's the poetry coming on?'

I smiled.

'Slowly, as always.'

'Pollio says you're working on an adaptation of Theocritus.'

'That's right.' The secretary's stool was behind me. I sat down. 'I've two poems completed and several more at the ideas stage. But it's a long job.'

He poured himself some wine and held the jug up enquiringly. I shook my head.

'How are you approaching it? The adaptation, I mean.'

'I'd thought of giving the poems an Italian setting. No explicit references. Just the general mood.'

Gallus rolled the wine-cup to and fro between his hands, frowning, as I had seen him do in the past when he had something to say that he knew would upset or embarrass me. Finally he said abruptly, 'You haven't considered introducing a political element?'

'How do you mean?'

'Just something Pollio and I were discussing. It'd be an interesting blend of genres, completely new, completely Roman. Treating political and social issues in a pastoral context.'

'What sort of political and social issues had you in mind?' I said sarcastically. I could see which way the conversation was tending.

'That'd be for you to decide, naturally.' Gallus backed off slightly. 'But poetry – really good poetry – of that type would be useful.'

'Useful to whom?'

Gallus's eyes shifted.

'It might help to clarify an ambiguous situation,' he said. 'Smooth the path for the forces of order. Explain things a bit more clearly in a way the educated classes could relate to.'

'You mean you want me for your court poet? To dignify what Octavian is doing in deathless verse?'

This was too direct. Gallus had the grace to blush.

'Not at all,' he said. 'We wouldn't ask you to go against your principles.'

'I'm glad of that,' I said, 'because the answer would have been no.'

'I didn't mean—' Gallus began, but I interrupted him.

'I don't write for penny-ha'penny warlords who murder people I respect.'

Gallus held up his hand, palm outwards, in an oddly placating gesture.

'Please, Publius,' he said. 'It has nothing to do with Caesar. Not personally. Think about it. And try to keep an open mind. Meanwhile I'll see what I can do about your father's farm.'

He stood up.

I stood up as well.

'You aren't trying to coerce me, are you, Gaius?' I said.

He looked hurt: genuinely hurt.

'No. Never,' he said quietly. 'I swear I'm not. Never believe that, Publius. We're friends and I'll do my best for you, whatever happens. But I can't help my convictions any more than you can yours. It was a genuine suggestion, one poet to another. Just keep an open mind. Please.'

'Very well,' I said, a little stiffly. 'You have my word.'

With that I left.

39

When I got back to the farm, there was a horse tethered at the trough by the barn. It was an army horse – that much was clear from the brand on its rump – but far too poor a specimen to belong to an officer. I shouted for the slaves, but there was no answer.

The house door was open. I went in, through the kitchen and into the living-room – and almost spitted myself on the point of a sword.

The man who held it wore military uniform: a legionary, probably about my father's age, although chunkier and muscle-hard. Behind him I could see my father and the two slaves backed against the wall. One slave held a blood-soaked rag to his arm.

'You'll be the son?' the soldier said. It was not a local accent. I judged that he was a southerner, probably Campanian.

I felt sick.

'That's right,' I said. 'Who are you?'

The sword was at my throat now. It looked very sharp, the edges honed almost concave.

'Name's Flavianus.'

'What do you want? Money?' Some deserter, I thought – although soldiers did not desert a victorious army. Perhaps he was in trouble of another kind.

He grinned and spat.

'Stuff your money. I want you off my land.'

'*Your* land?' I was so surprised that I actually laughed – a dangerous thing to do with a sword at your throat. The point bit beneath my chin, and I stiffened.

'That's right.' He looked at me with narrowed eyes. Then, obviously deciding that I posed no threat, he lowered the sword and stepped back. 'This farm's mine. I want you off it.'

My knees had begun to shake. Whatever happened, I knew, I must not show fear. I leaned back against the wall.

'Are you all right, Father?' I said.

'The bastard pushed his way in.' My father's voice was indignant. I envied him his courage. 'Titus here' – indicating the wounded slave – 'tried to stop him but he got cut.'

'He ran on to my sword,' Flavianus said.

'Nonsense. You stabbed him.' I forced myself to speak steadily: a rhetorical education has some value. 'That slave doesn't belong to the farm. He's mine. And if you've permanently damaged him I'm holding you liable.'

The soldier's eyes flickered. I pressed my advantage, injecting a note of authority.

'What legion are you?'

'The Alauda. Second cohort.'

'Centurion?'

'Decimus.'

'You know Cornelius Gallus?'

The soldier paled slightly. I could see that he was beginning to reassess his position.

'Yes, sir,' he said.

'Put that sword away.' He did so, with encouraging speed. 'I've just got back from Milan. I've had a word with my friend Gallus' – I dwelt on the word *friend* – 'and there seems to have been a mistake. He agrees with me that the matter should be investigated.'

'Oh, there's no mistake, sir.' Flavianus reached into his tunic and brought out a greasy, crumpled sheet of parchment. He held it out to me with a curious pride. 'See for yourself.'

I took the parchment and read it. He was quite right. It was a legal deed of transfer, ceding the property to him with immediate effect.

'This is dated the day after tomorrow,' I lied, handing the parchment back.

He frowned and peered at the crabbed writing – as I had hoped, without result.

'They told me today,' he said.

'That's not what it says there. We have two days' grace.' I stepped away from the door. 'I suggest you leave now and come back on the legal day. Unless, of course, the mistake has been rectified by then, as I have every hope that it will.'

He gave me a shamefaced look as he moved past me, and I felt almost guilty. After all, my father's loss was no fault of his, and a farm meant security in old age. If he lost this one there was no guarantee that he would get another.

'Very well, sir,' he said. 'Sorry about the fuss.'

I said nothing, and followed him out. Once I had seen him mount and ride off, I returned to my father.

'Well done, my boy!' My father showed his uneven teeth in a grin. 'That's got rid of him!'

I sat down on the bench. I was shaking uncontrollably, too far gone even to appreciate the unaccustomed praise.

'Only until he finds out I wasn't telling the truth,' I said.

The old man frowned.

'What d'you mean?'

'He was perfectly within his rights. He just couldn't read, that's all. The poor devil's illiterate.'

'You're saying he can turf me out? Just like that?'

'That's what I'm saying.'

'I'll die first,' my father said. 'Or I'll kill the bastard with my own hands if he sets one foot on my land.'

'It's no use,' I said wearily. 'The law will back him up. You can't fight the whole Roman army.'

He looked at me, his eyes bright with contempt.

'You coward,' he said slowly. 'You pissing coward.'

I was too tired to argue.

'That's as may be,' I said. 'But I've bought us an extra day, at least. The slaves will help you pack. I'll arrange for a wagon in Mantua. You can come back home with me.'

I think my tone surprised him, perhaps shamed him a little, too, for he was a just man, beneath the bitterness. He sat for a long time with his head bowed. Then, in a different voice, he said, 'I'm sorry, Publius. You did your best. It's not your fault.'

'I saw Gallus. He's willing to help, but it may take time.'

My father did not move. His almost sightless eyes were fixed on the floor at his feet.

'This farm's my life,' he said. 'You understand that, don't you? It would kill me to lose it. I'd be like a plant pulled up by the roots.'

'I know, Father,' I said. 'I know.'

We left for Naples the next day. My father sat hunched like a ragged crow beside the cart-driver, and did not look back.

40

Final preparations for war began with the new year – not before time, for Proculus had been right about the change in public opinion. The horror of the proscriptions had left a deep wound that was slow to heal; while to the injury of the land requisitions the triumvirs added the insult of a property tax to pay the mounting costs of the campaign.

Antony and Octavian had twenty-eight legions to the Republicans' nineteen. Eight they sent ahead into northern Greece, where Brutus and Cassius had based themselves. The remainder crossed the Adriatic during the early summer. Proculus had thought that they would be harassed by Pompey's fleet; but Pompey was too busy consolidating his own position in Sicily to concern himself with the welfare of allies.

Octavian played no part in the early campaign: the 'son of the Divine Julius' (Caesar had been officially declared a god at the start of the year) lay groaning with a colic at Dyrrhachium. Antony crossed over with the troops and confronted the Republican army. In September, Octavian joined him; and the two armies clashed at Philippi.

The first battle of Philippi was a muddled disaster for the Republicans. Brutus and Cassius were camped side by side to the west of the town, blocking the Egnatian Road. To the south lay a stretch of marshy ground which served to protect the camp from a flanking attack and safeguard its lines of communication. Antony, in an attempt to breach this, had begun to build a causeway, against which Brutus and Cassius prepared their own siegeworks. Antony suddenly attacked these, launching at the same time a frontal attack on Cassius's camp. He was completely successful. Cassius's troops were routed and his camp plundered. Not knowing that Brutus had attacked on his own account and actually taken Octavian's camp, Cassius thought that the battle was lost. In true Roman fashion, he killed himself, leaving Antony the honours of the field.

Antony. Not Octavian and Antony. Antony. His co-commander Octavian, if the rumour is true, was hiding somewhere in the marshes. He did not reappear until the following day, on foot, wet through, spattered with mud and without his cloak. When Antony questioned him, Octavian could only say that his doctor had had a dream instructing him (Octavian) to leave the camp before the battle. Where had he been in the meantime? Octavian wouldn't say.

Later, Antony was to taunt Octavian with this instance of cowardice, and the stain on Octavian's character persisted long after the civil wars were over.

Octavian is certainly a physical coward. I know that, from my own observations: he is, for example, terrified of thunder and will hide in a cellar until the storm is over. Yet the position is not that simple. Nothing about Octavian ever is.

Consider our instinctive reactions. If we pick up something too hot to hold – a bowl of scalding soup, perhaps, or a hot iron from the fire – we immediately let it fall. We do not think, If I drop this bowl the soup will spill, or If I drop this iron I may start a fire. There is no thought involved. The reaction is outwith our control.

Octavian is different. He can interpose the thought

between action and reaction. He may be a coward, but he has the ability to subordinate cowardice to self-interest. Take for example his conduct during Caesar's Spanish campaign, or in the second battle of Philippi, when he picked up a fallen standard and carried it through the thick of the battle. On these occasions, circumstances demanded that he show bravery; and show it he did.

I do not criticise, only observe. Perhaps his is true bravery; to conquer one's fear and bring it under one's rational control. I do not know. But his actions strike cold, and chime too well with a calculating nature. His cowardice before Philippi was less in character; but it showed that even inside Octavian there burned a spark of humanity.

With the death of Cassius, Brutus was left alone to carry on the struggle. Naturally more cautious than his colleague, he did nothing, in the hope that the approaching winter would make the enemy's position untenable: his fleet threatened their supply lines and the Egnatian Road was the only route to the south. However, a combination of desertions and pressure from his own officers forced Brutus to take action. On 23 October he launched his attack. The Republicans were completely routed, and Brutus, seeing that his cause was lost, took his own life.

Let me say at once that I approved of – still approve of – the verdict of Philippi. I am no Republican. No one can be who seriously considers the harm Republican government caused, and would still be causing if Philippi had gone the other way. In financing their campaign, Brutus and Cassius were completely ruthless. Together they bled Asia dry. When one particular city, Xanthus, refused to contribute, they placed it under siege. Rather than surrender to the Tyrannicides' tender mercies, the Xanthians set their city alight and committed mass suicide in the Market Square – men, women and children alike. That, to me, is damning.

A system of government which produces such a reaction is rotten at its heart.

Freedom may thrive on blood; but it is usually the innocent who shed it.

I have more sympathy for Cassius than for Brutus. Cassius, like Antony, had the saving grace of *choler* – I can think of no better word. He was the perfect Homeric hero, with all that hero's best qualities: bravery, impulsiveness, generosity and a keen sense of honour. Of course, he had also the Homeric hero's faults: pride, rashness, undiluted self-interest and a preference for instinctive, rather than reasoned, action; and these made him a dangerous anachronism. One may admire Achilles or Agamemnon as men, but one would not wish to live under them.

Brutus was different to Cassius. He was the anti-Octavian: like his enemy, a cold, self-righteous fanatic, but without Octavian's *rightness*. Octavian, when all is said and done, at least had right on his side. Brutus was merely dangerous, and the world is a better place without him.

41

Meanwhile, my father had recovered his farm.

It is illogical, I know; but that one sentence, for me, has far greater importance than all the events of the preceding chapter.

The news came early in May, in a letter from Pollio. Enclosed were the title deeds, made out to my father 'in perpetuity'. When I gave them to him, and told him what they were (he could not read them himself, being now quite blind) he wept, and kissed my hand.

Kissed my hand!

What are victories, or principles, set beside that?

My father had enjoyed his five months at Naples. At first he had wandered about the villa like a ghost – a clumsy ghost since, taken out of his familiar surroundings, he had to rely on the little sight left to him to make his way around. When the spring came, however, and the weather improved he spent most of his time in the garden, not sitting but working: planting, pruning and weeding by touch and smell better than I could do with my eyesight unimpaired. He never, of course, took part in our philosophical discussions – he felt that they were beneath him – but finding that Siro had a reasonable (if theoretical) knowledge of plants and agriculture he would corner him and try to catch him out. Which he did, on several occasions, to his great satisfaction.

I cannot say that, in these five months, we grew much closer: we were too different in temperament and interests for that. Yet by the end of them we were at least comfortable in each other's company, and he even, on occasion, called me 'son'.

With the arrival of the letter, all this came – pleasantly – to an end. There was no reason now for him to stay. Pollio had even provided slaves to accompany him north and work the farm: three Gauls and two Spaniards, previously state-owned, from Caesar's campaigns, together with a North African woman-slave to serve as housekeeper. I would have gone with them, but Siro fell ill towards the end of the month and, knowing that he would not recover, I stayed where I was.

The period was less productive in other ways. I had, as I had told Gallus, completed two Theocritan pastorals. A third was at the stage of being licked into shape. Turning back to this poem after our conversation, I discovered that it no longer worked, that I could no longer see it clearly, as if my perspective had shifted: if you are a poet yourself you will understand what I mean. I found that, almost against my own will, I was tinkering with it, introducing contemporary themes, even names.

That both frightened and faintly disgusted me. Before I was tempted to go any further, I shut the poem away in a drawer as if it were some dangerous animal, or a drug to which I was addicted, and did not look at it again for over a year. Oh, I wrote other poems, not very many, and not very good – but no pastorals. That was a conscious decision; but it only postponed the inevitable.

Imagine a colt, just captured, wind-wild, fresh from the plains. A stupid farmer will set the halter on it straight away, break its mouth with the bit and its spirit with the whip. He may tame it quickly, but the horse is ruined, fit only for carrying firewood or turning a mill like an ox. The wise farmer lets the colt run free about the paddock, feeds it grass and peas, when it will take them, from his own hand, until the horse has grown accustomed to the man-sight and the man-smell and does not see them as threatening. Then the farmer throws on to the colt's back a light blanket, and, little by little, accustoms it to carrying things until, finally, it is ready to bear a rider.

During these eighteen months, like the colt with a wise master I was left to canter around the paddock. My emotions were similarly confused. The simple fact was (and I can see this more clearly now, with hindsight) that I had found Gallus's idea of a blend between the real world and a fanciful Theocritan utopia fascinating. As Gallus had said, such a blend would be completely new, completely Roman; and it is not often we Latin poets can steal a march on the Greeks. I knew, too, that he honestly expected nothing in return for his help over the farm. The letter and the deeds had come from Pollio; and Pollio was Antony's man, not Octavian's. It was a beautifully tactful way on Gallus's part of divorcing politics from friendship. Last of all, and greatest, I felt an enormous debt for the only fondness my father had ever shown me. That, I would have given anything to repay. I baulked, not at the price, but at the currency. Round and round I went, kicking up my heels, shying away from the proffered handful of peas. Although I did not know it, I was being broken to the man-smell, the smell of power.

All this sounds, I am afraid, like a cheap plea for sympathy. Believe me, that is not my intention. No one can find fault with a horse-trainer who does his job, least of all when he does it well. A horse's worth lies not in himself but in how well he serves; and if, in the end, he throws his master, which of the two is blamed?

Siro died on 3 June. I grieved, of course, but he was happy to go: although his final illness had been a short one, he had been in considerable pain for several years. I cannot agree with Epicurus's maxim 'Long pain's easy borne/Strong pain soon over'. It conflicts too often with observed fact, and its patness suggests too great a desire for rhetorical balance over truth.

When Siro's will was opened, I found that he had left his villa outside Naples to me. I was embarrassed. Siro had no family, certainly, but he and Parthenius had been very close for many years. I approached Parthenius and suggested tactfully that I refuse the bequest. He smiled.

'Siro knew what he was doing, Publius,' he said. 'Let things be. I won't survive him long, and it would have come to you after me.'

That was the first indication I had that Parthenius, too, was ill. He was to outlive Siro by only a few months. By the time Philippi was fought, I had lost both my teachers.

Philippi was the final nail in the Republican coffin. There were the diehards, naturally: Pompey with his fleet in Sicily, Ahenobarbus with seventy ships and two legions in the Adriatic. But not being leaders of the calibre of Brutus and Cassius they had only secondary importance. The three-man junta, on the other hand, had shrunk to two – an ominous sign. Lepidus, always the lightweight of the alliance, had tried to make a private deal with Pompey while his colleagues were in Greece. To punish him, Antony and Octavian deprived him of his provinces and shared them out between themselves: the whole of Gaul and the east to Antony, Spain, Sardinia and Africa to Octavian.

The division reflected the warlords' comparative importance. After Philippi, Antony was unquestionably the dominant partner. It was he, not Octavian, who had beaten the Republicans. Over the campaign, the magic of Caesar's name had worn thin: the troops could see that, despite Octavian's claims, he wore the sacred mantle like a scarecrow. Octavian was no Caesar, and now everyone knew it. For him, politically, the war had been a disaster.

Antony then proceeded, as he thought, to turn the screw a notch tighter. While he went east, to deal with the shambles in which Brutus and Cassius had left the Asian provinces, Octavian was left in Italy to continue the grey task of conducting the land requisitions. Militarily, there was still Sextus Pompey to face; but Pompey had a fleet now of some one hundred and eighty ships, and his forces were growing daily before a constant stream of Republicans, dispossessed Italians and runaway slaves. An attack on Pompey would be dangerous, to say the least. Octavian could only grit his teeth and wait.

His opportunity to regain his lost military reputation came before the end of the year, and from a wholly unexpected quarter: Antony's wife Fulvia and his brother Lucius.

Lucius was a complete nonentity, with political aspirations. His consulship the year before (which he had from Antony) and the triumphal parade (also Antony's gift) to mark his victory over an obscure Alpine tribe had gone to his head. Declaring himself the saviour of the Republic, he launched a verbal attack on Octavian; and, encouraged by the degree of support, he persuaded Fulvia that armed revolt was in Antony's interests.

Octavian did not know whether to rub his hands for joy or tear his hair. If Lucius was acting with Antony's knowledge then Octavian was finished. To be safe, he sent a legion to guard the port of Brindisi, where any troopships must dock. Meanwhile his two commanders, Rufus and Agrippa, pursued Lucius to Perugia, put the town under siege and starved him out. He surrendered in February of the following year.

Octavian, of course, could not punish either Lucius and Fulvia or their supporters without offending Antony; not that it was important, for he had re-established himself as a general and embarrassed Antony into the bargain. However, the town was another matter. He took its senate of three hundred members, and all the Republican fugitives found within its walls, and put them to death.

I was in Rome the month after Perugia fell, visiting Gallus, who had extended business in the city. We had been browsing our way along Booksellers' Street in the Argiletum, and I was consulting Gallus on a copy of Meleager when someone called my name. Looking round I saw a small, round figure making its way towards us.

'Virgil! Thrown any good pots lately?'

Horace.

42 ∫

He had not changed very much from the boyish young man I had bumped into five years previously in Naples clutching his copy of Lucilius's poems outside Demetrius's bookshop, except that he was fatter, and his hairline was already receding. In another ten years he would be as broad (and as bald) as his Uncle Titus.

I performed the introductions. When Horace heard Gallus's name his smile disappeared. Gallus, if he noticed this, made no sign.

'Look, let's go somewhere for a drink,' he said. 'My treat. There's a decent wineshop off Cyprian Road.'

Gallus's knowledge of Rome's wineshops was encyclopaedic, matched only by his knowledge of the city's brothels.

Horace, I think, would have made some excuse and left. I mistakenly put this down to embarrassment: Gallus was, of course, an important man now in the city and Horace, as the son of an ex-slave, might feel socially outclassed. I should have known better. Horace had more cogent reasons for keeping his distance.

'An offer too good to miss,' I said, taking a firm grip of Horace's arm to prevent him escaping. 'Mind you, Gallus will still have more than his share. He always does.'

'I can pay for my own wine.' Horace was almost surly.

Gallus raised his eyebrows but said nothing. He led the way through the maze of alleys while I followed, still holding Horace's arm.

'How long have you been in Rome?' I asked.

'Only a few weeks.'

'Your father's with you?'

'He's dead,' Horace said shortly.

'I'm sorry to hear it,' I said. I was beginning to regret having forced Horace to come with us. He was obviously ill at ease and his manner, even to me, was truculent. 'Perhaps we could . . .'

I was going to suggest another meeting, an exchange of addresses; but just then Gallus turned round.

'Here we are,' he said, indicating a small wineshop near the corner. 'The best Alban wine in Rome.'

'It wouldn't be from your own estates, would it?' Horace said. He sounded almost sneering.

Gallus frowned and paused on the threshold.

'No,' he said. 'My father's estate's in Provence.' So what? his tone added.

'Mine had a farm near Venusia.' Horace had stopped too. 'He made a good country wine, nothing you'd drink. Rough but honest. Someone else makes it now.'

Gallus simply stared at him. He was not angry – Gallus rarely got angry – but I could see that Horace was beginning to annoy him.

'Look,' he said to me, 'I don't know what's going on, but I want a drink even if you and your friend don't. Let's talk it over inside.'

'Come on, Horace,' I said.

We went in and sat down. Gallus ordered wine and a plate of pickles.

'Now, what's this all about?' he said to Horace when

the waiter had gone. 'We've never met before to my knowledge and you're treating me like I screwed your sister.'

'You're on the land commission, aren't you?'

'Yes, I am. Along with several other people.'

'Two months before he died my father lost his farm. It was confiscated. By you and your friends.'

There was silence. The waiter returned, set down the plate and poured the wine.

'I'm sorry,' Gallus said at last. 'Really I am. But I don't make the decisions.'

'I see. But why not complete the cliché? You only carry them out.'

I was embarrassed, for both of them. This happened, I knew, quite frequently. Rome was full of men who had been deprived of their land by the requisitions and had drifted into town to find work and, if possible, redress the grievance. In the past two days Gallus had been accosted five times while I had been with him. He could genuinely do nothing, and it hurt him greatly.

On the other hand, I thought I had assessed Horace well, even on our scant acquaintance. He was not a complainer, he did not carry grudges, and above all he was fair. His father's loss must have hurt him deeply to bring about this reaction. Again I was struck by the parallels between my life and his.

'My father lost his farm too,' I said.

Horace looked at me in surprise.

'Your father? When?'

'Last December. Gallus got it back for him.'

'That was Pollio,' Gallus said quickly.

'It was both of you, and I'm grateful. I always will be.' I turned to Horace. 'Listen to me. I went to Gallus in Milan, told him what had happened. I had nothing to give in return, no claims but—'

'Shut up, Publius,' Gallus said.

'No claims but friendship. And Gallus told me he'd do what he could. There were no strings, no bribes, no promises. Just that.'

I could see Gallus shifting in his seat, but I carried on regardless. I was angry myself now.

'He got it back. It took him months, but he got it back. He's not responsible for the confiscations. If you want to blame anyone, blame Octavian.'

I stopped. My voice had risen over the general conversation, and I realised that the other customers were looking at me. I felt my face redden.

Gallus was laughing silently.

'Have you quite finished, Publius?' he said. 'If not, then shut up before you get us all arrested for treason.' He turned to Horace. 'Don't get me wrong. I agree with Caesar – the confiscations are necessary. But all the same, they're none of my doing. Not personally. Give me the details and I'll see if I can help.'

Horace shook his head.

'No. Thank you, but no. It's done now, and my father's dead anyway. I know it's not your fault, really, and I'm sorry I behaved so boorishly.' He held out his hand.

Gallus took it.

'Apology accepted,' he said. 'And if you change your mind . . .'

'I won't.'

'Very well.' Gallus, I could see, was relieved. 'Now drink your wine. Please.'

Horace drank, held the wine in his mouth for a moment, then swallowed. He smiled.

'You're right about the wine,' he said. 'It's excellent.'

I sipped at my own cup, and tactfully (as I thought) changed the subject.

'So what are you doing in Rome?'

'Working as a clerk in the Provisions Office.' Horace took a pickle from the plate and bit into it.

'I thought you were studying in Athens?'

'I was. Until the war broke out. Then I joined Brutus.'

I had forgotten how unsettling this young man's directness could be. There were certainly ex-Republicans in the city, but generally they kept a low profile, or lied. To admit that one had served willingly on the losing side, especially with one of the ruling junta at the same table, was unusual to say the least. Gallus, however, did not seem to mind.

'You fought at Philippi?' he said.

Horace nodded and drank his wine.

'I was on Brutus's staff. Although *fought* isn't exactly the word I'd use. *Ran* is more like the thing.'

Gallus laughed.

'You're exaggerating, of course.'

'Not at all. I threw away my shield and ran as fast as my legs would carry me.'

Gallus looked at him, his eyes twinkling.

'"No matter"' – he spoke the words slowly and carefully, in Greek – '"I'll get another shield just as good."'

We all laughed. The quote was from the early Greek soldier-poet Archilochus, who had also (or so he said) thrown his shield away in battle – the ultimate disgrace for a warrior, Greek or Roman. Horace looked a little discomfited, as well he might, having been caught out: I found out later that he had served with distinction. Far from throwing away his shield he had saved a friend's life and brought him to safety at the risk of his own. But to tell that story would not have fitted well with his own gentle self-mockery.

We talked poetry then. Horace, of course, had heard of Gallus in that context, too, and admired him, although not uncritically. His directness of vision made him an excellent critic, and his nature took the sting from any adverse criticisms he made – a quality as necessary, I have found, to a good critic as sound judgment and insight. Several times I was amused to see Gallus wince and nod his head in reluctant agreement.

Horace asked about my own poetry, but I put him off. Gallus acquiesced silently: whether or not he guessed about my struggles of conscience over Pollio's pastoral commission I do not know. I suspect he did. In any event, he was mischievously tactful. To change the subject, I asked Horace how his plans for Lucilius were progressing.

'Oh, I'm still thinking about it,' he said. 'Time's the problem. I have enough to do keeping body and soul together at the moment.'

'You don't think you're succeeding too well with the former?' I said slyly.

He grinned.

'And hardly at all with the latter. Yes, I know I'm getting fat, Virgil. There's not a lot I can do about it.'

'"Starve your poetry,"' Gallus quoted Callimachus. '"Cultivate a slender Muse."'

'Oh but my Muse is naturally fat,' Horace objected. 'Like Claudia Gemella.' Claudia Gemella was the large wife of one of the leading senators. She had artistic aspirations. We laughed.

Suddenly, Horace stood up.

'I'm sorry, I have to go,' he said. Then, to Gallus: 'Thank you for the wine. It was a pleasure meeting you, sir.'

We exchanged addresses. Since I would not be in Rome for long, I gave him details of the villa near Naples.

'Call on me soon,' Gallus said to him as he left.

'Thank you,' said Horace; but I knew that he probably would not. Gallus had too much to offer, and if Horace was jealous of anything it was his own independence.

He still is. That is yet another of his qualities that I envy.

News of Antony had come at the beginning of spring, with the reopening of the sea routes. He had spent the previous months, not in winter quarters with his troops at Pergamon, but in Alexandria as the private guest of Queen Cleopatra.

This is, I think, the first time I have mentioned Cleopatra; and as she is to figure largely in later events perhaps I should say a little about her. As with Antony, and for the same reasons, I find this difficult.

Perhaps you know the story of Melanippe? Melanippe was a Rhodian: rich, well born and cultured. She had the misfortune to attract the interest of an artist named Iphicles. For years he pestered her, following her about, sending her love-notes and expensive presents, and generally making a nuisance of himself. Finally he bribed her maid to let him into her house, secretly, while her father was away on business. Iphicles attempted no violence. He simply threw himself at her feet and declared his undying love for her.

At first Melanippe treated him kindly. She explained that she was already betrothed, and although she appreciated his feelings she could not reciprocate them. The best thing he could do, she said, was to leave quietly and forget all about her. Iphicles refused; and in the end Melanippe had no choice but to call her slaves and have him thrown out.

Iphicles went home and prepared his largest canvas. He

began by painting a true likeness of the girl, one that all would recognise. Then he proceeded to modify it. Her nose was a fraction longer than the average; he lengthened it still more, until it became grotesque. Her teeth were slightly uneven; he gave her tusks, like a Gorgon. Her eyes were a little close together; he painted in the eyes of a pig. Understand, he told no lies. He simply took what was imperfect and exaggerated it.

Then he hung the painting in the Market Square, where everyone could see it. When Melanippe heard, she hanged herself.

This, barring the details, is how Octavian treated Cleopatra. He told no outright lies, yet being the consummate artist he was, he twisted the truth to suit his own purposes; and he did it so well that it is difficult for me, now, to see the real woman behind the Gorgon mask. It is more difficult for you, who have grown up believing the mask to be the reality.

To begin with, then, the bare historical facts. Cleopatra was the daughter of King Ptolemy the Fluteplayer. At the age of fourteen she became joint ruler of Egypt with her younger brother, only to be ousted three years later by a palace revolution. In return for Caesar's help in regaining the throne, she became his mistress and bore him a son, Caesarion. At the time of Caesar's death she was in Rome, where she renewed her acquaintance with Antony.

She spent the civil war in Egypt, and her enemies claimed she had given support to the Republicans. This was false; but it provided Antony with an excuse to summon her to Tarsus. She arrived in state, dressed as the Greek love goddess Aphrodite, sailing up the River Cydnus in her royal barge. Antony – being Antony – put up no resistance. Before the week was out they were lovers, and he accepted her offer to spend the winter at Alexandria. Early in the new year, she gave birth to his son and daughter.

Cleopatra was not beautiful, but she did have a beautiful voice, husky and – so the rumour goes – incredibly seductive. She was highly intelligent (much more so than Antony) and an outstanding linguist. It is *not* true that the native Egyptians hated her, quite the reverse: she had a genuine sympathy with their culture, especially their religion, and spoke the language fluently, the first Greek ruler of Egypt to do so. After her death, the country rose spontaneously against Octavian, and even today Egyptians refer to Cleopatra simply as 'The Queen'.

It is not true, either, that she was a nymphomaniac. Her motivation was not sex but the need to preserve Egyptian independence. She had seen the old Hellenistic kingdoms fall like skittles to Rome, and she knew perfectly well that Rome coveted Egypt, both for the fabulous Treasure of the Ptolemies and for its rich grain harvests. Had it been possible in the modern world, she would have secured her country through a strong dynastic marriage. As it was, the best she could do was become the mistress of men who could guarantee that security. For this, Octavian branded her whore, and although this is unfair it is not entirely unjust. With both Caesar and Antony Cleopatra, as they say, made the running, and took her payment in power, not money. Yet if she was a whore she was an honest one. She stayed faithful to both Caesar and Antony while they lived, and to Antony's memory when he died. On her side, at least, their marriage was a legal and binding one, and she respected its sanctity. Had Octavian permitted Antony (as he could not have done) to keep the east, she would have been content with that. His claims that she was aiming at Rome's destruction and the transfer of the capital to Alexandria were pure scaremongering, directed at the Roman people.

The accusations of racial impurity and habitual drunkenness were simply untrue, and I pass them over without comment.

In the early months of the year Calenus, Antony's governor in Gaul commanding eleven veteran legions, died unexpectedly. On hearing the news, Octavian immediately went north. He announced himself the province's new caretaker and set his own trusted commander, Rufus, over its armies.

I have never been entirely happy with this. It is too pat. Calenus was in the prime of life, strong and healthy; and yet he died a sudden, natural death. If you recall the earlier Italian campaign against Antony, you will remember that the Senate gave the joint command to Octavian and the consuls, Hirtius and Pansa. Pansa, of course, was killed in action, Hirtius died of wounds. Now there was an unpleasant rumour current at the time that Hirtius's wounds had been poisoned: his doctor Glyco was in fact held on suspicion but released because of the lack of evidence. Hirtius's death gave Octavian the military muscle he needed to apply pressure on the Senate and establish his credentials with Antony. That, too, was . . . convenient.

As I say, I have no proof that Octavian was involved. But Calenus's death could not have occurred more opportunely. And it would fit Octavian's character.

The annexation of Gaul produced a political crisis. Antony took immediate action. He entered into negotiations with Sextus Pompey in Sicily and, more significantly, with Ahenobarbus, who commanded the remains of the Republican army in the Adriatic. They combined fleets and sailed for Italy, where they found Brindisi closed against them. Although this was probably not Octavian's idea, he hastily gathered an army and marched south. For several weeks, the two warlords glared at each other across what had suddenly become a military front line; and it seemed as if the civil wars were about to break out afresh.

44 ∫

In late September I was again in Rome, at Gallus's invitation. His house was on the western slopes of the Esquiline. It had belonged to one of the victims of the proscriptions, a senator with eclectic sexual proclivities and a complementary taste in art. Gallus found the combination amusing, but it embarrassed me acutely. I took one look at the floor mosaic in my room and asked for it to be covered over. Merely changing rooms would not have been enough. The rest were worse.

The day after I arrived, I was reading in the garden-courtyard when Gallus came out.

'You've brought a good mantle with you, I suppose?' he said.

I put the book down.

'Naturally,' I said.

'Go upstairs and put it on. We're going visiting.'

Gallus, in this mood, was exasperating. I remembered his last mystery trip to the theatre.

'It's not a play, is it?' I said. 'Or have you arranged an outing with Cytheris and one of her friends?'

Cytheris, if you remember, was Gallus's mistress, off and on (currently on). She had also been, in the past, the mistress of Antony and the oh-so-pious Brutus, which speaks well for her broad-mindedness and her sense of humour. I liked her, but in small doses. At present, she came a poor second to my philosophical studies.

'Oh, Cytheris would love to come,' Gallus laughed, 'but I doubt if she'd be very welcome. And her friends certainly wouldn't be. You, however, will love it.'

'You're not going to tell me where we're going?'

'Certainly not.' Gallus grinned. 'It's a surprise.'

I frowned. I knew all about Gallus's surprises.

He was waiting when I came downstairs.

'It's not all that far, but we must make an impression,' he said. 'The litters are at the door.' He looked at me. 'Virgil, *not* your bloody party slippers! We're not going out to dinner.'

I handed them to a slave with a sigh of relief. Whatever Gallus had in mind, it promised to be mercifully short.

We got into the litters. As Gallus had said, it was no great distance. I thought for an awful moment we were going to Proculus's house – now, of course, someone else's property – but we passed it, following the line of the old Servian wall in the direction of the Esquiline Gate. We stopped outside a large house and the slaves helped us alight.

'Where are we?' I asked Gallus as we climbed the steps.

'Where do you think?' He grinned. I did not.

'Gallus, I'd like to know now, please. Who have we come to see?'

'Cilnius Maecenas,' he said.

The front door opened as we reached the topmost step.

We were shown into the garden, and I decided that I need not have troubled over the mantle.

Maecenas, Octavian's cultural and diplomatic adviser and one of the most powerful men in Rome, was playing handball with three of his slaves. He was stripped to the waist and sweating like a pig.

'Gallus! *Delighted* you could come, my boy!' he said as we made our salutations. 'And this must be your friend Virgil, he of the glorious biceps.'

I glanced at Gallus, wondering how he would take this; but Gallus was laughing.

'Don't scare him off, Maecenas,' he said. 'He's only here because I didn't tell him where we were going.'

Maecenas pouted. He threw the ball to one of the slaves – a good-looking young African boy – and snapped his fingers. Two more slaves rushed over with thick woollen towels and began to rub him down.

'Very flattering,' he said. '*Very* flattering. And here was I thinking he'd come lolloping along behind you with his tongue hanging out simply *desperate* to meet me. Ah well,' he sighed. 'A harmless enough fantasy. Welcome, Publius Vergilius Maro, in any case.'

I must admit I did not know how to react to all this. I knew Maecenas's reputation, of course. He was a dandy, an epicure, a lover of beautiful things and beautiful people. Proculus would have loathed him – Proculus had no time for men of Maecenas's sort. And yet I found him intriguing. Despite his effeminate manner he had a strong face and shrewd, intelligent eyes that were summing me up even as he delivered himself of this nonsense to Gallus. More, for a man who loved to eat he looked remarkably fit. I thought of my Uncle Quintus (long dead now from apoplexy) and compared his pasty-white, blubbery appearance with Maecenas's muscular torso. Not a man to dismiss readily. Not by any means.

The slaves with the towels finished rubbing him down. A third slave (he seemed to have one for each small task) brought him a plain tunic, which he put on.

'Let's go inside,' he said, taking Gallus's arm and mine, and steering us back through the porch. 'I am hungry for poetry.'

The sitting-room was sparsely furnished, but in impeccable taste. The floor mosaics were the finest I had ever seen, while at the edge of the central pool crouched a bronze boy holding a frog in the palm of his hand. He was so lifelike that I half expected to see him breathe.

Maecenas noticed my interest.

'I found him in Athens,' he said. 'Isn't he beautiful?'

'Incredible. A Praxiteles?' Maecenas nodded, pleased. 'Who was the copyist?'

Our host's eyes widened.

'Oh, my dear boy!' he exclaimed (he was, I judged, only a year or two older than me). 'There are no copies in *this* house!'

I reddened, and mumbled an apology. Gallus chuckled. If it was genuine – and I was sure that it was – the statue must have cost millions.

A slave entered (not one of those from the garden) and stood waiting for orders.

'Wine,' Maecenas told him. 'A jug of the Setian. And bring some fruit juice for Virgil here.'

I was surprised and, I admit, flattered. Maecenas had obviously taken the trouble to learn more about me than my name. The fruit juice came in a heavy silver goblet, beautifully worked in the Corinthian style.

'Gallus tells me you're the most promising poet we have.' Maecenas held up his own goblet for the slave to fill. 'I've been on at him to bring you for months.'

I blushed again and drank my fruit juice. It was delicious, with an aftertaste of honey.

'Gallus exaggerates,' I said.

'Nonsense.' Gallus lolled back on his couch. 'You've got me beaten hollow already. And you haven't started yet.'

'You mustn't be so modest, Virgil dear,' Maecenas said. 'Modesty is all very well in the mediocre, but it's not for you. I hear you're working on a set of pastorals. Could we hope for a recitation, do you think?'

'I'm afraid I haven't brought them with me,' I said. 'In any case, there are only two so far.'

Gallus took out a scroll of parchment from the fold in his mantle and tossed it over. I opened it, read the first few words and looked up at him in surprise.

'You sent me it months ago.' Gallus was grinning. 'Go ahead. Read.'

I could not very well refuse without seriously insulting our host. The poem was the first of the series: a love-sick shepherd pleads his case to a spoilt young herd-boy. Maecenas listened smiling, his eyes closed, as I stumbled through the reading. By the end I was almost dead with embarrassment, and the silence was deafening.

'Charming,' Maecenas said at last, opening his eyes (I noticed they were lined with Egyptian cosmetic). 'Utterly charming. Simple, yet deceptive in its simplicity. I see what Gallus means. You base it, of course, on the sixth *Idyll* of Theocritus?'

I nodded. My throat felt dry as sawdust.

'The original has Polyphemus for its protagonist. Could I ask why you decided to replace him with an ordinary shepherd?'

'Polyphemus has connotations of savagery,' I said. 'In the *Odyssey* he's a monster. He dashes men's brains out and eats his victims raw. Polyphemus could never be "charming".'

'I see.' Maecenas nodded. 'You're quite right, of course. He is rather a boor.'

'Then again,' I went on, 'Polyphemus belongs to myth. I wanted my characters to be real people. Idealised, but real.' I indicated the bronze. 'Like your Praxitelean boy.'

'And their concerns to be real also?'

'That, too.' I was warming to my theme, and losing

my self-consciousness. 'How can a reader identify with a character unless he understands him?'

'Indeed.' Maecenas sipped his wine, and then asked casually, 'And had you considered a purpose at all for your poetry?'

I frowned. Out of the corner of my eye I saw Gallus stiffen.

'What purpose could there be,' I said, 'except to entertain?'

'Perhaps to inform,' Maecenas said softly. 'Even to educate. Both perfectly valid functions of poetry.'

I felt myself break out into a sweat: as a man who is afraid of heights will when he approaches the edge of a cliff and looks down into the chasm below. His head begins to swim; he is afraid, yet he feels an inexplicable desire to jump, to let the chasm have its way with him. Gallus, I noticed, was making surreptitious warning signs with his fingers; but Maecenas ignored them. He was still smiling blandly, and his eyes willed me to answer.

'That's true,' I said. 'Yet before he takes it upon himself to lecture the poet must be sure of his ground.'

'And if he were sure, would he consider it his duty, do you think?'

The room, Maecenas's smiling face, had become sharp and unreal. My head sang.

'He might,' I found myself saying. 'If he were sure. Only if he were sure.'

'Then we must do our best to convince you, Virgil, my dear.' Maecenas's voice was light and bantering, but his eyes were grave. I looked at Gallus. He held my gaze steadily for a moment, then signalled to the slave to fill his goblet. The tension in the room relaxed.

'You've heard the news, of course?' Maecenas turned to Gallus.

'About the trouble in the south?' Gallus frowned into his

wine. 'Of course. The Market Square's full of it. You think it'll come to anything?'

'I hope not. It's a misunderstanding, only that. No one wants war, least of all Caesar. And I hear there's even a certain amount of fraternisation across the lines.'

'Are you involved at all?'

'As a go-between, certainly.' Maecenas smiled. 'I leave for Brindisi tomorrow, in fact. Your friend Pollio,' he turned to me, 'will also be there, to represent Antony. I'm sure we can work something out. Italy has had enough of fighting. What she needs now is peace.'

'And Caesar' – I was diplomatic – 'can give her it?'

'With Antony's co-operation.' Maecenas could be diplomatic too. 'Plus the goodwill of all peace-loving men.' He stopped suddenly; his face brightened. In retrospect, it was a beautiful piece of acting. 'I've had the most *brilliant* idea, my dear! Why don't you come with me as my guest? To Brindisi? We can get to know each other better on the road, and Pollio will be there.' Then, when I hesitated: 'Virgil, I will be absolutely *mortally* offended if you say no! And I'm sure Gallus won't mind, will you, Gallus?'

Gallus looked at me, his eyes twinkling.

'Oh, no,' he said. 'I think it's a splendid idea.'

For a moment, time seemed frozen. I could feel both Gallus and Maecenas watching me, and the room was absolutely still. I looked down over the lip of the cliff into the chasm beneath, took a deep breath . . .

And jumped.

'Why not?' I said, my heart racing. 'Yes, all right. If you want me to, of course I'll come.'

I knew that chances were I would be dashed to pieces; but I suddenly felt the exhilaration of flight.

Caesar's Poet (September 40 BC–
September 19 BC)

45 ∫

If I were asked to draw a line, and say, This is the point at which I became Octavian's poet, I would choose that journey to Brindisi.

Maecenas persuaded me by discussing, not politics, but poetry. I discovered that I had been right not to under-estimate him. Not only did he have a thorough knowledge of literature but also a sincere appreciation of it – the two do not necessarily go together. I was surprised at first to find that when we were alone he talked naturally and seriously, without affectation. Once I was over my shyness, our discussions became enjoyably acrimonious, and I did not always have the best of them, by any means. Only on the subject of his own work was he less than serious, and that, too, impressed me: Maecenas wrote the most appalling drivel, but he knew it and could laugh at himself. He said it did not matter, and he was right.

We know each other better now – he was, until that last disastrous meeting only a few months ago, one of my closest friends for almost twenty years – but I still wonder which is the real Maecenas: Agrippa's 'chattering jay', my razor-brained critic, or Octavian's master of diplomacy and propaganda. All three, I suspect, and more besides. A senator once said, sarcastically, of Julius Caesar that he was 'all things to all men'. That is certainly true of

Maecenas, although not in the way the senator meant it of Caesar. For me, it was enough that he was my friend, and it would have been wrong to probe too deeply. In the course of that journey he won my respect (he has it still, although he would not want it); and if both he and Gallus believed that Octavian was Rome's only hope, then despite my private reservations I owed him my support, too.

Perhaps at this point I should clear up a possible misunderstanding. In his fifth *Satire*, Horace gives an account of a journey he, Maecenas and I made to Brindisi. This, I am sorry to say (since it is a marvellous slice of low life) is completely imaginary, although written with Maecenas's full knowledge and approval: a beautiful bit of tongue-in-cheek nonsense, rather like my Gallus poem (I will tell you about that one, in its proper place), that made all of us laugh when he read it. Maecenas would not be seen dead in an inn (and this is the point of the poem), let alone one with fleas. When he travels, his accommodation is arranged in advance either with some rich friend or with prominent local dignitaries; and even then he takes his own linen, for preference.

Our real journey to Brindisi was much more luxurious. We arrived on the last day of September; and there our paths immediately diverged since I was not, of course, involved in the negotiations themselves. Maecenas had arranged for me to stay with an acquaintance of his, a certain Appius Mucro, who was old, half blind and completely deaf. After welcoming me to his house and giving his slaves strict instructions to look after me, he courteously left me alone, which suited both of us very well. I did not see much of Pollio either. As Antony's second, he had more important things on his mind than socialising. I understood, and kept my own company.

Brindisi, although it is the major port for the east, is quite a small town. With the peace conference it was bursting at the seams, and the mood was almost – paradoxically – one of holiday. I could see what Maecenas had meant about fraternisation: the wineshops were full of soldiers and sailors from both Octavian's and Antony's forces, but there was very little trouble. The officers, too, seemed to be making no attempt to keep the armies apart. It was obvious that no one wanted war. From the soldiers' point of view there was little to gain: a fresh civil war would put money in nobody's pocket. In any case, the troops, too, had had their fill of fighting. Maecenas had been right. What Italy needed now was peace.

The day after my arrival, I set out to explore the town. I cannot remember exactly where I went, but I ended up, as you might expect, in the booksellers' quarter. I was examining a copy of Plato's *Laws* when I realised that I was being watched by a stooped, elderly man. As I looked up, he bowed: hand on heart, with a curious, bobbing motion.

'Forgive me for staring,' he said. 'I couldn't help noticing your interest in the philosophical works. Are you a philosopher yourself, by any chance?'

'I'm a student of philosophy,' I said. 'I wouldn't claim anything more.'

'But you are' – the old man indicated the book I held in my hands – 'a follower of Plato?'

'Of Epicurus,' I said.

He frowned.

'I have never understood,' he said, 'how any man can deny the existence of the soul.'

'Some find it comforting to believe that death is the end.'

He shook his head.

'Belief is one thing,' he said gently. 'Facts are another. The soul exists. Whether we choose to believe that or not is immaterial.'

I had not had a philosophical discussion for months – my

time had been taken up with poetry and other things. With a warm glow of anticipation, I replaced the book and turned to the attack.

We agreed, in the end, to differ. My new friend introduced himself. His name was Matthias, and he was by origin an Alexandrian Jew now resident in Brindisi. He invited me to his house nearby for a cup of wine.

I spent a very pleasant day with Matthias and Sarah, his wife. Although he had studied Greek philosophy, his main interest lay in the Jewish writings. I cannot remember many details of our conversation, except for one thing: a discussion of the Jewish prophecies concerning the Messiah (in Latin, 'Anointed One').

The Messiah, Jews believe, is a man sent from God to rescue them from their enemies, including, of course, ourselves. They do not know when he will come; but his coming will signal the beginning of a new era of prosperity and justice. The Messiah will be called Wonderful, the Counsellor, the Prince of Peace. In his time, the lion will lie down with the lamb, and wars throughout the earth will cease for ever.

As we sat in the autumn sunlight in Matthias's garden, and he read the prophecies to me, I could feel, even beneath his stumbling translation, the beat and fire of the language. Whoever he was, this Isaiah was a great poet; unless, as the Jews believe, he was what is greater, the mouthpiece of their god. When I left, after saying my farewells, his words left with me, and my ears still rang with them.

The next day, the peace treaty was signed. Under its terms, Octavian and Antony split the world between them, Antony taking the east, Octavian the west. Lepidus was to be left in possession of Africa, and the sentence of exile passed on Ahenobarbus revoked. Further, since Antony's wife Fulvia had died in exile at Athens, the pact was to be sealed by a dynastic marriage between Antony and Octavian's sister, Octavia.

They say that, when the news reached Rome, the celebrations surpassed any within living memory. Certainly Brindisi went mad that night. I have never seen anything like it, before or since, even including the thanksgiving after Actium. It was as though the whole town were one great wedding party, soldiers and civilians alike. There was no violence, no looting, hardly even any unpleasant drunkenness; and that was a miracle in itself. More, there was a strange, pervasive feeling in the very air of the place, a feeling that everything was going to be all right. I cannot put this any more clearly, nor can I explain what is inexplicable. It was simply a fact. If anything was needed to convince me that peace is the greatest gift the gods can give, that night was the proof, whatever happened after.

I retired early to my room; but not to sleep. I felt restless, as if a million tiny flies were crawling over my skin. I tried to read, but the letters would not stay still on the page or the words in my head. I got up, walked around, lay down again a dozen times; but always my eyes kept straying to the window. Finally I threw open the shutters and looked outside, over the city.

It was a magical evening, clear and alive with diamond-bright stars. Below me I could see the glittering of a thousand torches, moving and weaving through the narrow streets like fireflies, and hear the sussuration of voices like a beach full of pebbles stirred by the waves. I stood entranced for I do not know how long, letting the peace and contentment and pure joy of the night flood through me. I think I prayed, but I am not sure, nor do I know to which god. In any case, my cheeks as I turned away were wet with tears.

I cannot remember reaching for my pen and wax tablets, nor of writing what has become my fourth *Pastoral*. I have never written another poem like it and never could again. It came unbidden, complete and perfect as a fine-cut gem. Part of it was the night, part my memories of those rolling Jewish prophecies, part the signing of the treaty and the marriage settlement: but still, that was not the whole. There was Something Else that stood behind my shoulder and guided my hand as I wrote, and to this day I cannot tell who or what it was. I can only be grateful.

The poem celebrates the birth of a child; no ordinary child, but one who will bring back the Golden Age, the Years of Saturn when there were no wars and no hunger and no fear anywhere in the world; when man and nature lived as one in perfect harmony and the gods walked quietly through smiling fields. It celebrates peace and plenty and an end for ever to the bickering and the bloodshed and the million million sad, wasted tears of human history:

> For you, Child,
> The untilled earth will pour forth her gifts—
> Small at first, the smallest of giftlings:
> Trailing ivy; valerian the healer;
> Lilies, and the smiling acanthus.
> Goats will bring, with no man urging,
> Their milk-swelled udders swaying homeward.
> Lions
> Will hold no terrors for the sheep.
> Your very cradle, Child,
> Will pour forth flowers in rich abundance
> To welcome you . . .

As I say, I do not know where the poem came from. I did not write it, it wrote itself, and alone of my poems I altered not a single line. When it was done, I closed the tablets, laid them beside my bed, and went quietly to sleep.

46

The joy of Brindisi was short-lived.

This time, the fault lay with neither Antony nor Octavian, but with Sextus Pompey. He had, quite understandably, considered himself snubbed. Octavian and Antony, when they thought he might be useful, had each proposed an alliance. After Brindisi Pompey found himself out in the cold, packed off back to Sicily like a faithful dog who is surplus to immediate requirements but who his master knows will come back, tail wagging, when he whistles.

In the latter months of the year, Pompey set out to make his presence felt. From his bases in Sicily and Sardinia he began to launch raids on the Italian coast, threatening Rome's vital grain supplies. The cost of provisions escalated, and matters were made worse by the fresh taxation levied to raise cash for the new sea war. Finally, in mid-November, the Roman mob rioted and troops were called in.

It was clear that Pompey had to be dealt with, one way or the other. Realising that they were not yet strong enough at sea to risk an all-out campaign, Antony and Octavian decided on a peaceful settlement. They persuaded Pompey to accept Corsica, Sardinia, Sicily (legitimately) and the Peloponnese as a governorial province, in exchange for a pledge of good conduct.

The east was in an even worse state. Persia – the great

empire beyond the Roman boundaries – had invaded Syria, and Antony's ramshackle arrangements for the buffer-kingdoms at the eastern edge of Roman territory sagged and collapsed like a rotten tenement. Petty king after petty king went over to the invaders: Cappadocia, Commagene, Galatia . . . one after another. Worse, the Persian commander was an experienced Roman general, Caesar's renegade lieutenant Labienus. By the autumn, the situation had become critical. Antony set out for the east to take over the conduct of the war; and Italy enjoyed a whole year of peace.

I spent the year after the Pact of Brindisi between Naples and Rome. Now that I had come to terms with Octavian and Antony's plans for the state, I had begun in earnest on the pastoral poems. It was as if a blockage had been removed. I no longer baulked at the political content; in fact, like an ox who, once he has discovered the taste of salt, comes again and again to the lick, I began positively to enjoy the challenge. First of all, I discharged my debt by writing two poems on the confiscations. To these I added another, on Caesar's divinity (Antony had recently, at Octavian's request, become a Priest of the Divine Julius. The poem was thus a three-way compliment). These seemed to satisfy the craving, for the time being.

Here I should perhaps relate a story which is a warning to poets and critics alike: poets, because critics may read into a poem something they did not mean; critics, because they may, in their cleverness, credit the poet with an allusion which he never intended. Maecenas enjoyed the 'political' poems, but on reading one of the others (an uneasy blend of pastoral and Epicurean physics), he suddenly amazed me by dissolving into a fit of coughing.

'I'm not exactly sure, my dear boy,' he said, 'that I approve of the allusion here.'

I must have looked blank, for he added: 'The Silenus

figure. Antony may be fond of his wine and women, but he's hardly likely to enjoy being portrayed as a hung-over demigod. Especially one whose interests seem to include the natural sciences.'

I was relieved. I explained that there was no allusion to Antony, that if Silenus represented anything it was the philosophical union between the instinctive and the rational sides of the human spirit. Maecenas, I could see, listened to none of this. I had the impression that he was not displeased, and had filed the comparison away for future use.

I do not know if Antony himself ever thought I was being disrespectful, but I doubt it. It has been my experience that although compliments tend to get themselves noticed, people do not readily recognise when they are being criticised symbolically. Others notice, of course, especially those like Maecenas, who think easily in symbols; and sometimes they are too clever for their own good.

I wrote another of the poems about this time, or perhaps slightly later, I cannot now remember: a fairly short, tongue-in-cheek piece addressed to Gallus. I mention it because, in retrospect, it was a chilling foretaste of what was to come. In the wake of one of their violent but never very long-lasting quarrels, Cytheris had gone off to Milan with a young cavalry officer, leaving Gallus not so much disconsolate as at a loose end (he did not remain so for long). In the poem, I pictured him, near suicidal and ready to die for love, haunting the sylvan glades and vowing every kind of desperate act, while Lycoris (the name he used for Cytheris in his own works) tramped the frozen north barefooted behind her soldier lover. It was a pretty bit of Alexandrian nonsense, and both Gallus and Cytheris, when she finally returned, as I knew she would, had a good laugh over it. Yet the poem contained a kernel of truth – do poets, like prophets, have the power to see the future?

– and I remembered it later, when the time came to lament my friend in earnest.

Antony was away from Italy, except for a brief but significant visit, for the next two years. After pushing the Persians back across the border he set up his headquarters in Athens, where he lived with Octavia and their newborn daughter Antonia (no, there was no male child, after all, despite the optimistic prophecy contained in my fourth *Pastoral*).

Octavia is one of the few 'good' characters in my story. In her quiet way, she resembled Cleopatra.

I can see your eyebrows rise, but I mean exactly that. Not in looks (Octavia was far more beautiful), nor in character. Certainly not in her behaviour. Yet both women had an intense inner drive which united them. For Cleopatra, it was a love of her country, and of power; for Octavia, of her family and the old Roman virtues of constancy and fidelity. Both, in their different ways, loved Antony, and he responded to both in ways of his own. If anyone could have saved him from himself, that person was Octavia. During the two years they lived together, he was the model husband: sober, faithful, attentive. He even took to sitting in on philosophical lectures, which he hated – philosophy was very much one of Octavia's interests. However, the fault lay so deep in Antony's character that not even Octavia could dig it out. Like a man who, once he has tasted spiced wine, will no longer be content to drink plain water all his life, Antony was drawn away from her to Cleopatra; and she destroyed him. Even then, Octavia made no complaint. After his death she reared his children by the Egyptian queen as her own, until her brother had them murdered.

Meanwhile, Octavian himself had married, for the third and (hitherto) final time. His admirers say it was purely a love-match, but I am not so sure. Sex, for Octavian, was merely an extension of politics; and marriage with Livia gave him the entrée into respectable society which he badly needed, plus the added bonus of a wife with a talent for political analysis that almost surpassed his own.

To marry Livia, Octavian had to divorce his second wife Scribonia. He did so, the day she bore his daughter Julia, on the pretext that 'she nags me.'

I wish I had met Scribonia, who sounds interesting. I did meet Livia, and found her merely frightening.

While Antony was in Athens, and shortly before Octavian's marriage, trouble had broken out yet again with Sextus Pompey. This time the consequences were to be more serious.

47 ∫

I do not propose to describe the war against Pompey in any detail, but I must spend some time on it since it highlights Antony's relationship with Octavian, and Octavian's abilities (or rather lack of them) as an admiral. You see, like a lawyer, I am preparing my case. Very soon now Antony will become the horned monster, the devourer of children, who leads the whole yapping crew of beast-headed eastern gods against poor trembling Italy. Against him will stand Italy's champion, Caesar-Apollo, calm, strong, serene in his perfect marble coolness: Caesar the Python-Killer, the Destroyer of Demons. I would not take you into that blinded by the Authorised Version. There were faults (and failings) on both sides. I would have you see them clearly.

The trouble began over Sextus Pompey who rightly felt he was being squeezed out on to the political sidelines. Finally, he had lost patience and ordered his pirate fleets to raid the western Italian coast. Octavian sent messages to Antony asking for help. Antony came at once with part of his fleet, but by that time the reinforcements were no longer necessary. Antony sailed back to Athens in disgust. Then, as winter was closing in, Octavian himself was caught in a sea-battle off Cape Scyllaeum, and lost fully half his ships. Forced to swallow his pride, he appealed again to Antony; and again Antony came.

He came to Tarentum with his entire fleet. He also – fortunately, as it turned out – brought his wife Octavia. Meanwhile, however, Agrippa had been building new warships. Octavian sent a message to Antony telling him, once again, that his help was not required. Antony, understandably, was livid. This time he did not go home, and relations between the two deteriorated almost to the point of war.

It was then that Octavia took a hand. She went back and forth between her husband and her brother, explaining, excusing, patching up some sort of peace. Finally she brought the two together at Tarentum, and the thing was smoothed over. The two warlords renewed their pledges of mutual support, and Antony and Octavia returned to Greece.

Octavian wisely gave the sea command to Agrippa. By July of the following year, the new fleet was ready. Octavian had prepared a complicated plan of attack. Agrippa's task was to smash Pompey's fleet, while Octavian and Lepidus would invade Sicily from the Italian mainland and Africa respectively. The invasion was only partially successful. Lepidus landed his troops safely. Octavian allowed himself to be caught yet again, this time by a storm, and the damage set his plans back by a full month.

I should perhaps also say a little here about how Octavian was viewed at this time. It goes a long way towards explaining his concern later with intangibles.

First of all, he was developing a reputation for impiety.

After Cape Scyllaeum, Pompey had struck coins proclaiming himself 'Son of Neptune'. The storm that wrecked Octavian's fleet a second time was seen by many to confirm this; and Octavian's removal of the god's statue from the procession before the Games did not help matters. A good general simply did not do things like that. People remembered the tale of old Admiral Appius Claudius who, when the sacred chickens had refused to eat – the worst of all omens – had thrown them into the sea, shouting, 'Let them drink, then!' – and promptly lost the battle.

Secondly, Octavian was seen by many as totally incompetent militarily. There was an epigram current at the time – I cannot remember the poet – which touched him on his most sensitive spot. Being true, it was even more galling:

> Twice thrashed at sea, Caesar lost his ships.
> Thinking he had to win at *something*, he . . .
> Played himself at dice.

That sums it up nicely, as well as getting in a sly hit at Octavian's passion for gambling. Octavian, it was generally agreed, could not win a battle to save himself.

His impiety only made matters worse.

In August, Octavian launched another attack on Pompey, and again suffered a humiliating defeat, despite the fact that his colleagues had gained their objectives. This time the disaster involved him personally. In the course of the engagement his ship was rammed and sunk. Octavian clung to a plank and drifted ashore in the darkness, accompanied only by a single slave. Thinking that all was lost, he begged the man to kill him. The slave, fortunately for Rome, refused, and in the morning brought him safely – although rather wet and bedraggled – back to his own headquarters.

Agrippa had had enough. Tactfully but firmly, he requested that Octavian stick to what he was good at and leave the fighting to those who understood it. Octavian had no choice but to swallow his pride and acquiesce.

The final battle was fought off Naulochus on 3 September; and, with Agrippa commanding, ended in complete victory. The story goes that Octavian was not at all keen to take part – quite understandably so – and had to be physically rousted out of bed to give the order for the attack. Whatever the truth of that, Pompey was defeated. He fled with the remains of his fleet to the east, and was later executed on Antony's orders.

The death of Sextus Pompey marked the end of that particular civil war. It also cleared the stage of all but the two leading players. The next act of the drama was to be the final one.

48

Meanwhile I had found myself famous.

The *Pastorals* were finally finished and published, largely due to Maecenas's influence, although he was content to allow the earlier arrangement with Pollio to stand. In part, his reasons were diplomatic, since Pollio was known to be Antony's man, and anything which suggested a close relationship between Antony and Octavian at that time was highly desirable. The arrangement suited me, too, of course: although I had seen little of Pollio over the last few years we still corresponded regularly. I regarded him – still regard him – as one of my closest friends, and would have been very sorry indeed to have appeared ungrateful. Nevertheless, Maecenas made it clear, in the most tactful way, that the book of poems had his own and Octavian's backing; and this ensured their instant success.

I did not – do not – enjoy being a celebrity. Public readings terrify me: I have to concentrate hard if I am not to lose the thread and, as a consequence, panic. Total strangers stop me in the street and interrogate me about my work – quite naturally, as if they have a perfect right to do so. Often I find myself having, politely, to refuse pressing invitations to dinner accompanied by little 'presents' to ensure my compliance. The whole business causes me excruciating embarrassment. If I could stay at Naples and never set foot in Rome, I would be happy. Unfortunately that has not been possible. Now, of course, it is too late even to wish. I will not see either again.

I did find one advantage, however, in my new literary eminence, and that concerned Horace. We had met several times when I was in Rome and discussed, not only poetry, but life in general. Each time I was struck anew by how similar we were, and how unlike.

Think of a flawed mirror. It reflects and yet distorts, making a perfectly normal face ugly and preposterous, the nose swollen to impossible proportions, the eyes out of line or twisted in astigmatism. Reverse the metaphor, so that reflection becomes reality and reality reflection. Now, instead of making the beautiful ugly, the mirror beautifies the beholder's ugliness – slims and straightens the bloated nose, corrects the misalignment of the eyes. Horace was my mirror-image. In him I saw my own faults and imperfections smoothed away and turned into virtues.

I had tried, several times, to bring Horace and Maecenas together; but each time he set the idea aside.

'I'm my own man,' he would say. 'I've nothing to offer a patron that he'd be willing to accept, or that I'd be willing to pay. Thank you, Publius, but no.'

I persuaded him, at last, around the time of Tarentum.

I was staying in Gallus's house, as I usually did when I was at Rome. Gallus himself was away on business, and Horace and I were sitting in the garden, discussing a poem Horace had written some months before, on the same theme as my Messianic pastoral. In it he had taken the pessimistic view: true happiness, peace and order do not belong to this world at all. To find them, one must turn one's back on the world and seek out the mythical Isles of the Blest, the never-never land beyond the western ocean where gods and heroes live out their unvexed lives.

'You don't think, then,' I had said, 'that men can ever bring about the perfect society?'

Horace had laughed, rather bitterly.

'They haven't got very far up to now, have they? Human history's a dog's breakfast. Why should we expect things ever to be any different?'

'You really believe that?'

He became suddenly serious; turned his face away towards the chirruping sparrows in the branches of a plum tree.

'Perhaps not,' he said. 'Perhaps some day, far in the future, we'll drag ourselves out of this whole rotten, stinking mess on to solid ground, and take a proper look at the world. But we'll still need help, because with human nature being what it is we can't do it on our own.'

'We can try, surely,' I said. 'We are trying. Maybe this time it'll work.'

He turned to face me then, and his round, good-natured face was angry.

'*We?*' he said. 'Who's your we, Publius? Who d'you think is going to set the world to rights? Antony? That bastard Octavian you're suddenly so fond of?'

'Perhaps.'

He stared at me, shook his head.

'Oh no,' he said. 'Not Octavian. Not him. You know what his answer was to one poor bugger after Philippi, who had the nerve to beg for a decent burial? "Ask the vultures"! Good sweet Jupiter! I heard him myself. "Ask the vultures"! If that's the saviour you've pinned your hopes on, you can forget it as far as I can see.'

'Look, Quintus,' I said quietly. 'You believe the gods are at work in the world. Let them use what instruments they will.'

'Octavian's no divine instrument, he's a common-or-garden prick, and not a very clean one, either.' Horace could be crude when he was angry, and he did not mince his words. 'I want nothing to do with him. Nor, for that matter, with his bumboy Maecenas.'

I must have looked as shocked as I felt, for Horace was instantly contrite. He gave me a shamefaced smile.

'I'm sorry, Publius. I didn't mean that. I know Maecenas is a friend of yours.'

'He's also one of the most . . . literate men I've ever met. And Octavian may well be a common-or-garden prick' – I enunciated the words carefully, and Horace laughed – 'but he's Rome's only hope.'

'Poor Rome, then.' Horace poured himself a cup of wine from the jug at his elbow.

'Come and see him,' I said suddenly. 'Now.'

Horace choked and raised startled eyes from the wine-cup.

'Octavian?'

'Maecenas,' I said. 'Believe me, he's not what you think.'

'You mean he's not a bumboy?' Horace grinned.

'That's got nothing to do with it. I'm asking you, as a friend, to give *my* friend a chance. Will you?'

He held my eyes for a long time. Then he said slowly, 'Very well, Publius. Very well. But if he talks politics, or starts making offers, then I'll leave. Straight away, with no second chances and without a backward glance. And I won't ever come back. You understand?'

I found that my throat was dry, and gulped down some of my own wine.

'He won't,' I said. 'I promise you.'

'Only not right now.' Horace winked. 'I've got an appointment tonight with a Syrian girl I've been trying to make for months, and I wouldn't trade her for a dozen Maecenases. Or even one good poem.'

'Fair enough,' I said. 'I'll arrange something.'

We went two days later. I had warned Maecenas (not that he needed it) of Horace's conditions, and he did not disappoint me. I noticed, with an inward smile, that Horace had not bothered to change his mantle, and that it had a winestain on its topmost fold. Horace himself was as stiff as if he were paying a call on his worst enemy; but underneath the stiffness I could see that he was nervous.

'Don't worry, Quintus,' I whispered mischievously as we waited for the slave to open Maecenas's imposing front door. 'He doesn't bite.'

Horace grinned.

'He'd better not,' he said. 'He'd get rabies.'

Maecenas was in the garden, as he had been on my first visit – not playing ball this time, but reclining sedately on a couch with a set of wax tablets and a pen in his hands. He was wearing the simple tunic that I knew he genuinely preferred; he never, if he could avoid it, wore a mantle, favouring Greek dress wherever possible. When he rose to greet us, I was relieved to find that he spoke without his usual affectation.

'Horace! Glad you could come!'

Horace scowled, and mumbled something inaudible. I winced. Maecenas seemed not to notice.

'Make yourselves comfortable. The wine'll be along in a minute. Meanwhile I need your help rather badly.'

'What with?' I lay down on a second couch. Horace, after a certain amount of hesitation, took the third.

Maecenas held up the wax tablets.

'One of my wretched scribblings. I can't get it to work at all. I've been trying for days, but I only make things worse.'

This was news to me. I had spent several hours the previous day with Maecenas, and he had never mentioned that he was working on a poem. I began to smell a rat.

'Let's hear it, then,' I said. Maecenas shot me a covert smile.

'Very well.' He cleared his throat and began:

O Niobe, weeping like the willow-bough,
Bemoaning with a thousand tears thy pitiable lot!
Thrice three sons and thrice three daughters hadst thou
Until cruel Apollo and Artemis to death them shot . . .

I burst out laughing. I could not help myself. Horace stared at me as if I had gone mad. Maecenas stopped, a look of comical surprise on his face.

'What is the matter?' he said.

I could hardly get the words out.

'That's terrible!' I gasped. 'It's the worst bit of drivel I've heard in my life!'

Maecenas looked crestfallen.

'It's not very good, is it? But I was hoping you'd help me get it right.'

'No one could help you with that! It's like a one-legged cat! The best thing you can do is put it out of its misery.'

Horace's mouth, I noticed, was hanging open – and then I realised why. He had expected, whatever I claimed to the contrary, that I would toady to Maecenas; that, in exchange for his patronage, he exacted complete subservience and abject flattery. What he saw was the normally shy Virgil berating one of the most powerful men in Rome; and, more important, the said powerful man taking it meekly.

Which, of course, had been Maecenas's intention from the beginning.

'*You* don't think it's totally beyond help, Horace, do you?' Maecenas's pathetic appeal was masterly. I almost burst out laughing again; but that would have spoilt everything.

'Well,' Horace coughed. 'The metre's all wrong for a start.' He settled himself more comfortably on his couch.

'But it isn't a complete disaster. Let's see what we can do, eh?'

And together we took Maecenas's 'poem' in hand. By the time we had finished the ice had been broken.

I was wrong, as I found out later, in thinking that Horace had been completely taken in. Straightforward he might be, but he was no fool, and he had understood perfectly what Maecenas had been up to. However, the trick had appealed to his sense of humour, as well as to his good nature, and he did not resent it.

'If someone can go to that much trouble to put a guest at his ease,' he told me as we walked home, 'then he can't be all bad.'

'Then you'll come back again?' I said eagerly.

'Now I didn't say that exactly.' Horace grinned. 'I might eventually, on my own terms, if he'll have me . . .'

'Oh, he'll have you, Quintus!'

'. . . but not for the present. Give me time to think, and to make my point. I've got my pride too, you know.'

They became friends at last, of course, Maecenas and Horace. But although it took him only nine months to come round, where I had taken two years, he was never wholly Maecenas's man, let alone Octavian's. He remains to this day an unbroken horse: ready to remain on friendly terms with his masters, but unwilling to trade his freedom for a handful of peas.

As I said, Horace is my reflection made straight. I envy him.

49

The battle of Naulochus, as I told you, marked not only the end of Sextus Pompey but also of the present civil wars. However, there was still one short scene to be played before the curtain was drawn on the penultimate act; and that, as it turned out, was a comedy.

The principal actor was Octavian's erstwhile colleague Lepidus.

After Naulochus, Lepidus had been left, with Agrippa, to blockade Messina. Plinius, Pompey's lieutenant, had offered to surrender the town; and although Agrippa advised him to wait for Octavian, Lepidus accepted. He then joined his own legions to Plinius's. The next day, when Octavian arrived from Naulochus, Lepidus attempted to use the troops as a lever to demand restoration of his triumviral rights.

Five years before, he might have got his way. Now was the wrong time. The legions, sick of war and more than sick of Lepidus, refused to back him. Lepidus, devoid of their support, could only beg for mercy. Octavian gave him the honourable (and powerless) position of Chief Priest of the Roman State and packed him off to the provincial town of Circeii. That, effectively, was the end of Lepidus. He never saw Rome again.

Octavian then began the work of reconstruction. Most of the legions were disbanded. Discharged veterans were settled on small farms throughout Italy and the islands. Finally, late in the year, Octavian returned to Rome; and Rome fell over itself to vote him honours. He was the city's darling. Nothing was too good for him, and amid the celebrations his past was forgotten. In return, he showed that he, too, could be magnanimous: public debts were cancelled, taxes cut, and documents relating to the civil wars publicly burnt. He even hinted that, when Antony returned from his Persian campaign, the Republic would be restored. It was a time of glorious optimism; and Octavian was its hero.

During it I received my second commission; not from Pollio, or even from Maecenas, but direct from Octavian himself.

I was in Rome, as I always seemed to be in those days, when the summons came. I use the word with hindsight: it was merely an invitation to dine with Maecenas on the evening following, with the added incentive that my fellow-guest would be Marcus Terentius Varro.

I should say something here about Varro. Varro was an institution. In his long life (he was eighty that year) he had written over five hundred books covering practically the whole literary field: poetry and prose, history (natural and political), tragedy, works on etymology and religion . . . the list is endless, and exhaustive. He had also, in between times, managed a distinguished political career. I had never met him, but had always wanted to. Now it seemed that I would get my wish.

The slave took my cloak at the door and led me through to the dining-room. The couches were already filled. Maecenas wore a Greek mantle of Coan silk – thin, sheer stuff that shone like a butterfly's wing – and was decked to the eyeballs with jewellery. Facing him across the table was a spry old man whom I took to be Varro: bald as a coot, with a fringe of white hair above the ears, very correctly dressed in a stiff white mantle with a broad senatorial stripe. When I came in, he was holding forth about sheep-shearing.

The young man in the place of honour to Maecenas's left was Octavian.

I had not met him, either, yet I knew him at once – a slim, fair-haired young man, very good-looking, but delicate, almost sickly. I paused on the threshold, so suddenly that the slave who was escorting me cannoned into my back. Varro stopped talking, his hand raised like a marble statue's.

'Publius!' Maecenas got up quickly and *slid* (I can think of no more appropriate word) across the room towards me. His earrings tinkled and I could smell his scent, a blend of musk and roses that I found both overpowering and unpleasant. 'You got here at last! Charmed to see you, my dear boy!'

I realised with a sinking heart, as he hugged my shoulders, that he was playing the genial host; but, considering the circumstances, I made the necessary allowances.

'You know Varro, I suppose?' I did not, of course, but there was no gainsaying Maecenas in this mood. I nodded, and Varro grunted. 'And this' – Maecenas paused for effect – 'is our Very Special Guest, who is simply *dying* to meet you.'

The young man's gaze shifted to my face. I cannot describe, or analyse, that first look that Octavian gave me. It was ... complicit? proprietorial? possessive? All of these things. Certainly very personal, and very unsettling. The eyes themselves were arresting: a pale washed-out blue, almost grey, with ... *nothing* behind them. Literally nothing. They were like two frozen pools in a sterile waste of mountain snows; frightening in their emptiness.

Octavian smiled. His teeth were thin and uneven. In that face they seemed a mockery, like bow-legs on a statue of Apollo.

'Virgil. Delighted to meet you at last.' He did not offer to shake hands.

I stammered something. What, I can no longer remember.

Octavian indicated the empty space to his left.

'Sit by me. Please.'

Maecenas steered me to the couch, laid me down like a rag doll. Slaves appeared from nowhere. I held out my hands, automatically, and felt the chill of the water they poured over them.

'Varro was just telling us about his latest book,' Maecenas said. 'A manual of husbandry. Isn't that delicious?'

'You're supposed to read the thing, not eat it,' Varro growled, obviously displeased at being interrupted in midflow. I suspected that he was not altogether taken with our host.

Octavian laughed – a thin sound, with no humour, as if it were something he had learned to do because people expected it.

'Oh, Maecenas will eat anything,' he said. 'So long as it costs enough.'

'Perhaps I should have it written on peacock-skin, then,' Varro said. 'Or on the hide of a young donkey.'

That brought another laugh – from Maecenas this time. He had recently created a sensation at Rome by serving young donkey-flesh to his guests as a delicacy, and he was always ready to appreciate a joke at his own expense.

'Now you mustn't be cruel,' he said. 'Especially as I've gone to such lengths to make this dinner party a success.'

He clapped his hands, and a line of slaves brought in the first course: peahens' eggs in a nest of fennel, tiny salt fish swimming in a blue gelatine mould and a selection of raw vegetables with a light sprinkling of vinegar and fish sauce. Varro's eyes lit up greedily, and he helped himself liberally from the fish creation as soon as it was set down. Octavian, on the other hand, was as abstemious as I was, and picked at some hard-looking green olives which a slave had placed at his elbow. He did not drink much, either – I doubt if his wine-cup was filled more than once in the whole course of the evening.

'You were telling us about your farming manual, Varro.' Maecenas shelled a peahen's egg and dipped it in salt.

Varro raised his head and scowled at him. A bead of gelatine glistened on his chin.

'It's not a manual. I've better things to do than teach clod-hopping bumpkins how to farm.'

Maecenas shot me a sideways grin as he popped the egg into his mouth.

'Then what exactly is it, pray tell.'

Varro waved his spoon.

'A treatise. Your gentlemen-farmers nowadays don't know one end of a mattock from the other. Their bailiffs rob them blind.' He jabbed the spoon savagely into the mould and heaped his plate with more of the quivering jelly. 'Someone's got to teach them their ABCs. Not like fifty years ago. Farmers knew what they were about then, even if they did have money. They didn't need telling.'

'You think there's a need to educate people in agriculture?' Octavian asked.

'Of course.' Varro regarded him balefully, his jaws moving (I wondered if perhaps he had lost most of his teeth). 'The better classes, at any rate. Don't you?'

'Oh, certainly.' Octavian selected a radish, stared at it for a moment, then delicately bit the end off. 'Especially now that things are settling down. We need to encourage a more countrified outlook.'

Varro mumbled something that sounded like, 'Countrified my arse!' but I may have misheard him.

'What we want,' Octavian was talking to Varro, but looking at me, 'is to give a voice to the old country values.

Italy's had enough of wars and destruction. It's time to rebuild, take stock, get back to the important things. The simple peasant virtues that made Rome great. Cincinnatus on his farm, laying aside the dictator's mantle to plough his own acres. An encomium of the Italian countryside, of honest sweat and toil. Wouldn't you agree, Virgil?'

I started, almost spilling my wine. Perhaps it was the effect of Octavian's voice – it was certainly pleasant, almost hypnotic – but I found myself agreeing totally. He was right. That was just what Italy needed. Not encomia on leaders and battles, not literary masterpieces of polished excellence, but a celebration of the quieter things, the little, peaceful concerns of ordinary folk that were, in the long run, far more important.

'Yes,' I said. 'I do agree. Very much so.'

'Well, don't look at me, Caesar,' Varro grunted. 'I've got enough on my plate.' As if by association, he spooned in another mouthful of jelly. 'Good little fish, these. What are they?'

'Baby eels,' Maecenas said. Varro nodded approvingly.

'Catch them young,' he grinned (I had been right about the teeth). 'That's the trick!'

'Your pastoral poems have made quite an impression, I hear.' Octavian was still looking at me intently. 'I've read them myself, of course, and they're excellent. Absolutely excellent.'

'Thank you, Caesar.'

'Perhaps you'll read some for us later.' It was a command, not a question, and as such needed no reply.

'They simply breathe the Italian countryside, don't they?' Maecenas smiled. 'When I read them I can almost smell the goats.'

Varro and I laughed – his laugh was like a creaking gate. Octavian merely smiled. Perhaps he had only a little laughter to give, and did not wish to squander it.

'They are completely perfect,' he agreed. 'You have a rare talent, Virgil.'

'Thank you.'

He selected an olive and carefully cut the stone out with the point of his knife.

'Do you have anything else on hand at present?'

'Not really, Caesar. I had thought of a miniature epic. Something in the style of Calvus's *Io*.'

'The subject?'

'I hadn't decided. But I have my doubts. Epic, even miniature epic, seems a little too . . . grand for me.'

'Well, perhaps in time.' Octavian frowned. 'How about something along the lines we were discussing?'

'A work on agriculture?' I looked across at Varro. 'That would be the raven competing with the swan, surely.'

Varro laughed.

'Never mind my white hairs, boy,' he said. 'And don't think I'd be offended. I've read your stuff, and it isn't bad. A bit lacking in guts, but there, you can't have everything.'

'But I know nothing about farming.'

'You're a country boy, aren't you, Publius?' Maecenas smiled at me. 'Your father still farms at Mantua, so you tell me.'

I do not think it was deliberate. I honestly do not think that. Yet I was suddenly reminded that, if my father still had his farm, the man I had to thank lay on the couch beside me. I still owed a debt – to him, to Maecenas who was my friend; and, just possibly, to Rome.

'Yes, he does,' I said.

'We're not interested in a manual,' Octavian put in (I noticed that *we*). 'No more than Varro here. Call it a pamphlet.' Maecenas shot him a warning glance, but he ignored it, repeated the word carefully. 'A *political* pamphlet, addressed to the cultured classes, explaining what we're trying to do, to bring about. Do you understand?'

'Yes, Caesar. I understand.'

He must have noticed something in my voice, because he said, almost apologetically, 'It's for peace, Virgil. We're not asking you to glorify me, or harm anyone else. We want you to do this for peace.'

'I said I understand!' I spoke sharply, more sharply than I meant. Certainly too sharply for politeness. Varro tutted, and reached for a peahen's egg. Maecenas frowned. Octavian merely nodded.

'Good,' he said; and turned to Maecenas. 'Now what about this dinner you promised us? I'm hungry!'

I noticed that he had not asked whether I had accepted the commission or not, and his assumption that I would chilled me. Was he so sure that I would do whatever he asked? Or did he know me better than I knew myself?

Perhaps, I thought, both of these were true; and that thought was the most chilling of all.

The slaves served the main course. I ate as little as politeness allowed (although I still suffered later from indigestion). Then I made my excuses and left early, to think about the poem which was to become my *Georgics*.

50

I have not mentioned Antony for some time.

I left him, I think, in Athens with Octavia, after the Peace of Tarentum. Antony (and who can blame him?) was having second thoughts about his colleague. Twice he had come to Octavian's support, and twice he had been snubbed. Now, under the terms of the treaty, he had lost a large part of his fleet in exchange for a promise of troops that was never made good. Antony was, if nothing else, an honest man. He kept his word, and expected others to do the same. Octavian, he was finally beginning to realise, was not to be trusted.

The other cause of friction between the two was a more personal one.

For two years Antony had lived with Octavia as a model husband; yet Antony and Octavia were like the opposing elements of fire and water. Coexistence became first difficult, then impossible. Antony, ruled by his emotions, could not live up to his wife's high standards.

Let us be clear about this. Octavia was no prude, nor was she a shrew. If Antony had taken a mistress at Athens, Octavia would no doubt have grieved, but she would not have reproached him for it: she had not an ounce of jealousy or spite in her. At first, her mere presence was enough to shame Antony into virtue. Finally, however, his true nature triumphed. He used her pregnancy and the approaching Persian campaign as an excuse to send her back to Italy; and when she was gone, he summoned Cleopatra to Antioch. There, he married her.

Antony's marriage to Cleopatra did not go against the letter of Roman law. Marriage with a non-citizen is not legal, and technically Antony had merely taken Cleopatra as his official mistress. Yet it was a studied insult, since Octavia was Octavian's sister, and to marry Cleopatra he had put her aside. Nor could he claim that he did it out of policy. If he had needed money for his Persian campaign (which he did not) he had the legions to take it, and Cleopatra could not have stopped him. No, the marriage was a personal one, unconnected with politics. Antony simply did not care.

Nevertheless, it did have a political effect, apart from the insult to Octavian. As far as the east was concerned, it was legal and binding; and Antony proceeded to make his new wife a wedding present of huge chunks of Roman territory: Chalcis, central Syria, coastal Palestine, Phoenicia, Cyprus . . . *that* could not be ignored.

As the playwright Menander says, whom the gods wish to destroy, they first drive mad. If Antony had wished to force a confrontation with Octavian (and I do not believe that he did, at this point), he could not have chosen a better way, barring outright attack, than this marriage with the Egyptian queen. Nor could he have played into Octavian's hands more thoroughly.

If Antony had conquered Persia, perhaps things might have been different: he would at least have had something to set against Octavian's victory over Sextus Pompey. As it was, the campaign was disastrous. Poorly planned from the start, in execution it was a total failure. By the time winter had set in, Antony had lost fully a third of his men. The retreat to the coast was horrific. His troops had no food, no blankets, no boots even, and Antony was forced to beg for supplies from the largely unsympathetic king of Armenia. He was only saved by the prompt intervention of Cleopatra herself, who sent a fleet to rescue his shattered army.

He spent the rest of that year recovering his strength in Alexandria. It is a measure of his continued belief in Octavian (or perhaps of his short-sightedness) that he sent letters to Rome asking for the four promised legions. Octavian, of course, did not send them; but he did send the ships from Antony's loan that had survived Naulochus – which he knew Antony did not need.

Octavia offered more practical help. Having begged two thousand men from her brother, she brought them to Athens together with several shiploads of supplies. Antony accepted them, but told her to mind her own business and sent her back to Rome. The next year, he set out on a further campaign against Armenia. This time he was more successful, and at the end of it celebrated a triumph.

When the news reached Rome, it caused a major scandal. Triumphs are awarded only by the Senate, and they take place in Rome – *only* in Rome. Antony celebrated his Armenian triumph in Alexandria; and it was presided over, not by the Roman Senate and People together with Jupiter Best and Greatest, but by Cleopatra, seated on a golden throne and robed as the goddess Isis.

Worse was to come. Following the triumph, he made a speech ceding the entire Roman east to his two children by the Egyptian, and declaring the young Caesarion Caesar's legitimate son in the place of Octavian. It was a direct challenge. Antony was placing himself at the head of the Hellenistic east in opposition to Octavian's west; and if any doubt remained of his intentions then the form of Cleopatra's oath, 'as surely as one day I shall give judgment from the Capitol', swept it aside. Antony had made his choice. He had claimed sole leadership of the Roman state, and war was inevitable.

After the *Pastorals* were published I found Rome more uncomfortable than ever. Not only did I become too well known, but because of my friendship with Maecenas (and through him Octavian) many people felt, quite wrongly, that I had some influence with the ruling junta. I was constantly being pestered by petitioners – total strangers – whom I could not help. Only in one case did I break my own rule of not asking Maecenas for any favours, and that was because the recipient was emphatically *not* a petitioner.

Maecenas would, I am sure, have been delighted to help Horace without prompting from me. The stumbling-block was Horace himself. He had kept to his word; and when he finally did agree to call on Maecenas again it was only because he felt himself sufficiently secure financially to accept friendship on equal terms.

I had, of course, told Maecenas of Horace's father's loss of his farm, and for some time we had cast about between us for some way of making it good. Just before I left for Mantua, we finally succeeded. Maecenas owned a small property in the Sabine hills east of Rome, not a recent purchase from the land clearances but part of an estate which had been in his family for two generations. It was in a very poor condition. The tenant farmer who rented it was childless and too old now to keep the place up.

Maecenas approached Horace and tactfully suggested that Horace might take it on, stressing that the present occupier would be well taken care of financially and was quite happy with the arrangement. He would not hear of rent – the farm hardly paid for itself as it was. Perhaps Horace would be so good as to take it off his hands and do everyone a favour in the process . . . ?

Horace, to my surprise and delight, accepted. We went there together, all three of us. Maecenas had not exaggerated – the farm was in a terrible state, rank with weeds, its fruit trees and vines unpruned, fences rotten or missing, equipment scanty or worn out. The farmhouse itself was almost a shack. Its roof leaked, its walls were riddled with holes and the inside looked as if a herd of pigs had been wintered there. The place was a complete mess.

Horace took it all in and, literally, beamed.

'It's perfect,' he said to Maecenas. 'Give me a few months and we'll see what we can do.'

He was as good as his word. I visited him the following year and found it as tight and pleasant a little farm as you could wish for anywhere. In a way it was symbolic of what I and Maecenas and Octavian were struggling for on a larger scale: the rebuilding of Italy. Seeing what Horace had accomplished gave me even more heart for my own task in writing the *Georgics*. If they could help, even a little, in bringing about similar changes throughout Italy then they were worth all my poor efforts.

Horace is still there, seventeen years later, on his Sabine farm, sturdy and independent as ever. As I have said before, I envy him.

Shortly after my meeting with Octavian, I left Rome for Mantua. I had received news that my father was dying.

It was not unexpected. He had been failing now for years, and could hardly get around even with the help of a slave to support him. There was nothing specific, as there had been with my mother. He was simply worn out, like an old shoe, and happy to go. We spent three weeks together, and during them we made our peace.

I remember one particular evening, the last, as it turned out. We were sitting outside under the trellised vine, and a light rain was falling – hardly more than a mist. All around us were the earth-smells: the scent of herbs, the rich, brown smell of the earth itself and, cutting across them from the steading beyond the kitchen garden as the breeze shifted, the acrid, throat-catching tang of the goats. I had been talking, what about, I cannot now remember, but it was nothing important. My father was turned to me in profile, his sightless eyes closed, breathing in the scents, listening, I knew, not to me but to the little sounds of his countryside: the faint tinkle of goat-bells, the song of the night-birds, the occasional rustle of some small animal. Suddenly he moved his head to face me.

'You think it goes on, Publius?' he said. 'All this? After we die?'

The question took me by surprise: it was not the sort of question my father would normally ask. But I knew what he meant.

'Some people believe it does,' I said.

'Do you?'

I was silent for a moment.

'No,' I said. 'Not me.'

My father smiled.

'Then I'm sorry for you.' Then, after a while: 'Do you know what I believe?'

'No. Tell me.'

'I think we're part of it. Not separate. Part of it. Part of the land, of the rain, of the scents. When we die, we go back. There's no separation, ever again. We *become* the land, and it is all of us, all of us that've ever been.'

I had never heard him talk like this before. Perhaps he knew it was his last evening, and had already let go. I said nothing, and waited.

'And the land is all we have,' he went on at last. 'A child's cord is cut at birth, but if we cut the cord that joins us to the land we wither and die like a tree without roots. We can cover the earth with cities, or strive for any of a hundred different things, but it always comes back to that in the end. Without the earth under our feet we're nothing.'

'It's getting cold now, Father,' I said. 'Let's go back inside.'

'Just a little longer.' He closed his eyes again and turned his head away. 'You've been a good son, Publius. By your lights. I'm sorry I haven't been as good a father.'

'You made me what I am. You couldn't have given me more.'

His mouth twisted.

'"You made me what I am,"' he said bitterly. 'Well, that's certainly true, and I'm sorry for it. But what are you, Publius? Where are your roots? What do you believe in?'

'Let me get you a blanket.'

He sighed.

'No, that's all right. I'll come in now. You're right, it's turned cold and the evening's dead.'

He got up slowly and I moved to help him. As I took his elbow, he gripped my arm and turned his empty eyes on my face.

'Don't desert the land,' he said. 'Hold on to it, whatever happens. The land's your priority, your only priority, son. Remember that.'

I found him next morning, when I went to wake him, dead in his bed. He must have died early in the night, for he was stiff and cold. I tried to close his eyes, but the lids had frozen, and his sightless eyeballs watched me as I wept above his corpse.

When the news of Antony's speech at Alexandria reached Rome, there was a public outcry. Octavian sent him a strongly worded letter taking him to task for his liaison with Cleopatra and his treatment of Octavia. Antony replied in kind, telling Octavian that it was none of his business. He also, more significantly, sent letters to the Senate, offering to lay aside his triumviral powers if Octavian would do the same. This, of course, Octavian could not have. It was essential that Italy see him both as her leader and as her champion against the arch-fiend Antony; and Octavian immediately began working to bring this about.

That, long before it was formally declared, was the start of the real war. It was a war that suited Octavian admirably: a war of ideas, not of weapons. The fight against Antony was to be a personal one. 'Italy' and 'Caesar' were to be made synonymous; and to further this Octavian set about creating in the minds of Italians a pride in their national identity. Note, I do not say 'Romans': it contributed in no small degree to Octavian's success that he saw Italy as a single entity, and he based his strategy on conveying this to the people and linking himself with it indissolubly. At Rome herself, he and Agrippa, largely at their own expense, embarked on a public building programme to beautify the city and improve her amenities; and Maecenas saw to it that, although the benefactors were suitably modest, everyone knew where the money came from. Octavian also began to instil a pride in the traditional religion, restoring old temples, making costly dedications and lending his support to the priesthoods. In banning eastern religions from the city he was, in effect, clarifying the line between 'Italy' and 'Caesar' on the one hand and 'the east' and 'Antony' on the other.

Imagine an artist who wishes to paint a picture to hang high on a wall, far above people's heads, yet which must be perfectly visible and comprehensible from below. First of all, he simplifies his subject, reduces it to its basic components. Then he lines them in: crude shapes devoid of detail, that do not confuse with their complexity – distorted, perhaps, to allow for the angle of viewpoint. Finally he adds the colours, hard primary colours, or simple black and white, with no half-tones or mergings of one colour with another. Taken down from the wall, and viewed closely, such a picture would be ludicrous, a child's painting that offends by its lack of subtlety and poor draughtsmanship. Replace it where it is meant to be hung, however, and it strikes more truly than the finest work of Zeuxis.

That was how Octavian conducted his war against Antony, in its initial stages. It was a strategy of genius. It brought all of Italy behind him, and Antony, although he tried his best, had no answer to it.

By the new year, everyone knew that war was imminent. The consuls were both Antony's men and, after throwing down a challenge to Octavian on his behalf, they left Rome taking a large part of the Senate with them. On the face of it, this was a blow to Octavian: if he were to represent himself as the champion of the Roman state, then how could he justify the defection of both chief magistrates and much of the governing body? In fact, it made Antony's task far more difficult. Where Octavian had been at pains to have his own position clear-cut, Antony now found himself with a dilemma. He could lead his Roman supporters as a Roman magistrate, or his eastern allies as a Hellenistic king, but he could not do both. Whichever he chose, he was bound to offend the other party. This was to be crucial.

The year was spent in preparations. Antony gathered a huge fleet and called on his client-kings to mobilise their own troops. Cleopatra provided money, an immense amount, but only a fraction of the fabled Treasure of the Ptolemies held in Alexandria. She was already the major cause of friction between Antony and his Roman allies, but she refused to leave; and as she was paying most of the bills she had her way.

Then Octavian suddenly changed his tactics. He targeted Cleopatra as the prime foe. Antony became the innocent dupe, bound to her will by drugs and sorcery. In late May, almost on cue, Antony himself lent his enemies a hand by finally divorcing Octavia.

Although Octavian milked the divorce for all it was worth, his outrage was quite genuine. With the possible exception of his new wife Livia (and I am not sure even about her), his sister was the only person for whom he felt genuine affection; perhaps because she was everything he was not. Yet it had another effect even more damaging. Two of Antony's foremost supporters, Plancus and Titius, took it as a sign that Cleopatra's hold over him was now unbreakable, and in disgust defected to Octavian. They revealed that Antony had deposited a will with the Vestals in Rome; and Octavian, not scrupling under the circumstances to take it by force, made the terms public.

Most of the clauses came as no surprise, confirming as they did the grant of kingdoms to Cleopatra's children by Antony and acknowledging Caesarion as Caesar's heir. But there was one which was new and, in the eyes of the ordinary Roman people, outweighed all the rest.

Antony asked that at his death he be buried with Cleopatra in Egypt.

I do not know if this was an invention of Octavian's or not. Certainly it could have been, since no one but Octavian read the will; yet Antony never denied it, and it has the ring of truth. It seems a small thing, I know, but it had immense significance. In effect, Antony had disclaimed his Roman heritage. He had cut himself off from Italy; and in revenge Italy cut herself off from him.

Even Octavian, I suspect, was taken aback by the violence of the reaction. There had been some grumbling over increased taxes for the war. That ceased. It hardly needed Octavian's campaign of vituperation against Cleopatra to fan the flames, or even much prompting on the part of his secret agents to guide people down the path he wished them to go. First Italy, then the provinces joined together to swear an oath to Octavian of personal allegiance and solidarity. It was a tremendous vote of confidence, an open mandate for war. Octavian (or Maecenas) may have helped to engineer it, but in the last analysis it was Antony's own doing. He had not only dug his own grave, but jumped down into it and pulled the soil on top of himself; and Octavian needed only to stamp it flat to complete the job.

He did this before the end of the year. In an ancient and impressive religious ceremony not seen for generations, robed as a priest of the war goddess, Octavian declared on Rome's behalf a Holy War; not against Antony, which might have clouded the morality of the issue, but against the woman who had corrupted him: the drunken, beast-worshipping witch-whore Cleopatra.

The last stage of the war had begun.

53 ∫

The Actium campaign justified all Italy's expectations, and proved that Octavian had finally come of age as a strategist. Before the sailing season was properly under way, he had transported his troops across the Adriatic and established a beach-head on the coast of Epirus in northern Greece.

You notice, of course, the discrepancy here. Octavian had crossed unopposed, and there had been no intervening sea-battle. What had happened to Antony's numerically superior fleet?

I discovered the answer much later, in a rare (and thankfully brief) conversation with Agrippa. I doubt if I will mention Octavian's close friend, admiral and erstwhile heir-designate again at any length in the remaining part of my story. We did not get on well; he classed me with Maecenas – whom he despised – as an effete unpractical scribbler, too clever by half and a natural degenerate. I saw him as a muscle-headed semi-illiterate boor with too great a sense of his own importance. No doubt there were faults on both sides. At least we respected each other's abilities, which on his side were considerable.

I cannot remember the exact circumstances of that talk. We had found ourselves fellow-guests of some notable in Brindisi. I was returning from a trip to Athens, he was on his way to Egypt on official business, and we were both detained for several days by adverse weather. The atmosphere was uncomfortable, the conversation stilted, but both of us felt it our duty to maintain the common politenesses.

Agrippa was a big man, heavily muscled, with a broad, jowly face. He reminded me of these dogs that peasants rear for bull-baiting. Maecenas once said – he was only half-joking – that Agrippa could hold only one thought in his mind at a time, if it were simple enough. I would not wholly agree. He was a superb tactician, and in military matters far superior to any of his rivals or colleagues, Antony included. Only in the broader fields of strategy and politics did his military skills let him down. Agrippa was no Caesar, not even an Octavian.

We were, as I said, fellow-guests. I was sitting in the solar, making some notes from a philosophical text, when he entered. He had not expected to see me, and was visibly taken aback; in fact, for a moment I thought he would march straight out again. Finally, however, he drew up a stool and sat by the window, glaring out at the rain.

'Pissing weather,' he growled.

I took this for an opening conversational gambit, and agreed pleasantly. We said nothing more for some time. Agrippa fidgeted with a large ring on his right hand. I noticed his fingers were broad and stubby, the nails black and broken.

'You coming or going?' he said at last.

'Coming. I'm just back from Greece.'

'Pissing country. Nothing but ruins. I wouldn't give you tuppence for it.'

'Athens has its points.'

'So they say. The north was enough for me.' He laughed – a short, barking laugh. 'Mind you, I was busy at the time.'

I laid aside my book.

'So I've heard,' I said. 'Along with several other people.'

He glanced at me suspiciously to see if I was making fun of him, but I met his eyes with a look of bland innocence.

'Oh yes,' he said. 'You were safe in Italy at the time, weren't you, Virgil? Along with Maecenas. Taking care of things like good little housewives while the men did the work.'

'Someone had to do it.' I was unruffled. 'Not that I was concerned personally.'

He grunted and scratched his barrel chest. I could see this was not going to be a jolly get-together unless I steered the conversation into more congenial waters.

'I've always wondered,' I said, 'how you managed to catch Antony on the hop like that. Was it luck?'

'Luck be damned,' he growled. 'Ahenobarbus sold him out. Caesar'd had it arranged for months.'

This was complete news to me. Ahenobarbus had been Antony's commander of the fleet, responsible both for giving warning of a crossing and stopping Octavian's troops from landing. I knew that he had gone over to Octavian later in the war – he died shortly afterwards – but not that he had thought of it so early on.

'Ahenobarbus was a traitor?'

'I don't like that word. He saw sense, certainly.'

'Why? Why did he do it?'

Agrippa shrugged.

'Who cares? It's none of my business. Couldn't stand that bitch Cleopatra, I expect. Like a lot of them. Thought Antony was betraying the Roman state.' He enunciated the words carefully, with a twist to his mouth. 'These sodding Republicans were all alike. Too pious for their own good, and brains in their arses.'

'Did Antony know?'

'Probably. But there wasn't much he could do about it, was there? He had enough problems keeping his shower together, and Ahenobarbus was well in with the nobs.' He stood up abruptly. 'Looks like it's clearing. Think I'll have a stroll down to the harbour, get some fresh air, see how the ship's doing.'

'I'll see you at dinner, then,' I said.

He looked down at me, frowning; then he nodded and went out.

He did not reappear that evening, or indeed on many other occasions while our enforced companionship lasted. Perhaps he preferred to dine on hard tack and bilge water with his friend the captain.

Agrippa was right about Antony's difficulties in holding his army together. The problem, of course, was Cleopatra. If she had withdrawn to Alexandria and left him to fight it out alone, the result might have been quite different. As it was, he was stuck on the defensive. He could not invade Italy with her beside him – his Roman allies would not have stood for that – nor could he force her to leave, since she was his main source of money and supplies; besides, the eastern allies would have seen it as a slight. He could only encourage his enemies to come to him and, having caught them between his own forces and the sea, either starve them into submission or smash them where they stood.

In the end, he did neither. Agrippa moved south and took Patras and Corinth, severing Antony's own lines of supply. In the north, the local allies on whom he was depending went over to Octavian, while his fleet was of little help since he refused to provide it with soldiers (perhaps because he did not trust Ahenobarbus?) As the noose tightened and food ran short, the bickering and desertions began. Recognising that his position was rapidly becoming untenable, Antony fell back on Actium.

The battle of Actium – the last, decisive battle – was fought on 2 September. Antony had six squadrons – about three hundred and fifty ships – plus one more (Cleopatra's) to protect his rear. Aboard were some thirty-five thousand men. Agrippa, commanding Octavian's fleet, lay further off the coast, waiting for the prevailing wind to shift to the north-west, as it usually did around midday. When the wind changed, both Antony and Agrippa moved – Antony under oars, Agrippa using sail. They clashed, and ships were sunk on both sides.

At that crucial moment the three squadrons to the left and centre of Antony's line suddenly deserted; and a further two, their avenue of retreat blocked by Cleopatra, raised their oars in surrender. At a single stroke Antony had lost his whole fleet, except for the remains of his personal squadron – some forty ships, currently engaged with the enemy – and Cleopatra's. Transferring from his own damaged craft to Cleopatra's flagship, he abandoned the battle and ran for safety. The remaining ships, seeing their leader gone, gave themselves up.

The next day Octavian sent the news back to Rome by the fastest available cutter. Most of Antony's surviving ships he burnt as a thank-offering, having first detached the bronze rams from their prows and set them up as a victory monument. There only remained the question of Antony and Cleopatra themselves; but their fate was a foregone conclusion.

54

It was to be several months before that fate was sealed. Octavian had to move cautiously. He was facing now, not Antony, who was a broken man, but a far more dangerous adversary, Cleopatra herself.

I had a slave once, a certain Simon, from the mountains to the north-west of Pella, the Macedonian capital. His left arm, from elbow to wrist, was a red, wrinkled mass of scar tissue (I got him cheap because of it). When I asked him how he had come by such a terrible wound, he told me the following story.

Before he was taken as a slave, he had been a hunter. One day he and some friends started a lioness. Simon got in a cast of his javelin and wounded the beast in the side. The lioness escaped, but she was badly hurt and he followed her meaning to finish her off. She ran down a narrow corrie and disappeared into a cave at its end.

Simon's friends were for giving up. They had no torches with them, nor did they have the stomach to follow a wounded lioness into her lair. Simon, however, thought differently. The animal, he knew, was seriously weakened, probably already dead or dying. Also, the cave was narrow, little more than a fissure in the rock. If he advanced with his spear held out in front of him the lioness would have no room to manoeuvre and would, if she attacked, spit herself on the point. Besides, he wanted to finish the job. Despite his friends' warnings, he went in.

The fissure was a shallow one, and even without a torch he could see the animal crouching against the far wall. With her were three cubs. Simon knew then that he had made a foolish mistake, but he had no time to rectify it. The lioness sprang, straight on to the point of his spear. Being designed for boar, it had a crosspiece a quarter of the way down the shaft. Somehow she managed to reach past this with her claws and lay open Simon's arm like a fishmonger filleting a sturgeon.

Simon's friends, hearing his screams and realising what had happened, dragged him back. The lioness was already dead, pressed hard against the crossbar. She had forced the spearhead right through her body and out at the back halfway down her spine. Its iron blade protruded a full handspan clear of the pelt.

Simon said he had been lucky not to have died himself. His friends had tied the arm above the big vein tightly with rope and got him home safely; but although the wound healed in time the tendons had been severed and his left arm was useless.

The two situations are not exactly parallel: Octavian was far too clever a huntsman to get himself mauled. Yet in other respects the metaphor holds good. Cleopatra was brought to bay in her own land. For herself, she had little hope: Octavian could not allow her to keep the throne, even if he spared her life. Her children were another matter, and she was ready to go to any lengths to defend them. Having transferred the royal treasure to her own mausoleum and piled about it dry kindling and jars of oil, she barricaded herself in. Unless Octavian gave the Egyptian crown to one of her children, she said, she would throw down a lighted torch.

Octavian was in a quandary. He could not afford to lose

the treasure – he had made too many promises to too many people that depended on it. But neither could he leave Antony's or Caesar's son on the Egyptian throne. Somehow, Cleopatra had to be got out.

Meanwhile, Antony was already dead. When he and Cleopatra had reached Egypt hc had stayed behind to resist Octavian's advance. Now, deserted by his few remaining troops, and thinking that Cleopatra herself was dead, he had fallen on his sword. Octavian gave permission for him to be taken to the mausoleum, and he died in Cleopatra's arms. She mourned him like a true wife; and her grief was more sincere, I suspect, than any Octavian was capable of.

The stalemate was resolved by a member of Octavian's staff, Proculeius, together with my friend Gallus, who was rapidly becoming one of his most trusted lieutenants. While Gallus talked to Cleopatra through an iron grille in the wall, Proculeius and two others slipped through a window and overpowered her. She was led away and kept under house arrest in her own palace.

For what happened next I have only Gallus as an authority, and that when he was drunk: wild horses, I suspect, would not have dragged the story out of him otherwise.

We were at Rome, a few months after Cleopatra's death. Gallus had just been appointed prefect of Egypt, and we were celebrating before he left. I, of course, was quite sober, but Gallus had accounted for at least two full jugs of wine and had reached the talkative stage.

We were discussing Cleopatra's death.

'Caesar couldn't kill her, see?' Gallus stared at me with owl-eyes over his twentieth wine-cup. 'He wanted her dead. The army wanted her dead. 'grippa wanted her dead. Sodding *Rome* wanted her dead. But he couldn't do it. Couldn't kill last queen of Egypt.'

'Why not?' I said.

Gallus rolled slightly on his couch, belched.

'Thought she'd curse him,' he said. 'Curse of the Pharaohs. Thass why he let her be buried like she wanted, with Antony. Shit-scared of her death-curse.'

It sounds incredible, I know; yet the more you think about it the more possible – even probable – it becomes. Octavian is very superstitious. He is always careful, for example, to place his shoes on the floor correctly before going to bed, and will never conduct important business on the ninth day of the month or set out on a journey immediately after a market day. He believes totally in precognitive dreams and omens, and in the power of magic. And Egyptians are very skilled over things like curses.

'Still, she had to die,' Gallus went on, 'so he had a private talk with her an' they came to an agreement.'

'What was that?' I asked. Gallus simply stared, his eyes goggling. 'Gallus! What was the agreement?'

'Carrot 'n' stick,' he said. 'Caesar'd spare the kids if she killed herself 'n' let her be buried beside Antony. If not, they'd all walk in his triumph 'n' be strangled afterwards.'

'But he did kill them. The boys, anyway,' I said.

Gallus shrugged, roused himself, poured more wine. It slopped over the rim of his cup and ran like blood across the table.

'She was dead by then, Publius,' he said. ''Sides, they were old Julius's 'n' Antony's. He couldn't let them live, whatever he told her.'

'So what happened?'

Gallus drank slowly, set his cup down and wiped his mouth.

'We were ordered to keep clear of her,' he said. 'No Roman guards, jus' Egyptians. Sat there twiddling our thumbs, waiting for her to get it over with, but she wouldn't. Finally Caesar got fed up waiting, told her they'd be leaving for Rome in three days' time. God knows what he'd've done if she'd called his bluff, but she didn't. Got someone to smuggle in that damned snake in a basket of figs.' He grinned. ''N'that was that. Good riddance.'

'Why the snake? I mean, a dagger would've been easier, surely?'

Gallus looked blank for a moment. Then he laughed.

'Not jus' any snake,' he said. 'Not jus' any snake. Asp. Egyptians believe 's messenger of thingummy . . . sun god. Get bit by asp 'n' you're a god.' He tried to snap his fingers, but he was too drunk. 'Jus' like that.'

'Did Octavian know?'

''Course he knew! Whole thing was a set-up, I told you. Only slip he made was he got cold feet at las' moment. Decided she'd probably curse him after all, thought he'd better keep her alive as long as possible. So he sent for a snake-priest to suck the poison out. Too late, of course, an' he wasn't supposed to know anything 'bout it. But where superstition's concerned Caesar isn't rational.' He grinned at me, raised his cup. 'Don't tell him I told you, will you?'

So there you are. Believe it or not as you please. It fits the facts, certainly, and more important it chimes with Octavian's character. But I have no proof, beyond what Gallus said; and, were he alive today, I have no doubt that he would deny everything.

55

By the late spring of the year following Cleopatra's death, the *Georgics* were largely finished. I had planned them in close consultation with Maecenas, and both he and I were pleased with the result.

They were in four books, covering the various aspects of farming: crops, trees, animals and beekeeping. As far as the content was concerned, some of it came from my father and memories of my own childhood, but the larger part, I confess, I took from Varro's *Countryside Book*. Despite his abrupt manner, he himself helped me considerably, and I was glad that he lived long enough to see the work finally published.

As for the poetic side, my obvious model was Hesiod; yet from the start I could not bring myself to use him. He was both too great to bear imitation and too dark for my purposes. I thought for a long time before choosing Lucretius.

My reasons were not altogether straightforward, as you might expect: writers on agriculture do not normally choose philosophers as their models. Yet before he was a philosopher, Lucretius was a poet; and not only that, but an inspired poet who could breathe fire into your belly and tighten the muscles of your throat as you read him. He was what I needed. If I could do for Octavian what Lucretius had done for Epicurus, and put fire into the bellies of others, I could rest content.

The second reason was personal. I chose Lucretius as a kind of exorcism.

I do not know which attracted me first to Epicureanism: the doctrine itself or Lucretius's poetry. Both came together, bright and clean as a single sword-flash. Then I met Siro, wisest and kindest of men. If Epicureanism was good enough for him, and for my other teacher Parthenius, I decided, then it was good enough for me, and I thought no more about the matter. If this sounds too simplistic, then I am sorry. As far as I am concerned it is the truth.

Since Siro's death, I had come to examine my beliefs more critically. First there was my love of poetry. That was not strictly against the Epicurean canon – witness Parthenius, and Lucretius himself. My growing involvement with politics was more serious, and completely against Epicurean strictures: Siro, I know, would have been horrified. Yet again this was a venial sin: many Epicureans managed to combine politics with philosophy.

The main charge against me, however, was my changing attitude to the gods, and the fate of the human soul. Here I had no defence. The gods exist for Epicureans, but they have no interest in mankind. They inhabit the pure air between the worlds, and are busy with their own concerns. This I could no longer accept. What I believed exactly, I am not quite sure; but recent events had convinced me that the gods – particularly Jupiter – had not totally abandoned us, and were at work through Octavian.

As for the soul, I no longer had a firm opinion. Perhaps it was that last conversation with my father; but I felt that I wanted to believe in its survival. That, too, was heresy to an Epicurean.

And so I chose Lucretius. In using him I was retracing my steps, sloughing off the philosophical skin that I had, not outgrown (to think that would be arrogance), but found no longer fitted.

I was putting the final touches to the *Georgics*, as I said, the year that Octavian returned to Italy after settling matters in the east. He arrived at Brindisi in the early summer; and almost immediately fell ill. Too weak to proceed straight to Rome, he spent some time at Atella in Campania. Towards the end of June I received a message asking me to join him, and to bring along a copy of the poem.

Octavian was staying at one of Maecenas's country villas. I was relieved to find that Maecenas was also there: the thought of a private reading to the ruler of the Roman world unnerved me completely. On the other hand, I discovered that I was to be part of his cure, and expected to read the whole work – the *whole* work – to him over the next few days. A great honour, no doubt, but one I could have gladly foregone. Either my voice would give out, I thought grimly, or my nerve would break and they would take me home raving in a closed carriage.

Seven years had passed since our last (and only) meeting. Octavian had not changed much physically, although he showed clear signs of his recent illness: his face had a gaunt, yellow look and his wrists were thin. I noticed, too, that he wore woollen leggings despite the summer temperatures – he was sensitive to cold – and, on the rare occasions he ventured outside, a heavy military cloak.

The reading went well. Fortunately, Octavian preferred his medicine in small doses, and in any case we were continually interrupted by official business. It was not until the last book that things went terribly wrong.

I had decided (without telling anyone) to close the work with a short tribute to Gallus; and I had just begun reading this part when I felt the atmosphere change. I looked up. Octavian was sitting tight-lipped, staring at Maecenas, who was frowning.

'That,' Octavian said, 'will have to go.'

'I'm sorry, Caesar?' I thought perhaps I had misheard.

'There will be no mention of Cornelius Gallus.'

That came out flat. I simply stared at him. Maecenas started to say something, but Octavian silenced him with a look. He was not angry – Octavian was rarely angry, or at least rarely showed his anger – but coldness seeped from him as from a glacier.

'Could I ask why, Caesar?' I was ashamed to find myself trembling. 'Gallus is my friend. I thought he was your friend, too.'

'Some things go beyond friendship.'

'I'm sorry, I still don't understand.'

'Gallus has . . . overstepped himself, Publius,' Maecenas put in smoothly. 'Become' – he tried a smile which did not work – 'a little too large for his boots.'

'In what way?' I said. I was genuinely puzzled. Gallus was no traitor; and treachery was the only explanation I could see for this reaction.

'He's been acting . . . well, rather foolishly recently.' Maecenas glanced at Octavian, whose expression was set like chiselled marble. 'On that last campaign of his. There was some nonsense about an inscription and some statues. As if the victory was all his doing.'

'And wasn't it?' I asked.

'That's not the point. Gallus is a subordinate, after all. And the whole thing was extremely . . . self-congratulatory.'

I was beginning to see.

'You mean he should have given the credit to Caesar?' I said. 'Although Caesar was nowhere near Egypt at the time?'

How I dared, I cannot tell you. It was a combination of outrage on Gallus's behalf and on my own, as a poet.

'That is exactly what he should have done,' Octavian said. 'For the good of the state.'

The anger must have shown on my face, because Maecenas held up a placating hand.

'You must understand, Publius, that generals can no longer be allowed to take too much glory to themselves. Self-aggrandisement was the ruination of the Republic.'

'So they must give the credit to those who don't deserve it?' I snapped.

I had gone too far. Octavian's face was chalk-white.

'You've been told the reasons, Virgil,' he said. 'That should be enough for you. Whether you accept them or not is your own concern, but what I say goes. You will take that passage out.'

I sat absolutely still. The book slipped from my lap and rolled across the tiled floor. Maecenas was looking at me in mute appeal, Octavian merely . . . looking. I drew a deep breath.

'Yes, Caesar,' I said quietly. I think I could have killed him then.

'Listen, Publius.' Maecenas laid a hand on my arm. 'It's nothing personal. But we can't have this spirit of glory-seeking any longer among the army commanders. It's too dangerous nowadays.'

'Dangerous to whom?' I was trying not to look at Octavian, but it was he who answered.

'You know your history, Virgil. Generals become successful. They build up a mystique among their soldiers. Soon they're more important to the men than the state itself, and then they start elbowing for power. Before you know it, Rome's in the middle of another civil war. Better not to allow the process to start in the first place.'

This made perfect sense, of course, especially delivered in Octavian's flat, measured tones. I had known it for years. But somehow, coming from him, it rang false.

'Gallus is not a traitor,' I said. 'You can reprimand him officially if you like, but with all respect, Caesar, you have no right to tell me that I cannot pay *my* friend a private compliment in *my* poem.'

'But it's not a private poem,' Maecenas said gently. 'It's a public statement of official policy. You can't get away from that, Publius.'

I noticed my hands were gripping the arms of my chair so tightly that the knuckles were white. Consciously, I relaxed them, and flexed my fingers.

'Very well,' I said. 'You can write your own public statements from now on.'

Octavian became very still.

'Come now, Virgil,' he said. 'Don't be a beetroot. It's too small a thing to quarrel over. After all, the passage is only a dozen lines.'

'Let it stand, then.'

'I can't do that.'

I said nothing. Maecenas, I noticed, had a look of alarm on his face.

Octavian got up and walked over to the far wall, which was painted with a picture of Perseus holding aloft the Gorgon's head. I noticed, in my detached mood, that our lord and master limped: an old wound, perhaps, or a congenital weakness. He stood for a long time in silence, staring at the picture.

'I need you, Virgil.' Octavian's back was still turned towards me. 'I have the present, but I need you to give me the future. Help me. Not for my own sake, but for the sake of Rome.'

There it was. The appeal that I had hoped he would not make, phrased in terms I had hoped he would not use. It was unanswerable.

'Very well, Caesar,' I said. Only that; but I hoped he would not press me further.

Octavian nodded. He was still looking at the picture. Beside me, I heard Maecenas let out his breath.

'Good.' Octavian turned round at last and tried a smile. Again I was struck by the thinness and unevenness of his teeth. 'You do understand, don't you?'

'Oh, I understand, Caesar,' I said. 'I understand perfectly.'

'I hope so. I really do hope so.' He hesitated, then went on in a stronger voice: 'In any case, I wanted to discuss another project with you.'

'And that is?'

Octavian's eyes rested on me for a moment, then shifted away.

'I want you to write an epic.'

'The story of Aeneas.' Maecenas was watching me much as one will watch a skittish horse for signs that it will bolt.

I turned to him.

'Another *public statement*?' I asked sarcastically.

Octavian made a curious motion with his hand; as though he were warding off a blow. He still refused to look at me.

'I told you,' he said. 'I need you to give me the future. You're a great poet. Perhaps the greatest Rome has ever produced. We – you and I together – have the chance to build a perfect world. I can control men's bodies, even their minds, but only you can give me their hearts.'

I sat still and said nothing. Even Maecenas was looking discomfited at the unmistakable pleading in Octavian's voice.

'I won't live for ever, Virgil.' Again, his back was to me. 'I'm not strong, I may not last even another ten years. I want my work to live after me for others to take up. You can write a poem that men unborn will listen to and say, Yes, that's right, that's how things should be. That's how we want to live. Will you do it, Virgil? Please?'

'What about your past?' I heard myself saying. 'The killings. The backstabbings, the lies. Your own shortcomings. You want me to justify *those*?'

When he turned, at last, I swear there were tears in his eyes.

'Forget them,' he said. 'Forget the past, it's not important. What I did was necessary. Virgil, please! I need you to justify me, not for my own sake but for Rome's.'

Maecenas, I noticed, had turned away and was examining another of the paintings: Priam and Achilles. He might have been distancing himself from Octavian's plea, but I suspect that, like me, he was merely embarrassed.

Octavian and I stared at each other for a long time. Then I lowered my eyes.

'Very well, Caesar,' I said. 'I can't promise you the future, but you will have your *Aeneid*.'

56

I did not begin the *Aeneid* at once. Before a word could be written, I had an immense amount of planning – and thinking – to do.

Had Octavian not specified Aeneas, I would have chosen him myself. Although he has no direct connection with Rome, his son Iulus is the ancestor of the Julian clan, to which Octavian belongs. More, Aeneas has an impeccable Homeric pedigree, and so using him enabled me to make explicit the necessary link between Homer and Italy, the old world and the new.

Aeneas's story, too, fits. Together with his aged father, he flees from Troy at the gods' bidding, to found a new and better state in the west. After undergoing many dangers, he reaches Carthage, where he is detained by the beautiful Queen Dido. Caught between love and duty, he hesitates; but duty triumphs and he sails on, to Italy. There he is greeted by the king, Latinus, as the prophesied leader from overseas who will marry his daughter and make his kingdom great.

Latinus's daughter has, however, been promised to another man, Turnus. Turnus persuades the Italians to fight against Aeneas and his Trojans. Finally Aeneas is victorious. Trojans and Italians are united as brothers, and the gods' purpose fulfilled.

You see the possibilities: the underlying themes of divine intent, piety, religious obedience and the conflict between duty and self-interest that were so germane to Octavian's purpose. You see also the sheer scale of the thing. Octavian was demanding that I become no less than a second Homer. What his *Iliad* and *Odyssey* had been to two hundred generations of Greeks, my *Aeneid* would be for Rome. Through me, Octavian and what he was striving to create was to be made immortal: the divine yardstick against which all future behaviour would be measured.

Do you wonder that I felt inadequate?

Had I been Octavian's man, body and soul, the task would have been awesome enough. As it was, I was fettered by my own reservations, my own opinions of Octavian as an individual. And, as any poet will tell you, a fettered poet is no poet at all, let alone a second Homer.

I must make my position clear, even at the risk of repeating myself, for clarity here is vital. First of all, I was convinced – *am* convinced – that what Octavian was attempting was right, that he had heaven's mandate to build a new world; and I still hope so, although I am no longer so sure. If it had been possible, I would have given him my full support, unreservedly; but that I could not do. If I had tried, the poetry would have run slack and sour, become second-rate, useless. I could only try to compromise, to retreat into poetic allusion and allegory. My true opinions would be there, embedded in the poem, couched in terms that were unambiguous if looked at sideways with a biased eye, but which otherwise could be dismissed as embellishments or poetic fancies.

This sounds complicated, I know, yet I cannot put it any more simply and retain the sense. Let me, instead, give you an example.

I had promised Octavian that I would remove the lines at the end of my *Georgics* in praise of Gallus. In the event, I replaced them with a passage on the death of Orpheus.

You know the story, of course. Orpheus's wife Eurydice is bitten by a snake and dies. Orpheus, the divine singer, goes down to Hades to bring her back. His song drags tears even from the iron eyes of Pluto, god of the dead; and he is permitted to lead back his wife, on condition that he does not look at her until they regain the upper world. At the very edge of Pluto's kingdom, Orpheus turns, and loses Eurydice for ever. Orpheus then takes to the woods, lamenting his wife. He offends the Bacchants, the savage women-followers of Dionysus, and they tear him to pieces. His scattered body drifts down the River Strymon; yet still he sings, mourning for his lost wife.

Now consider Gallus, in the light of the story. Gallus, too, is a poet, a singer. He, too, offends a pitiless god and is destroyed because of it, although his poems survive him. Finally, as a signpost to the reader, I tamper with the myth itself. My hero, at this point, is a certain Aristaeus, who has lost his bees through Orpheus's anger. The original fault (I say) lay with this Aristaeus: it was because he was pursuing Eurydice, intent on rape, that she stood on the snake. Now, anyone with a knowledge of myth will realise that this is nonsense. Traditionally, Aristaeus had no connection whatsoever with Eurydice's death, or with the Orpheus myth.

You see now, I hope, what I mean. On the surface, a pretty story with a learned allusion (did Aristaeus try to rape Eurydice? Does Virgil know something we don't? What a clever poet he is!). Nothing overt, nothing explicitly stated. Yet the truth is there, and – if you have the key – it is unambiguous.

The dangers, of course, were obvious. I knew that if Octavian ever found out I could expect no mercy. Nevertheless, the *Aeneid* could be written in no other way, and the *Aeneid* was more important, in the end, than either my own life or Octavian's pride. I counted on three things: one, that I could keep the more obviously critical passages from Octavian until the work was finished; two, Octavian's own vanity, which would recognise the surface praise but not the underlying criticism; and three, the eventual complicity of Maecenas. He, I was sure, would miss nothing.

In choosing this path, I was consciously charting a course between Scylla and Charybdis. Perhaps I was wrong. Certainly my decision has been the death of me. Never mind. I have done all I could, and if in the end it has not been enough, I am too tired, now, to care.

Let me tell you, before I close this chapter, what happened to Gallus. Let me tell it quickly, as a surgeon hurries through an operation to spare his patient what pain he may.

Octavian recalled him to Rome, where he was charged with maladministration. A deluge of sycophantic accusations followed. He was deprived, by decree of the Senate, of his property and condemned to exile. Octavian stood aside: debarred from intervening, he said, by the harsh moral demands of his high office. In despair, Gallus took his own life. I was with him when he died, and closed his eyes before going back to my books, and the task of immortalising his murderer.

You see, now, how difficult it was to write my *Aeneid* and to give Octavian the future he so badly needs. Death, when it comes to me, will not be unwelcome. Nor will it be undeserved.

Little remains to tell, now, except for the end.

The remaining years were, for me, a period of growing disillusionment. Perhaps I had unconsciously hoped for too much. Perhaps I had hoped for the Golden Age to be ushered in to the blare of trumpets, and for all my doubts to be magically resolved. It did not happen like that. Of course it did not, although I wished it to, above all else: we are all children still, and love to believe in fables.

After Actium, Octavian was everyone's hero. He had united Italy and given her, for the first time, a sense of identity. His lavish spending on public works, funded from the spoils of his Egyptian war, had made him popular with the common people. Better still, he had brought peace. Most of the legions had been disbanded, and the doors of the Temple of Janus, which always stand open in time of war, had been closed for the first time in living memory. Rome was poised on the threshold of an age of peace and prosperity such as she had never known in the course of her history.

Then, amid the glory and the trumpets and the quiet peace that followed them, people began to compare Octavian with Caesar. Like Caesar, he had been voted honour after honour. Like Caesar, he held the supreme power and backed it with his armies.

Caesar, in the end, had failed. Was Octavian simply another Caesar?

Octavian was well aware of the dangers. By holding on to the highest public office of consul and depriving the leading families of their traditional rights, he had set himself on the same fatal course as the dead dictator. There had been one conspiracy already – that of young Lepidus – and there would be others. Somehow he had to find a way of retaining power while seeming to give it away.

He solved the problem at the start of his seventh consulship. In a 'surprise' speech perfect in its hypocrisy he restored the Republic to the care of the Senate. Then he allowed his friends, with carefully scripted spontaneity, to vote him back the powers he had laid down, in a different form. I will not go into details – they are complicated, and do not matter much to my story. Suffice it to say that, although I approved the necessity of his action, I was sickened by the form it took; and I remembered the trials of Milo and Cotta.

In gratitude for this proof of Octavian's respect for Republican tradition, the Senate of its own will named him Augustus. The name was ideal, and Octavian and Maecenas went to great pains in choosing it. Its overtones were almost divine, and severed for all time the link between the imperfect warlord Caesar and the perfect helmsman of the Roman state. O brave new world, O godlike Augustus, who has restored on earth the golden days of Saturn, when truth and justice will reign for ever!

I am being unfair, I know. After all, what could I expect? I had prayed for stability, and now that I had it could only grumble. If hypocrisy is the price we must pay for stable government, then should we not pay it gladly? Perhaps all sound political systems depend, at base, on deception, even self-deception. I do not know. But it is one thing to be deceived unwittingly in a good cause, and another to recognise the deception and yet applaud the deceiver as divine.

There occurred one more incident about this time which, I will not say increased my disillusionment, but certainly reminded me of my own ambivalent moral position. It had nothing to do with politics. It was completely personal.

I was in Rome, staying with Maecenas while I gathered material for my *Aeneid*. We had just breakfasted, and I had made my excuses as usual and was preparing to go to my room to start work when he plucked at my sleeve.

'Don't disappear straight away, Publius,' he said. 'I thought we might go on a little visit this morning. I know you're busy, but it won't take long.'

'Where to?' I was not too well pleased: I had work to do, even if he had not.

Maecenas shrugged.

'Just a visit,' he said. 'Don't come if you don't want to.'

I knew then that it was important. Maecenas is never offhand over trivia.

'Very well,' I said. 'So long as it doesn't take all day.'

'Oh, it's not far,' he assured me. 'Just round the corner. And I'm sure you'll enjoy it.'

Had I known our destination, I would not have gone; would have begged him to forget the whole idea if he valued our friendship. As it was, I did not know until we arrived at what had been Proculus's house.

Maecenas led the way up the familiar steps.

'Who lives here?' I asked.

He gave me a grin which I can only describe as mischievous.

'Wait and see,' he said.

His slave knocked on the door. I suppose I had half expected Proculus's Helenus to open it, but of course the porter was a stranger: a young man in a green tunic. He bowed; and Maecenas, to my surprise, instead of asking if the master was at home walked straight through the lobby into the living-room and sat down in what had been Proculus's chair.

'Well?' he said to me as I followed him in, totally bemused. 'Aren't you going to offer your first guest a drink?'

I must have stared at him like an idiot, because he laughed suddenly, stood up and clapped me on the shoulder.

'It's yours, you fool! Publius, it's your house! A little thank-you present from Augustus and myself.' And then, when I still said nothing: 'What's wrong, Publius? I thought you'd be pleased.'

Of course, he could not have known. Proculus was already dead when we met, and after his death I had had no connection with the house. It was not Maecenas's fault. Yet I felt the irony keenly: Octavian had killed Proculus and taken his house. Now, not knowing its significance, he was giving it back to me. For services rendered.

To Maecenas, it must have seemed as if I had gone mad. I left him standing and walked out, back through the lobby and into the study. Maecenas followed, a picture of innocent confusion. I stopped, and looked around me.

'They've cleaned up the blood,' I said.

'What blood? Publius, what's wrong with you? Don't you like it?'

He was my friend. The gift was both honest and generous, and I knew I could never tell him.

'It's very nice,' I said. 'Just what I've always wanted.'

I spent the night in the study, on the couch where Proculus had died, hoping perhaps to make my peace with his ghost. But there were no ghosts, save within my own head.

I have worked on my *Aeneid* for seven years. Since I began it, Rome has slipped back further and further into anarchy. To be fair, this is not altogether Octavian's fault. In a way, I would have been happier if it had been, if he had shown himself an unworthy tyrant. Call it, if you like, the fault of human nature and (how I dread the phrase!) the expression of divine will. Perhaps Horace is right, and the Golden Age is a myth, or lies in the far future. Perhaps the gods are playing with us, holding out their hands only to snatch them back as we reach for them. I do not know. But in the past few years there have been conspiracies, civil unrest, riots, bloodshed, just as there were before Octavian took all power to himself. Natural disasters, too, which would suggest that the gods are not, after all, on his side: three years ago the Tiber flooded, causing widespread destruction and bringing in its wake famine and pestilence. Pressure has been mounting on Octavian to become, like Caesar, sole consul, even dictator. Up to now he has resisted; but how long can that continue? How long, in fact, can Octavian himself continue? His health is bad – has always been bad. He has been near to death, as far as I know, at least twice, and there is no one to follow him but Agrippa, who would be disastrous for Rome. If Octavian dies soon, as I think he must, the darkness will return, and human nature will reassert itself.

What will be the good of my poems then? And what price their venal poet? Infamy? Or merely laughter?

Softly, Virgil. Softly. What's done is done. Finish your tale, and let the future look after itself. You will have, at any rate, no part in it.

I revealed my plans to no one, showed my growing poem to no one. Octavian was at first indulgent, then pressing, finally insistent, but there was little he could do. I never refused outright to let him read the manuscript – to do so would have aroused too many suspicions – but I dragged my heels as much as I dared, and read or sent to him only the most innocuous passages. Maecenas was more difficult. As a patron – and, more, as a friend – he had the right to my candour; but I could not strain his loyalty to that degree and (let me admit it) was not confident of his support. Fortunately, he was content with what I showed him, and did not press me further. I was helped, too, by the fact that latterly he and Octavian were not quite as close as they had been. Although the rift was political and did not concern me I was – perhaps selfishly – grateful for it. The strait between Scylla and Charybdis had become terribly narrow, and I no longer trusted myself as a pilot.

The crisis came two months ago, in July of the present year. It was precipitated partly by my own stupidity and partly by the officiousness of my secretary Alexander.

I have not mentioned Alexander, or indeed any of my slaves by name: it is curious that, considering how important a part they play in our daily lives, we hardly ever think of slaves as individuals. Alexander was the gift of my friend Pollio who, after Actium, had retired to Rome and given up politics to pursue his literary studies. He had been with me for several years, and I trusted him implicitly: although a slave, he was highly educated (perhaps too much so for his own good, for he was a very vain young man) and had poetical aspirations.

I was at my villa, working on the last book of the poem. Feeling a headache coming on (I have become increasingly susceptible to them, these last few years) I decided to take a break and walk for an hour or so by the seashore. Foolishly, I left the manuscript open on my desk, and the desk itself – with the rest of the work inside – unlocked. When I returned, Alexander met me at the door. He was smiling the particular smug smile he favours when he thinks he has done something clever.

'Oh, you're back, sir?' he said. 'Cilnius Maecenas has been waiting for you for ages. You'd better go straight through.'

A chill wind touched the nape of my neck.

'Straight through where?' I said.

Alexander frowned; as if anyone could be so stupid as not to follow his meaning.

'To your study, of course. I showed him in there as soon as he arrived.'

Why I did not slap his silly face, I do not know; but he saw my expression and stepped back.

'Have I done something wrong, sir?' he said, mock contrite. 'I'm ever so sorry.'

'You fool,' I whispered. 'You bloody fool!'

I crossed the lobby and threw open the study door.

Maecenas was sitting at my desk, a scroll of the *Aeneid* in his hands. He looked up frowning as I came in.

'I didn't expect you until tomorrow,' I said.

'The roads were good.' He laid the scroll down. Our eyes met, and I knew that my secret was a secret no longer. 'Publius, what have you done?'

I shrugged, tried to pass the thing off with a joke.

'It serves you right. People who read other people's letters never hear any good of themselves.'

'This,' he indicated the manuscript, 'is no letter. You've ruined us all, yourself included.'

I sat down and clasped my hands to stop them shaking. I

had dreaded this moment for years. Now that it had come, it brought with it a sense of unreality.

'I had to do it, Gaius.' I had never, I think, used his first name before, and I saw him blink. 'I had to tell the truth somehow. Otherwise there would have been no poem.'

He shook his head, not in denial, but with incomprehension; and said nothing.

'It was the only way,' I said. 'Besides, it won't show.' I might have been talking of a winestain on a mantle. 'Not if people aren't looking for it.'

'Augustus will have to know,' he said at last. 'I can't keep this from him.'

I nodded. My throat was dry. Maecenas stood up. He did not look at me.

'Do you hate us that much, Publius?' he asked softly. 'And have you so little faith that we're right?'

'I don't hate you,' I said. 'I want to believe in what you're doing, but I can't. Not completely. I've helped you all I can. You have all I can give.'

He turned, as if to say something. Then he thought better of it, and moved towards the door. On the threshold, he paused.

'I wouldn't like to be in your shoes when Augustus hears of this. He doesn't much like traitors either.'

I'm not a traitor! I wanted to shout. *I'm only a poet!* But the words stuck in my throat, and in any case he had gone.

I shut myself in my study for the rest of the day and wrote a few letters: a long one to Horace, several shorter ones to other friends, and a last – difficult – one to Maecenas. Then I began to put my affairs in order and plan what to do in the little time that remained.

I sailed for Greece three weeks later.

To my friends, I passed the thing off by saying I intended to stay abroad for three years, working on a final draft of the poem. This, in a way, was true. I had decided that I might as well be hung for a sheep as a lamb. If Octavian did not like the *Aeneid* as it stood, then I would write it to please myself, as a poet; getting rid of much of the pious humbug and placing a greater emphasis on the human drama. Perhaps Octavian would allow me to fade into obscurity, especially since I had signalled my desire to stay away from politics by spreading the rumour that, once the *Aeneid* was finished, I intended to devote my life to philosophy.

To Horace, however, I told the truth. He is, after all, the better half of myself, and will understand. I also left instructions that, if anything happened to me while I was away, any copies of the *Aeneid* left behind in Italy (and there are some, of the more innocuous books) should be burned. The complete manuscript, of course, I took with me.

Finally, in my will, I left what I have always regarded as Proculus's house on the Esquiline, plus half my estate, to his son Lucius. In a way, it was a sin-offering; totally inadequate but all the return I could make to a man I looked on as my second father. Another quarter went to Octavian: he was always greedy where money was concerned, and I thought that perhaps he would be content with that and allow the other bequests to stand. To my literary executors Varius and Tucca (Octavian's men, both) I gave permission to publish anything that I had previously published, but no more. It would not stop them from publishing the *Aeneid in toto* should Octavian order them to do so, but I hoped that circumstances would make that impossible.

That hope, I am afraid, is as dead as I soon will be. Octavian has his poem safe, and I wish him joy of it.

Maecenas's letter must have reached Pergamon shortly before I set out, and been specific enough to bring Octavian to Greece on his fastest galley. He was waiting on the quayside at Piraeus when I disembarked. There was no arrest – he did not even have his honour guard with him – but both of us knew that my flight was over.

'Well, Virgil,' he said cheerfully as we shook hands. 'You didn't expect to see me here, did you?'

'No, Augustus. What a pleasant surprise this is.'

His entourage smiled, nodded as we played our parts. Then, the farce played out, Octavian draped an arm round my shoulders and led me to his carriage.

I had expected, when we were alone, that he would allow the mask to slip, but he did not. He made no reference to Maecenas's letter at all. The only reproach to pass his lips was that I had planned to 'deprive him of my company'.

'I'm sorry, Augustus,' I said. 'We great poets need to be alone sometimes. To refresh our spirits and restore our souls.'

'Couldn't you restore your soul a bit closer to home?' he said. 'Hey, you old devil?'

I stayed silent. Outside the curtained carriage windows, the sounds of the port gave way to street cries and the rumble of carts.

'Come on, Virgil! Cat got your tongue? Why the hell did it have to be Greece?'

I have noticed, these last few years, that Octavian's speech has become more and more rustic: he sounds at times like a caricature Sabine peasant swapping pleasantries over the pigsty wall. Perhaps he feels that it makes him more endearing, more democratic. Personally, I find it artificial and extremely tiresome.

'Does there have to be a reason, sir?' I asked.

He frowned.

''Course not,' he said. ''Course not, you beetroot! Why should there be? You can go where you like, as far as I'm concerned.'

'Then I can stay?'

The frown deepened.

'Perhaps some other time, Publius,' he said. 'I'm needed in Rome, and I'd appreciate it if you came back with me.'

'Right now?'

He glanced at me, then away again at the closed curtains of the carriage.

'I'm not in a great hurry,' he said. 'A day or two won't make much difference.'

A day or two. When I had planned to stay for three years!

'In any case, the ship's not ready yet,' he went on. 'Sprung a plank on the way over, so the captain tells me. It's nothing serious, but we may as well have it fixed. Can't mock Neptune, eh?'

He turned, and looked me full in the face. And I knew.

I knew that he knew, and was telling me that he knew.

At the beginning of my *Aeneid*, Neptune calms the storm that has wrecked Aeneas's fleet and flung him up on the Carthaginian shore: a reminder (covert, of course) to my readers of Octavian's own shipwreck before Naulochus and his insults to the god's statue at the Games.

'No, Augustus.'

He grunted.

'It's a dangerous practice, Virgil. Mocking gods. It gets you nowhere. Nowhere at all.'

'Yes, Augustus.'

That was all he said. We finished the journey in silence.

I cannot dignify what I experienced over the next few days even under the term of 'house arrest' although, of course, I was Octavian's guest at the palatial mansion which the Athenian archon had made available to him. Being free to come and go as I pleased – where could I have run to? – I attended several lectures at the Academy, did a spot of sightseeing, visited old friends and said my tactful goodbyes. It was all very civilised.

On the fifth day, I took a trip to Megara to look at the walls which the Athenians had built during their war with Sparta. It was a hot afternoon, and I had made the mistake of leaving my hat at home. I walked about the town for a while then, feeling thirsty, stopped by a freshet for a drink. The water was icy cold – it must have come from a spring deep underground – and went straight to my stomach. On the way back I felt the beginnings of a chill; and by early evening was shivering uncontrollably. Octavian, uncharacteristically, noticed at once.

'What's wrong with you, Publius? Spot of tummy trouble, eh?'

'Just a slight chill, Augustus,' I said (my teeth were chattering). 'I'll be fine in the morning.'

'Better have Musa take a look at you.' He beckoned a slave over and sent him to fetch the doctor. 'He'll fix you up in no time.'

Musa was a Greek, and one of Octavian's most trusted attendants. He had, by a process of his own involving cold baths and compresses, saved Octavian's life a few years previously. Octavian never travelled without him.

'I'm all right, Augustus,' I said. 'I only need a good night's sleep.'

'Nonsense!' Octavian smiled, showing his thin teeth. 'We've got to look after you, Virgil. Anyway, the ship's ready, and we sail tomorrow. Don't want you to die on us before Brindisi, do we?'

I shivered; and it had nothing to do with my chill. I knew then that he had marked me for death.

So what is it, then? The poison Musa is giving me? Belladonna, probably; deadly nightshade, Proserpina's flower. That would, I think, produce the desired symptoms. I may ask him directly – Musa – the next time he comes to give me my 'medicine'. Or perhaps I should ask Octavian himself. It cannot matter now, and I would be interested to see his reaction. If any.

I must be grateful, I suppose, that I have been lucid enough to write. Either Octavian is in no hurry (for all his claims to be urgently needed at Rome, we are dawdling on this voyage) or he is afraid to make the manner of my death too obvious. I suspect the latter.

Why, then, do I not kill myself, you may ask? Cheat Octavian of the fruits of his final hypocrisy – final, at least, as far as I am concerned – in the knowledge that when we reach Italy he will have the embarrassment of unshipping not a living poet but a cold corpse? Or better still throw myself into the sea and leave him with no poet at all to show, living or otherwise? That last, certainly, would be to apply poetic justice to myself with a vengeance – my brother Marcus's vengeance. Oh, yes, I have seen him, these last few nights, with the weed in his hair and his half-gnawed face turned towards me in the light of the cabin lamps. He at least would welcome a death by water, and I would not grudge him it.

The truth is, I do not care any more. To inflict death on myself despite Octavian would be, at best, a small victory, not to say a mean one, like a child who, if he cannot have his way, refuses to eat his dinner although he is hungry. I have no interest in small victories. Compared with the book which you now hold between your palms (if indeed you do hold it), such victories are meaningless.

Besides, even if I wanted to kill myself now this task of mine is done, how could I do it? Not by willpower alone, and I have no other means. I have no dagger like Proculus, or, like Gallus, a razor to slit my wrists; let alone a snake, like the Egyptian queen, to make me immortal with its venom. The cabin door is locked; and if it were not I would be stopped before I reached the thwarts. Epicurus may hold that a man tired of life may choose to leave it like a spectator whom the play has ceased to please; but Epicurus did not have a prisoner in mind. No, let Death come when he comes. At least he will come in his gentlest guise, as he did at Odysseus's ending, or at my father's. And who can ask for more than a gentle death? Not I, certainly: it is more than I deserve.

I have asked, of course, for the manuscript of the *Aeneid*, so that I can burn it (it disappeared with the rest of my baggage when I docked at Piraeus). Equally, of course, the request has been ignored. Never mind. Octavian will find that excisions are not possible without damaging the poem irreparably, and he dare not allow that. He must publish and be damned – or, if not damned, at least slightly singed.

I have only one fear remaining for, as I have said, I do not fear death: that you, my reader (if indeed you exist!) are still blinded by the glamour of the Augustan myth. If so, then I have failed, finally and for ever. Octavian may bring in the Golden Age after all (and I pray that he does!), or he may be leading us down yet another of history's blind, blood-spattered alleyways. I do not know, but it makes no